"You actually intend to let me leave without making me a *very* happy man?"

"I know. Sad, isn't it?" Rory patted his hand. "Life is full of one disappointment after another."

He leaned his forehead against hers. "But it doesn't have to be, Miss Rory."

"It does if you're figuring on me going upstairs with you." She drew away.

Garth clasped her hand. "What are you afraid of, Rory?"

She batted her eyelashes. "I'm afraid I'll enjoy it too much, and will want to make it become a habit—but you'll no longer be here to satisfy me, so I'll have to settle for lower quality." She stood up. "Time to dance."

Garth got to his feet and took her in his arms. "Make jokes if you want to, honey, but can't you feel the excitement when our bodies touch?" he whispered. "At least let's go someplace where we can be alone without a dozen pairs of eyes on us."

"I don't think so; there's safety in numbers."

"Don't you trust yourself, Rory?"

"Of course I do."

He grabbed her by the hand. "Then come on, honey, we're getting out of here."

Praise for Ana Leigh's passionate Frasers novels

THE LAWMAN SAID "I DO"

"Winning . . . A very 21st-century light romance in a 19th-century setting."

—*Publishers Weekly*

"Quirky characters and witty dialogue fill the pages of this entertaining novel. . . . This will appeal to many audiences, from fans of the Old West, to readers who enjoy a good romance, to those who like books rich in humor."

—*Booklist*, starred review

"This novel is filled with funny moments and moments of poignancy. . . . Leigh is a wonderful writer who tells a great story."

—*Romantic Times*

THE FRASERS: CLAY

"[Ana Leigh's] strong characters and their biting repartee and tender emotions touch readers' hearts, while the hardships of western travel are brilliantly portrayed in this tender, exciting western."

—*Romantic Times* (4.5 stars)

"Delightful repartee and scenes of comic relief abound. . . . The pacing moves along nicely and allows the readers to laugh and cry as the plot progresses to an especially heartwarming ending that leaves one anticipating the sequel. . . . Pick up a copy . . . and join in an historical adventure of grand proportions."

—Romance Reviews Today

"This intriguing western romance stars two fine protagonists [who] struggle not to fall in love while the reader chuckles at their failure. . . . A fine tale."

—Harriet Klausner, The Best Reviews

Also by Ana Leigh

The Lawman Said "I Do"
The Frasers: Clay

HIS BOOTS UNDER HER BED

The Frasers

ANA LEIGH

POCKET **STAR** BOOKS

New York   London   Toronto   Sydney

An *Original* Publication of POCKET BOOKS

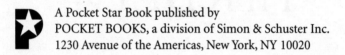 A Pocket Star Book published by
POCKET BOOKS, a division of Simon & Schuster Inc.
1230 Avenue of the Americas, New York, NY 10020

ISBN-13: 978-0-7394-7621-5

POCKET STAR BOOKS and colophon are registered trademarks of Simon & Schuster Inc.

Cover design by Anna Dorfman/cabin photo by Frank Krahmer/
    Masterfile
Book design by Davina Mock

Printed in the United States of America

*I Dedicate This Book to the Terrific Gals
of Our Tuesday Bridge Club*

Betty Bertram	*Bernie Willkom*
Jan Fertl	*Gladys Port*
Gen Seidl	*Phyl Wallock*

*and
Marge Tarantino*

A Grand Slam in Any Suit

*We may not be young enough to be desperate
housewives, gals, but thank goodness we're old
enough to be bridge-playing grandmas.*

1

Buckman, California
1867

Her partner reeked of booze, bad breath, and body odor, but for two bits a dance she could tolerate it.

The door swung open, and the man in the doorway made Rory's bored glance change to one of curiosity. He was well kempt compared to other strays that wandered into the Grotto, and he had to be a stranger in town to come to this dump instead of the Palace down the street, where the clientele was better heeled and the liquor wasn't watered down.

Rory watched with interest as the man crossed the room to the bar. She had learned to tell a lot about a man from the way he carried himself. This one walked tall, self-confident and relaxed, but at the same time generating an "I'm-not-looking-for-trouble-so-don't-piss-with-me" aura. She figured him for one of those tall Texans who often passed through town.

To Rory's relief the dance ended and she thanked her partner, rejected his offer again to go upstairs, and strolled to the end of the bar for a closer look at the new arrival.

The stranger was taller than the other men along the bar, and from her vantage point she saw that his profile bordered on perfection. His thick, dark lashes swept high cheekbones, which flowed into a straight nose and a firm jaw that reflected generations of patrician breeding.

This guy was no saddle tramp, all right; so who was he and what was he doing here?

As if sensing her stare, he turned his head. Their gazes locked, and a hint of merriment flashed in his brown eyes as he nodded.

Rory smiled back and was pleased to see him pick up his drink. She was certain he intended to move to her side when Shelia, one of the saloon's prostitutes, sidled up to him and slipped her arm through his.

"Hi, good-looking."

"Evening, ma'am."

"You can call me Shelia, honey. And what do they call you?"

He grinned, his teeth a brilliant white against the several days growth of whiskers that darkened his jaw. "Usually depends on who's doing the calling, Miss Shelia, but my mama always called me Garth."

"And what does your wife call you, handsome?"

"I don't have a wife, Miss Shelia."

"You got a last name, Garth?"

"Fraser. Garth Fraser."

"Well, Garth Fraser, I don't believe any man as good-looking as you should be drinking alone. How about buying a thirsty gal a drink? I'm so dry, I'm spitting sand."

"We sure can't have you doing that, now can we? Bartender, the lady's thirsty."

Rory had been wrong; he was no Texan. His soft-spoken, pleasant Southern accent caused her to close her eyes and conjure up fantasies of cotillions and flower-scented gardens.

The stranger glanced over at Rory with a lingering look and an apologetic smile; then Shelia turned him back to face her and slipped her arms around his neck.

"Maybe you'd rather finish your drink upstairs, handsome."

"The thought's crossed my mind."

"Mo, give us a bottle," Shelia said. "Me and good-looking here are gonna head up to my room."

"Like I couldn't figure that out." Mo slid a capped bottle across the bar. "Five bucks, pal."

"Five bucks! Pretty expensive for a bottle of watered-down whiskey, Mo," Garth said with a friendly smile.

"I ain't runnin' no charity house, pal. Besides, you'll get your money's worth; Shelia's included in the price."

"How about a hot bath? Is that included in the price, too?"

"Four bits more. And for another four bits—"

"I bet I know; Miss Shelia will bathe me." When Mo's thick lips curled in a smirk, Garth added, "I thought the war abolished slavery."

"You Johnny Rebs oughta know, considerin' how you got your asses kicked."

Fraser's friendly grin disappeared. "How would you know, *pal*? You probably never budged from behind that bar during the whole godforsaken war."

Garth tossed the money on the bar, grabbed the bottle, and slid his arm around Shelia's shoulders. "Come on, Miz Shelia, we'll wash each other's backs."

Rory watched the couple climb the stairs. Just her luck! If Shelia hadn't come along when she did, she would have gotten the price of a couple of dances out of him.

"Slow night," she said when Mo came over to her.

"That fella at the other end of the bar said he'd pay double if you'll go upstairs with him."

She glanced in the direction Mo indicated. The man was the same one she'd been dancing with when Fraser had come in.

"When Hell freezes over," Rory said.

"You'd think you were the queen of England, or somethin', lady. How much are you holdin' out for?"

"Love, Mo. That's my price, and I'm not settling for anything less."

Mo snorted. "There ain't a woman alive that can't be bought. You included, your royal highness."

"I'm tired of having this argument every night, Mo. We agreed no whoring. All I'd have to do is hustle drinks and dance with the customers, and I could keep half of what I earn."

"I said that because I knew your looks would bring in a lot of guys. You got any idea how much we could make if you'd start giving them more than just a dance?"

"Sorry, boss." She walked away and sat down at a corner table.

Lord, how she hated this town! She'd been working at the Grotto for a month, and would have moved on if Pop hadn't taken to bed with another attack of congestion. No one liked her. Mo was upset because she wouldn't whore, and the girls resented her for the same reason.

Well, no way was she going to become a prostitute.

She hankered to fall in love with a decent, hardworking man who loved her, and settle down and raise his children. Surely one of these days she would meet up with such a man. And if he was as sightly as that Fraser fellow, that sure would sweeten the pot.

Rory reached for the copy of *Grimm's Fairy Tales* that she was reading. Books were her only relief from her humdrum life. When her mother died, she not only had lost the woman she worshiped, but the only teacher she'd ever had. It had been her mother who had taught her ciphering, and how to write and read, and introduced her to the wondrous world of literature.

Rory read anything she could get her hands on, from the King James Version of the Bible to Benjamin Franklin's *Poor Richard's Almanack*.

But novels were her favorites. Be it Cooper's *Last of the Mohicans* or Emily Brontë's *Wuthering Heights* or her sister Charlotte's *Jane Eyre,* she devoured them all, delighting in Elizabeth Bennett's and Mr. Darcy's battle of the sexes in Jane Austen's *Pride and Prejudice,* or the mastery of Charles Dickens's words in *A Tale of Two Cities.* But nothing thrilled her like Sir Walter Scott's tales of jousting knights and fair damsels.

For the next couple of hours, she sold dances and read her book.

When two new arrivals entered, a shudder rippled her spine. Rory remembered seeing them the previous week. There'd been something about them that gave her a chill; an aura of evil. Both had mean stares, and never looked a person in the eyes. The shorter of the two had a skeletal-appearing face that gave him a ghostly look. Rumor had it that they robbed and shanghaied drunks for unethical sea captains.

After exchanging a few words with Mo, the two men sat down at a table in the corner. No matter how she tried, Rory couldn't keep her eyes off the creepy pair. For the next thirty minutes they spoke to no one, including each other, nor did they attempt to play cards or show an interest in any of the girls. They just sat there silently, drinking slowly, as if waiting for someone.

She shivered again and felt goose bumps prickle her arms as if "Satan, hisself be walkin' on me grave," as her Irish mother had said whenever something scared her. Rory decided to leave.

She stopped at the bar to purchase a bottle of whiskey to take back to her father. She was worried about Pop. He was getting up in years, but insisted that what he lacked in youth, he made up in cunning. Since her mother had died, he had taken to drinking his meals, rather than put some decent hot food into his stomach. That was why she couldn't leave him. At least at times she succeeded in getting him to eat.

At that moment, Shelia and Garth Fraser came downstairs. He was unsteady on his feet and obviously had drunk the better part of the whiskey he'd taken upstairs.

So he was just like all the other tramps after all, she thought in disgust. Men came in all sizes and shapes, but underneath they were all alike.

Once again he caught her eye and smiled and tipped his hat. He was a charmer, all right. Rory nodded and then turned her back to him.

As Rory settled up with Mo for the evening, she saw the bartender make eye contact with the two men and nod slightly in the direction of the departing Fraser. They got up quickly and followed him.

Rory's suspicious nature was a gift from her mother and had guided her successfully through what might have been some disastrous situations in her twenty-four years. She didn't have to step in a pile of horse manure to know that something smelled rotten—the two men were up to no good, and it looked like her boss was in cahoots with them.

Give it no mind, Rory O'Grady, if you've nay got a stake in the pot. Besides, drunk or sober, Garth Fraser struck her as a man who could take care of himself.

She stepped outside. The smell of the sea from a nearby inlet permeated the rising ground fog that swirled around her knees and ankles. In the distance, the clang of the bell on a moored buoy carried to her ears. She glanced skyward just as dark clouds drifted across the face of the moon. "Aye, Mum, I know: 'Tis a bad sign," she murmured.

Due to the late hour the street was deserted, but she was able to make out the figure of Fraser and the two men following him. Clutching her whiskey bottle in one hand, she tightened the shawl around her shoulders, and started to scurry the short distance to her rooming house.

Then her conscience got the better of her. She couldn't abandon Fraser to whatever fate those two blackguards had planned for him. Ignoring her common sense, she spun on her heel and followed them. Within minutes, the rising fog would engulf the town, swallowing whatever light remained in the moonless night. Rory could barely distinguish the figures, but still she hugged the dark shadows to make certain she'd not be seen.

Within seconds she lost sight of them entirely, and were it not for the gruff sound of a man's voice, she would have bumped into them.

"As soon as you finish tying him up, Skull, we'll tote him into our shack. Then I'll go and get the captain."

Holding what appeared to be a blackjack, the speaker stood over Fraser, who was trussed up like a roped steer with his arms tied behind his back and his ankles bound together.

Grunting, the two men lifted Fraser and carried him into a nearby shack. Rory inched closer and peeked into the window.

"Hurry, he's beginning to stir," the larger, gruff-voiced man declared. "Here's his gun. If he wakes up, you'll need it."

"You mean I should shoot him, Bates?" Skull asked.

"No, stupid! Keep it trained on him. That'll keep him from tryin' to escape."

Rory slunk back into the shadows when the man hurried away. As soon as she was certain he was gone, she moved over to the shack and peered into the window again. The glow from a candle inside enabled her to make out the bound figure of Fraser on the floor in the corner. Skull was standing over him with a pointed pistol.

"If you want to stay alive, mate, jest stay still."

"Can I sit up? This is uncomfortable," Fraser said.

"Okay, but don't try anything."

"Why didn't you just take my money and leave me?" Fraser asked, shifting to a sitting position.

"We've got better plans for you, mate. You're goin' on a long sea trip."

So her suspicions were right; they intended to shanghai him. She had to do something, or it would be too late to help the poor man. She heard footsteps and slipped back into the shadows just as Bates reappeared. When he went inside, she returned to the window.

"The captain and crew's ashore," Bates said. "There's only the bo'sun on duty. He said we'd have to carry him on ourselves."

"How're we gonna do that?" Skull riled. "The man weighs two hundred pounds at least. We can't carry him to the ship."

"Then we'll walk him there."

"And what makes you think I'll be obliging enough to do that?" Fraser asked.

Bates's mouth twisted into a cruel smirk as he pulled a wicked-looking knife out of his boot. " 'Cause it's better than havin' your throat cut."

"That's a good point," Fraser agreed calmly.

"And so has this knife, mate, so don't try anything foolish."

Bates cut the rope binding Fraser's legs and hauled him to his feet. Sliding the knife back into his boot, he opened the door and snarled, "Let's get movin'."

Fraser stomped his feet several times to get the circulation back in them, then Skull shoved him to follow. Fraser stumbled into Bates and knocked him off balance. Seizing the opportunity, he kicked Skull in the knee.

Doubling over with pain, Skull dropped the gun and clutched his knee. Fraser used those few seconds to try to take off, but the two men quickly recovered their footing and wrestled him to the ground.

Except for the grunts and sounds of the blows, no man spoke as they thrashed and struggled, but due to the proximity, no one was able to deliver a felling blow.

Considering he'd been inebriated, Fraser was managing to do a fair job of fighting them off, but it was two against one, and it would only be a matter of time before they'd succeed in overpowering him.

Fraser managed to stagger to his feet and shove Skull aside with such force that the little man stumbled backward, crashed into the table, and struck his head on the leg. He slumped to the floor unconscious.

Rory had been watching Bates and saw the weasel reach for the knife in his boot. She grasped the whiskey bottle firmly in her hand, darted into the shack, and just as the scoundrel was about to sink the knife into Fraser's back, she smashed the bottle over his head. He pitched forward unconscious.

Prepared to deliver another forceful kick, Fraser halted when he saw the new addition to the fight was a woman.

Rory picked up the fallen knife and freed his bound hands. Shaking his wrists, Fraser went over and recovered his pistol. He slipped it into the holster he wore on his hip, and then picked up his hat.

"I owe you a debt of gratitude, Miss—"

"Time for introductions later. Let's get out of here before these two wake up." She grabbed Fraser's hand and they raced away.

"Where are we going?" he asked when they passed The Grotto.

"Where it's safer."

They reached the rooming house and stole quietly into her room. She locked the door and lit the lamp.

"Excuse me, I'll be right back," Rory said. She went into the adjoining room and closed the door.

Walking over to the figure in the bed, she placed a hand on his brow. "How are you feeling, Pop?"

"Fair to middling. And after a wee nip of me medicine, I'm sure I'll be feeling a lot better. Would you bring me the bottle, darlin'?" His wide Irish grin always melted her heart.

"Whiskey is *not* medicine, Paddy O'Grady," she declared as she poured a dosage of liquid onto a spoon.

"Aye, darlin', but it kills the bitterness of this vile-tasting medicine the doctor forces me to drink."

"It's for your own good, Pop. And it's working, isn't it? You hardly coughed last night at all. Open your mouth."

His countenance scrunched up in displeasure as he swallowed the potion and shook his head. " 'Tis brewed by the devil himself. Better to let a swarm of blood-sucking leeches drain the blood from me!"

"Medicine's advanced beyond the Dark Ages, Pop, so stop acting like such a baby. You can get along without whiskey for one night."

"Are you telling me you didn't bring me whiskey?"

"I bought it like you asked, but I accidentally broke the bottle. I don't have any more money to replace it."

"And that thieving bartender wouldn't be trusting us for the cost of another bottle!"

"I didn't ask him. We had words again over my refusing . . . to work one of the rooms."

Paddy clenched his fist and shook it in the air. "That heathen son of the devil! When I get out of this bed, I'll be telling him so."

"Now don't get yourself all worked up, Pop, or you'll start coughing again."

A twinkle returned to his eyes. "Maybe there's a few drops left in me bottle to soothe the tongue of an ailing man, darlin'?"

Rory went over to the table and turned the whiskey bottle upside down. "Sorry, Pop, not a drop." She went back to the bed, tucked in the blanket, and bent down and kissed his forehead. "Get some sleep now. I'll talk to Mo tomorrow. I'm sure he'll give me a bottle on credit. Good night, Pop."

"Good night, darlin'." He sighed. "But how's an ailing man to sleep without his medicine?"

2

Garth clutched his aching head, sat down on the bed, and took off his boots. He unbuckled his gun belt and slung it over the bedpost, thinking about the night ahead with the spunky little blonde who'd saved his life. In the dim glimpses he had of his rescuer, he'd recognized the blonde he'd seen at the bar in the Grotto. Who could forget those blue eyes?

He remembered going upstairs with a redhead named Shelia, who most certainly had lived up to his expectations. But things got hazy and bizarre after that.

Granted he had drunk a little too much, but that whiskey had been so watered down that there was no sting to it—or at least he thought so at the time.

He remembered leaving the Grotto, but everything got foggy from that point on. His aching head and body made it clear he hadn't escaped unscathed but at least he had escaped. The one thing he remembered clearly was that those two SOBs who jumped him had intended to shanghai him, and most likely would have killed him if this woman hadn't come to his aid. It took a lot of courage for her to do that. Those two men were rattlesnake mean. Lord knows what they might have done to her if they'd had the chance. He owed the gal a damn sight more than just a thank you.

The thought of making love to her now had his groin aching; he'd wanted her the first time he looked at her. He stretched out and closed his eyes. What was keeping her? She didn't have to fancy up for him. His head might be hurting, but the rest of him was at full attention and ready for duty.

It's no wonder he liked women so much; what was there *not* to like? God sure had the right idea when he created a woman—even if she got her and Adam's rear ends kicked out of Eden.

Of course, he had good cause to feel as he did. Garth thought warmly of his beloved mother, of his adorable sister Lissy; the fortitude of Emmaline, his brother Will's wife who had lost her youngest and oldest sons during the war. Then he grinned, recalling the image of Becky, the irrepressible Yankee his brother Clay had married. Amazing women, all.

Especially the two ladies he'd met tonight, he thought with a smile, then yawned.

What in hell was keeping that woman? he wondered as he slipped into slumber.

*   *   *

Rory was surprised to discover Fraser fast asleep on her bed. She supposed it was just as well, though, with those two scoundrels undoubtedly hunting for him. More than likely they'd return to the Grotto, or try to find out if he'd rented a room in town for the night. Since she and Fraser hadn't exchanged even a word at the Grotto, this would be the last place they'd look for him.

She picked up the boots he had tossed aside and tucked them neatly under her bed. He never batted a single one of those long eyelashes throughout the whole process.

For a long moment she stood looking down at him. He sure was handsome. And even better—he didn't stink. That put him high on the totem pole, to her way of thinking.

He's just another drifter passing through, Rory, so don't get your hopes up. Just the same, he seemed like a nice-enough fella.

Rory picked up one of the pillows and grabbed the comforter from the foot of the bed, then blew out the lamp and went into her father's room, where the man who'd claimed he'd get no sleep was snoring away. She spread the comforter on the floor and took off her shoes.

For a long while she lay awake thinking about how easily Garth Fraser's life might have changed, or even ended, if Bates and Skull had succeeded with their foul deed.

"You're a lucky man, Garth Fraser," she murmured, "and you owe me a big favor."

But whether he'd ever return the favor or not, Rory was glad she'd intervened. It was satisfying to know she had followed her conscience rather than take the easier and safer way out.

Garth awoke the next morning and lay drowsily assembling the events of the previous night in his mind. As his head began to clear, the pieces of the puzzle took shape: leaving the Grotto, the attack, and his rescue by the woman. He'd had his fair share of close calls during the war, but shanghaied! God forbid. He'd *never* had a desire to sail a boat, much less go to sea for an extended time. The sea was more to his brother Jed's liking. During the war Jed had sailed on a privateer, running much-needed supplies through the Yankee ships blockading the Southern ports.

Garth had made a few necessary trips on the James River on a paddleboat or barge, but only when he couldn't persuade one of his brothers to do it for him. Horseback was his love. He and his horse Boots got along just fine.

He sat up in bed with an urgent call from Nature to relieve himself of all that whiskey he'd drunk last night. Seeing no chamber pot, he unlocked the door and scanned the hallway, then hurried to the door marked PRIVY.

"Good morning," Rory greeted when he returned to the room. She continued to plump up the pillow on the bed.

"Good morning."

Why couldn't he remember making love to her? They must have shared her bed last night, but he hated to think he'd slept through it and missed the best opportunity he could ever hope for.

She sure was a pretty sight. Her blond hair was swept up to the top of her head and her face was scrubbed clean of the makeup she wore in the Grotto. Her plain homespun blue gown with a white collar added brightness to those blue eyes of hers. He'd woken up in the bed of a pretty woman more times than he could remember, but this one had to be about the best-looking one yet. He sat down on the edge of the bed and put on his boots.

"How are you feeling this morning?" she asked.

"Name's Garth Fraser, ma'am," he said.

"Yes, I know. Mine's Rory O'Grady."

He smiled at her. "It's a pleasure to meet you, Miss O'Grady. I'm beholden to you."

"That was some beating you took last night."

"Guess I'll survive. The message just hasn't reached my head yet."

Garth picked up his gun belt and strapped it on. "What did they hit me with?"

"It looked like a blackjack. I think all that whiskey you drank last night might be contributing to your misery, too, Mr. Fraser."

He winked at her. "You may be right. Call me Garth, Miss Rory O'Grady."

She felt a tug at her heart at the way his tongue curled around her name, and she smiled at him. He was an easy man to like. A real charmer, all right.

"So why did you do it, Miss O'Grady? You could have been hurt."

"I saw them following you and figured they were up to no good."

"Do you know anything about them?"

"About as much as you do. The big one's Bates and the other one is Skull. That's what they called each other last night."

"Did you ever see them before?"

"They came into the Grotto one night last week. Didn't speak to anyone. After a couple of drinks, they got up and left. Then they showed up again last night. Same thing. They just sat, not saying anything to anyone. When you came downstairs, they got up and followed you out. Rumor has it they shanghai strangers traveling alone."

"Guess it's more than a rumor," Garth said. "Why hasn't the sheriff arrested them?"

"The sheriff!" Rory scoffed. "He's as crooked as they are, and probably in cahoots with them. I'm thinking Mo might be, too. But I don't think any of the girls are, because they're the ones who told me about Bates and Skull."

"Well, you saved me from a long sea trip, Miss Rory. I don't know when I can repay you, but you can be sure I will someday when I hit it big."

"Don't tell me you're a gambler, too. You men are all alike, always betting on winning that big pot."

"I'm not talking about gambling, Miss Rory. There's more than one kind of way to get rich."

She laughed. "Indeed. The *big* gold mine that's just awaiting for you to pick up the nuggets."

Garth chuckled. "Could be."

She gaped in shock. "It *is* that, isn't it? Holy sweet Mary! I sure had you pegged wrong, Garth Fraser. Figured you had something better under your hat than just a head good for smashing blackjacks over."

"Ah . . . about last night. Right now I only have a few dollars, but you're welcome to them."

" 'Tis a kindly offer, but why would I take your money?"

He glanced toward the bed. "You mean we didn't . . ."

She felt the heated flush of rising anger. "We certainly *didn't!*"

His smile of relief was just as irritating. "Then let me at least pay for the broken bottle of whiskey."

"You can be certain I'm doing just fine without your charity, Mr. Fraser."

He threw back his head in laughter. "You know, Miss Rory O'Grady, I find it delightful how you slip in and out of a brogue whenever that pert little nose of yours gets out of joint."

Rory blushed and took a deep breath to regain control. She'd worked too hard to rid herself of the brogue to get careless now. Glancing up at him, she tried to ignore the effect his engaging grin had on her.

"The whiskey was put to a better use than it would have been here," she said. "Now if I were you, Mr. Fraser, I'd get out of town first thing this morning in case those two scoundrels are still around."

"I'm not afraid of them. Now that I'm aware of what they're up to, I can take care of myself. But what about you? It's not safe for you to remain here. They'll want to get even with you for helping me."

"Neither of them saw me, so I'll be safe. I'll go back to work tonight, and no one will be the wiser."

"Why are you working in a dump like the Grotto anyway?"

"Because they didn't need my services at the Palace."

"I mean, why sell yourself for a couple bucks?"

Despite his friendly tone, she resented the remark. Who was *he* to judge what she had to do just to keep a roof over her head? Much less a fancy Southern mansion like that soothing Southern accent of his reflected.

"I am not a prostitute, Mr. Fraser. Maybe you should address your question to Miss Shelia, since I didn't hear you turn down her offer."

"Then why ... what ..." he stuttered.

"I hustle watered-down drinks and listen to men's tales of woe, and if they're willing to pay twenty-five cents, I dance with them. That's all *any* man gets from me: a sympathetic ear or a dance."

Rory squared her shoulders, picked up his hat, and opened the door. "Now, I'd appreciate you getting your ungrateful rear end out of here."

He came over to her and clasped her by the shoulders. "Rory, I'm sorry. I didn't mean how it sounded."

"Please leave, sir. I'm sure your mother didn't raise her son to ignore a woman's wishes, whether a lady or not."

For a long moment he stared down at her, and her pride made her hold the stare.

"You're right, Rory, she didn't. So I'll leave as you wish."

Transfixed, she watched the slow descent of his mouth toward hers and knew she should turn away. But she couldn't. Call it helplessness, call it curiosity, or call it what it rightfully was—desire. From the moment their gazes had met in that barroom, she had thought about this kiss.

She parted her lips.

From the first touch of his lips, sweet sensation spiraled through her. The kiss was slow, exciting, and she responded with fervency she never suspected she was capable of. He broke the kiss only long enough for them to draw a much needed breath, and as he reclaimed her lips, her head and body swirled with aroused passion.

She struggled for coherence under his drugging kisses when he swept her up in his arms and carried her to the bed.

"Put me down," she ordered.

"My very thought, ma'am." He laid her down, then unbuckled his gun belt.

"No, you don't understand," she protested in a choking whisper.

"Understand what?" He sat on the bed and pulled off a boot. It hit the floor with a thump.

"You can't do this."

"Oh, baby, you've got that wrong." He leaned over and kissed the tip of her nose. "A little headache isn't enough to stop me."

His other boot thumped to the floor, and he got up and pulled off her shoes. "Now let's get that dress off you."

She slapped his hands away when he lowered himself to her and reached for the buttons of her dress. "Get off me, you big oaf! If you don't listen to me, I'm going to scream," she warned.

"After last night it's a little late for modesty, isn't it?"

"Nothing happened last night."

"Why are you whispering, honey?"

"I don't want to disturb my father. He's in the next room."

He jerked up his head. "Your father is what?"

"You awake, darlin'?" a voice called out from the adjoining room.

"Yes, Pop, I'll be right in as soon as I finish dressing."

Garth rolled off her with a groan. "I don't believe this." He began to pull on his boots as she scrambled off the bed.

"Get out of here!" she hissed, arranging her disheveled hair.

Within seconds he stood up and came over to her. "This isn't the end between us, Rory. We have a debt to settle, and I'll not say good-bye until we do."

"We have no debt to settle, Garth Fraser. Just be careful, and watch your back. And I hope someday you'll find that treasure you're seeking."

The excitement of his kiss still lingered, but she dared not give in to a yearning for more. She shoved his hat into his hands and closed the door.

*   *   *

Garth intended to get back to the very enticing Miss Rory O'Grady as soon as he took care of his unfinished business with Bates and Skull. He had a pretty good idea where the shack of the lowdown scum was located.

After several blocks, he was certain he recognized the shack and peered into the window. It was the same cabin, all right, but it was empty. He tried the door and found it unlocked, so he went inside. There were no clothes or packs, so he assumed they'd left town. Just to be certain, he checked at the livery and found out the two had never boarded horses there. He tried the stage office with the same results: neither one had left on the morning stage. He even inquired about them with the local sheriff, and got only a suspicious look in return.

Could they still be in town? He decided to check out the saloons.

Later that evening, Rory felt her heartbeat quicken when Garth came into the Grotto. She hadn't seen a sign of him all day, and she had believed he'd taken her advice and left town.

Mo poured him a drink. "Heard you had some trouble last night."

"Yeah. How did you hear about it?"

"The sheriff," Mo said. "He said you're looking for Bates and Skull. Have any luck?"

"Not yet. How well do you know them?"

"Well enough to know you've got the wrong two in mind. Bates and Skull were here last night all evening. Had to kick them out when I closed up."

"Is that right? Got anyone who can back up that story?"

Mo glared at him. "Why would anyone have to? My word's always been good enough for the folks around here, Fraser."

"Think I'll check out your story with that blonde at the table over there. I remember seeing her here last night."

"Won't do you no good, Fraser. She left about the same time you did."

"Rather hear that from her."

"Keep this up, Fraser, and I'm gonna start taking it personal."

"Take it any way you want, pal. I know Bates and Skull tried to shanghai me, and I take that *very* personal."

"You've as much as called me a liar. That could be a big mistake."

Garth downed the shot of whiskey and threw a coin on the bar. "It wouldn't be my first one, Mo."

He walked casually over to Rory and sat down. "You were right about Mo. He's in on it. He just told me Bates and Skull were here all evening last night. I told him I was coming over here to ask you about them, so go along with me and start shaking your head as if you don't know anything. Just hold to the story that you left early last night, and went straight to your room and bed. That way they won't suspect you helped me."

"That's good of you, but if I thought they suspected me, I wouldn't be sitting here now. I've got more sense than that."

"I've looked everywhere today trying to find those two. They probably left town."

"Did you think to try that ship anchored out there?" Rory asked. Aware that Mo was watching them intently, she went along with Garth's suggestion and shook her head as she spoke. "What are you trying to do, Garth? Get yourself killed? Get out of town while you're still able."

"Good girl," he said, and stood up. "I'll leave you, so he'll buy the act."

Garth started to walk away just as the piano player announced his arrival with a loud treble on the keys.

"Hey, cowboy, sorry I couldn't be of any help, but for twenty-five cents I'll dance with you," Rory called out, loud enough for Mo to hear.

Garth stopped and turned back to her. "Now, why didn't I think of that?"

Rory stood up and slipped the coin he handed her into a velvet pouch pinned to her gown.

What a difference from the other men she'd danced with, she thought as he glided her across the floor. No furious arm jerking, no trampling on her toes. His movements were so smooth that she closed her eyes and gave herself up to the music. The provocative scent of male and musk aroused her senses, and the warmth of his body was exciting. This intense physical awareness of him was too dangerous to encourage— but too exciting to discourage.

Too soon, Gus ended the song, and she opened her eyes and returned to her real world of a smoky bar- room with the odor of cheap cigars and a cacophony of raised voices, clinking glasses, and clattering boots on the wooden floor.

"It's getting noisy down here, Rory. Why don't we continue our drinking and dancing upstairs?"

"Sorry, Mr. Fraser, but I've told you I don't go upstairs," she replied when Mo came over to the table to refill their glasses.

"If you want more than dances and drinks, I suggest you move on. You're discouraging my other customers."

"That's no way to treat a money-paying customer," Mo grumbled.

"Matter of fact, I don't feel much like dancing anymore. I'm tired; I think I'll go home," Rory said.

"It would be my pleasure to see you safely to your door, Miss Rory," Garth said.

"I'm quite capable of seeing myself to my door, Mr. Fraser."

"My mama would turn over in her grave if she thought a son of hers wouldn't escort a lady to safety."

"From what I've heard, you're the one who needs an escort, Fraser."

Garth broke into laughter. "Maybe you're right. But I'll see you home just the same."

She shrugged. "As soon as I square up with Mo."

She dumped the contents of the velvet pouch on the table and divided it. Mo scooped up his half.

"You running your own business on the side?" Mo asked.

"What does that mean?"

"All this talk about saving yourself for the right man. I'm thinkin' you might be whorin' at your place."

"Sure, with Pop right in the next room," she scoffed.

"Since when would Paddy turn away from the chance to make an easy buck?"

She wanted to scratch the leer off his ugly face. "Aren't you a little confused, boss? You're the pimp—not Pop."

Garth followed her out the door.

3

Once again a misty fog shrouded the night. Drops of moisture coated her bare arms, and Rory was unable to thwart the shiver that riffled through her.

"Cold?" Garth slipped an arm around her shoulders and drew her protectively against his side. She cuddled gratefully against the welcome warmth of his body, and suddenly felt warm—very warm.

"Delivered safe and sound," he said when they reached her door. "I guess this is where we say good night, Rory."

"The least I can do is invite you in to get rid of the chill—but don't think it's more than that."

"That's an offer too good to refuse," Garth said, and stepped in behind her.

After lighting the lamp, Rory hurried over to the

door of her father's room for a quick inspection, then closed the door and rejoined him.

"Pop's asleep," she said.

"How's he feeling?"

"He seems to be over the worst of it, and insists he's getting out of bed tomorrow." Smiling fondly, she shook her head. "Oh, he's a terrible patient. He won't take one word of advice and will not admit he's getting too old for the shenanigans he once tried."

"How old is he?"

"He admits to being sixty, which makes me believe it's closer to seventy. In the past ten years he seems to have lost a year every time his birthday was mentioned."

Once again she shook her head of blond curls that his fingers were itching to get into. The intimacy of the dim lamplight, her nearness, her faint scent of lavender began to arouse him.

"Well, I guess I better leave."

"Where are you staying, Garth?"

"I thought I'd bed down at the livery where my horse is stabled."

Rory arched a curved brow. "You're the last person I'd expect to bed down in a livery."

"Why do you say that?"

"You don't act like the other saddle bums who pass through town."

"Is that so? What's so different about me?"

"Your bearing, manners, and education. You're no cowboy, Garth Fraser. That accent of yours reflects thoroughbreds, not mustangs, and maybe a dairy cow or two, not a cattle herd."

He folded his arms across his chest and leaned back against the wall. "Very intuitive, Miss O'Grady."

"I don't need intuition to know you don't smell like a cowboy. They all smell like horses; I swear none of them have ever seen the inside of a bathtub."

"As long as there're streams and rivers, a man doesn't need a bathtub. I found that out enough times during the war and the trek west."

"Well, I *do*," Rory declared. "Nothing feels as good to me as sinking into a tub of hot water."

"Dare I hope that's an invitation, Miss Rory O'Grady?"

"Definitely not."

"You don't know what you're missing," he teased. "I've been told I'm a great back scrubber, honey."

"No doubt, but I'm in no need of a back scrubber."

"Well, maybe next time." He picked up a book lying on the table. "I've noticed you with a book when you're not dancing. Do you enjoy reading?"

"Yes, I do. But due to little time and money, I have few opportunities to buy a book."

"Well, when I hit my strike, you'll be able to buy all the books you want."

"Oh, of course! Your gold mine." She chuckled in amusement. "How could I have forgotten?"

"You don't believe it's going to happen?"

"Do you have any idea how many men pass through here believing they'll hit the big strike? For over twenty years, miners have dug and scraped every ounce of gold possible out of California. What makes you think there'd still be some left for you?"

"Because my uncle sent us a map." Garth dug the map he had drawn from memory out of his pocket.

"If there was gold there, why didn't he mine it?"

"He got sick and died before he could, but he sent us a map marked where he staked a claim. Trouble is, we didn't get it until three years after he died."

"And did he send you proof that he filed the claim?"

"No. According to the doctor, Uncle Henry was feverish before he died."

"And maybe he was feverish when he sent you the map. This could all be a figment of his imagination. For heaven's sake, Garth, your uncle wasn't the only miner. Surely by now, another one would have discovered this bonanza, found it deserted, and mined it for himself."

"I don't think so. See this?" He pointed to an **X** on the map. "From what I've read about the big strikes in California, this area wasn't among them. Uncle Henry wrote that it's up in the mountains, way off the beaten path."

"That could mean the strike wasn't as big as your uncle thought, and whoever might have mined it didn't strike it big."

"You didn't know my uncle. Uncle Henry had been mining most of his life and could practically smell gold."

"If you're that sure about it, why haven't you claimed it sooner?"

"By the time I finished school and the military academy, the war broke out. My brother and I came west when the war ended. Then when I struck out to find the mine, he asked me to come back and give him a hand building his house."

"And where is he? Does he have gold fever, too?"

"Not Clay. His dream was opening a winery. Besides, he got married, fell in love, and now has a son."

"Isn't that just like a man? Marries, and then falls in love. I'm curious, was it with the same woman he married?"

"Of course! It's a long story that you'd probably enjoy hearing, but it's late, so I'll leave and let you get to bed." He folded up the map and slipped it back into his shirt pocket.

"How long do you intend to remain in town?"

"Since I'm convinced my two friends are gone and since the ship sailed on the morning tide, I figure there's no further threat. I thought I'd hang around for a day or two, maybe try my luck at poker."

Rory shook her head. "And I thought maybe you were different. No wonder you're sleeping in the livery."

"Not necessarily. The livery doesn't have bedbugs."

"No, just the smell of horses and manure."

"Yes, but horses don't bite when I'm sleeping like those cursed, blood-chomping bugs do."

She sighed deeply. "You're hopeless, Fraser. There's no sense in trying to reason with you. You can sleep here tonight. I can assure you there're no blood-chomping bugs in my bed."

His heartbeat quickened and arousal speared his loins with the heat and speed of a lightning bolt.

Slipping his arms around her, Garth drew her to his

chest. "I hope there's a lock on that adjoining door. Lord, how I want you, Rory." He lowered his head to kiss her.

She shoved him away. "What do you think you're doing?"

"I thought . . ." Reality set in at the indignation on her face, and he dropped his arms. "Not again!"

"Didn't I make it clear to you that I'm not a whore?"

"Yes, you did. That's why I had no intention of paying you."

"I'm sorry you misunderstood my offer. I didn't mean we would sleep together. I'll sleep in Pop's room on the floor again, like I did last night."

"I wouldn't think of taking your bed. I'll take your offer to stay for the night, but *I'll* sleep in your father's room."

"It didn't bother you last night. Why should it now?"

"Last night I fell asleep. You should have wakened me."

"With Bates and Skull still lurking around, I was afraid to let you leave. You were still drunk."

"I'm not drunk now, so give me a pillow and blanket." He winked. "I just hope my brothers never hear about this."

Paddy awoke and was surprised to hear a man's voice coming from Rory's room. His daughter was a fine, decent woman, and she had never brought a man home until now. He got out of bed and put his ear to the door to listen.

So this was the Fraser fellow she'd prevented from being shanghaied. When Rory had told him about the incident that morning, he could tell the stranger had made a big impression on his daughter.

Paddy was about to interrupt them when he heard Fraser mention a map of a gold mine. Any quick way to get rich appealed to him, and for a few years after Rory was born he'd tried gold mining; but the little bit of gold he'd discovered was not worth the hard labor it took to mine it. He was skillful enough at cards to at least keep a roof over their heads.

Kneeling, Paddy peeked through the keyhole and saw Fraser return a folded paper to his shirt pocket.

When their conversation turned to Fraser spending the night, he figured the time had come to make his presence known. No drifter was going to bed the daughter of Paddy O'Grady. Then he grinned when he heard Rory's rejection.

That's me daughter. You do your sainted mother proud, darlin'.

When he heard Fraser declare he'd sleep on the floor, Paddy curled his lip in displeasure. Nobody had asked him if he liked the arrangement. Shouldn't he have the say of it? Hearing them saying good night, Paddy scurried back to bed and pretended to be asleep when Fraser came in.

Long after the man fell asleep on the makeshift bed on the floor, Paddy lay awake on guard. There was no way this stranger was going to sneak into the other room and compromise his daughter.

*   *   *

Rory had caught up on her missed sleep and Garth was gone when she awoke the following morning.

"Did he say he was leaving town?" she asked Paddy.

"He didn't say." Her father tipped up her chin and she saw pity in his eyes. "He may be a fine man, darlin', but you know his intentions are improper."

"I know, Pop; I just enjoyed being around him. He's a refreshing change from the men I'm used to."

"Ah, darlin', one of these days a fine man like him will come along and see what a proper wife you'd make." He picked up his derby.

"Where are you going?"

"To stretch me legs. It's been two weeks since I've been up and about."

"If you wait until I dress, we can have breakfast together."

"I'm not hungry. I'll see you later, me dear."

"Well, take it slow, Pop, until you get your strength back," she warned.

"That I will, darlin'." He kissed her on the cheek and left, whistling.

A sudden growl in her stomach reminded Rory that she was hungry, so she dressed quickly and hurried to the diner.

As she lingered over a final cup of coffee, her thoughts were on Garth and Pop's words to her. Would the right man ever come along? She felt the rise of resentment. Of course she could never be good enough for Garth Fraser; after all, she was nothing but a cheap saloon gal in *his* eyes.

*   *   *

Garth had returned to Rory's rooming house, and when no one answered his knock, he'd spent the next quarter of an hour searching for her. He finally located her in the diner.

For a long moment he watched her through the window. She looked like a schoolgirl, with her face scrubbed clean and her long hair tied back with a blue ribbon. He felt the heated surge to his groin. Every time he saw her, his desire grew greater.

She appeared to be deep in thought as she gazed into space and raised a cup to her mouth to sip from it. The sight of it evoked a memory of Lissy and Becky sitting at the kitchen table, the morning he said good-bye to them several weeks ago. Despite that tough façade she presented, Rory was very much like them.

Sure, she was used to a different kind of life, but she wasn't any less vulnerable and feminine. And she probably harbored the same kinds of dreams as his sister and his brother's wife. And all three weathered whatever life threw at them with an amazing innocence—and a damn lot of grit.

Rory fascinated him. He liked her humor and the sound of her laughter. And every time he looked at her, his groin told him that wasn't *all* he liked about her. Yeah, he wouldn't mind sticking around for a couple more days—but right now, getting hung up on a gal didn't fit into his plans. A good time was all he had in mind.

Her expression suddenly changed, and he couldn't help grinning, because whatever she was thinking caused her to thrust that pert little chin of hers up in the air.

He opened the door and went inside. "Good morning, Miss O'Grady," he said with a wide smile.

"Good morning and good-bye." She resumed drinking her coffee.

"I've been peeking in store windows looking for the prettiest girl in town. I finally found her. May I join you?"

She glanced up at him. "Did I ever mention I can't abide cheery people in the morning until at least my second cup of coffee?"

He removed his hat, pulled out a chair, and sat down. "And how many cups have you had?"

"Only one."

He motioned to the nearby waiter.

"Pop said you left early," she said after the waiter refilled her cup.

"I'm an early riser."

"I usually am, too. I don't know what got into me," she said.

He leaned back in the chair and stared at her.

Finally she sighed and put down the cup. "Okay, what's on your mind, Fraser?"

"I was thinking how cute you look this morning."

"Cute?" She laughed infectiously. "Nobody's called me *cute* since my mother died. Don't tell me that line worked for you before, Fraser?"

"Well, how else would I describe you? Curls the color of cornsilk, eyes as blue as a summer sky, and cheeks as rosy as a . . . ah . . ."

"Rose," she gibed. "Please, Fraser, I just ate; give me a chance to digest my food."

"You feel like taking a walk, Rory? "

"Where to?"

"Some peaceful place where we can be alone."

She arched a brow. "And you only have talking in mind?"

"Why would you doubt it? I do have talking *in* mind, but since I met you, I'll admit I always have another thought *on* my mind. Afraid to take the risk?"

Despite her common sense, Rory was flattered by his continued attraction to her. And since she enjoyed his company, she felt confident enough to be reckless when she saw the challenge in his brown eyes.

"I know just the place," she said.

She led him to a shaded hillside overlooking the ocean, deserted except for some seagulls sunning themselves on the rocks below. They sat down and for a long moment gazed at the waves crashing against the rocks.

"It's nice here," he said. "Kind of as if you're in a different world, isn't it?"

"I discovered it a couple of weeks ago," Rory said. "I come here every day now to escape for a few hours. Just the seagulls, the ocean, and me."

He stretched out and tucked his hands under his head. "Do you ever plan on settling down, Rory?"

"Certainly. And I hope it will be sooner, rather than later. But I don't think I'll be that lucky. What about you?"

"Much later, rather than sooner. I'm just getting started," he said. "Where are you planning on going when you leave here?"

She gazed pensively at the blue waters of the Pacific. "Wherever the road leads, I guess. Do you have a wife or sweetheart waiting for you back in Virginia?"

"No wife. No sweetheart. I never came near to wanting either. Now the war's over, my folks are gone, and my brothers and sister have gotten on with their lives, so now I can get on with mine. What about you, Rory? Ever been married or in love?"

"No."

"How long do you expect to move around with your father?"

"I always figured on doing so until something or someone came along that appealed to me more. That hasn't happened yet, so I'll stick with Pop until it does. He and I get along well, and we're both pretty much our own person." Her eyes danced with deviltry. "Although he does accuse me at times of being as bossy as my maternal grandmother."

"What happens if you fall in love or get married?"

"Then I guess we'd have to go our separate ways, because I doubt a husband would want him to live with us, any more than Pop would be willing to give up his wandering ways. He's a nomad at heart—and very set in his ways. I love him dearly, though, and his illness really has me scared. I wish he *would* decide to settle down, but it's not his nature. Whatever you do, don't mention your gold mine to him, or he'll grab a pick and be off with you. You're both dreamers."

He sat up and she sensed what he was about to say. Before he could, she said, "So, you're getting ready to leave. Today or tomorrow?"

"Tomorrow morning."

"I could tell you were holding back something you didn't want to tell me. Why not? For the past two nights, I've been telling you to get out of this town. As soon as Pop gets his strength back we'll be saying good-bye to this place, too, and believe me, it will be the happiest day of my life."

"I hate to say good-bye to you, Rory."

She forced a smile. "You'd have to sometime anyway, so better sooner than later. Besides, you're not going to find gold in this town."

"How can you be sure? I might be looking at it right now."

Her eyes flashed with amusement. "Those are pretty sweet words, Garth Fraser, but I'm still not going to go to bed with you."

"I'm not saying it just to get you into bed, Rory; I mean what I said. There's something very different about you from the other girls I've met in saloons. And even though we've known each other for just a short time, I want you to know you can always count on me as a friend."

"Although I believe you're sincere, Garth, I think some of what you feel is more gratitude than friendship."

He picked up her hand and clasped it between his own. "Of course I'm grateful to you; you saved my life. But I meant what I said. As much as I want you physically, I want you as a friend just as much."

She laughed lightly. "So *that's* why you went upstairs with Shelia."

"Will you forget that, please? My brain was between my legs, Rory."

"I already figured that out—and it still is." She slipped her hand out of his.

Garth clutched his hands to his chest dramatically. "You wound me, lady. It's my heart that I'm thinking with now. Surely you must have a soft spot for me. How can you just say good-bye and that's the end of it, when you know how much I want to make love to you?"

"Some good-byes are more painful than others, and I admit I've come to like you very much—but I have no intention of letting you make love to me. So please don't make this any harder than it is."

He threw his hands up hopelessly. "Okay, I admit it. I had a score to settle with Bates and Skull and some unfinished business with you. So I sure wasn't going to run away. There's no doubt they're gone now; and try as I might, it looks like I'm not getting anywhere with you, either—so I guess I have no excuse to hang around any longer. But I expect to have the last laugh when I hit my strike and split it with you for saving my life."

"And just how do you expect to find me if you do?"

"Not if, *when*, I'll be so rich then, I'll be able to put a dozen bloodhounds to sniffing your trail."

She laughed gaily. "Well, I'll look forward to it. And you surprise me, Mr. Fraser. I didn't expect you to surrender so easily."

He rolled over on his side and pulled her down beside him. "Lady, if you're flirting with me, I could read a lot into that statement."

"Such as?" she asked, with a coquettish toss of her head.

Lying back, he pulled her across him and searched her face with a seductive gaze. "Like I said, we've some unfinished business, Rory O'Grady. And I'll find you again wherever you go."

"Even when you're as rich as Croesus," she teased.

"Richer," he murmured.

"You *are* making this good-bye painful," she whispered. Dipping her head, she kissed him.

"Oh, God, baby," Garth murmured, when she broke the kiss and raised her head. He slipped his hands into her hair and pulled her back.

"Don't get your hopes too high, because it won't do you any good. We've got company," she said breathlessly. She nodded toward two children who had appeared on the top of the hillside above them.

Garth sat up in disbelief. "Why, Lord? What did I ever do to deserve this?"

4

Later that evening as he waited for Rory, Garth sat in on a poker game with Paddy O'Grady and several other men. Within the hour he won over fifty dollars.

Seeing Rory come into the Grotto, Garth didn't want to waste any more time on a poker game. This would be their final night together, and he hadn't given up hope of getting her into bed.

"Deal me out." He shoved back his chair and picked up his winnings.

A belligerent, "You leaving?" came from a whiskey drummer named McGill, who had lost continually since they sat down.

Smiling good-naturedly, Garth said, "Mr. McGill, a beautiful woman just came in, and I have a tremendous urge to dance with her."

"Ain't right for you to leave, Fraser, without giving me a chance to win back some of my money."

"Sorry, Mr. McGill. And if I were you, I'd quit before you lose any more. Good luck, sir. You need it."

Garth moved over to Rory's table and laid down a dollar. "I believe this puts me on your dance card for the next four dances, Miss O'Grady."

"Pop having any luck in that poker game?" she asked as they circled the dance floor.

"He's doing real good for himself. See that drummer in the checkered vest? Not only is he the worst poker player I've ever seen, but he's been drinking steadily since he sat down. Booze and cards don't mix. I won fifty dollars from him, and your father at least twice that."

For the next hour Garth monopolized all of Rory's time. They danced or sat talking. If anyone approached her to dance, Garth would declare he had claimed her already, and they'd get up and dance again.

"You realize, Rory, I'm leaving first thing in the morning," he said when they sat back down.

"And I wish you a pleasant and safe journey," she said, amused.

"And you actually intend to let me leave without making me a *very* happy man?"

"I know. Sad, isn't it?" She patted his hand. "Life is full of one disappointment after another."

He leaned his forehead against hers. "But it doesn't have to be, Miss Rory."

"It does if you're figuring on me going upstairs with you." She drew away.

Garth clasped her hand. "What are you afraid of, Rory?"

She batted her eyelashes. "I'm afraid I'll enjoy it too much and will want to make it become a habit, but you'd no longer be here to satisfy me, so I'd have to settle for lower quality." She stood up. "Time to dance."

Garth got to his feet and took her in his arms. "Make jokes if you want to, honey, but can't you feel the excitement when our bodies touch?" he whispered. "At least let's go someplace where we can be alone without a dozen pairs of eyes on us."

"I don't think so; there's safety in numbers."

"Don't you trust yourself, Rory?"

"Of course I do."

He grabbed her by the hand. "Then come on, honey, we're getting out of here."

Suddenly, cursing, McGill got up from the poker table and staggered over to them. "I remember you. You were at the poker table. That old man cheated me."

"I don't think so, McGill."

"You in cahoots with him?"

"I'm not in cahoots with anyone. You're just a rotten poker player," Garth declared, clearly irritated by McGill's intrusion.

He was on the verge of succeeding in his goal with Rory and wasn't about to let this loudmouth drunk interfere with his plans. "Now if you'll excuse us, McGill, the lady and I were about to leave."

They moved past him, then Rory froze in her tracks when McGill yelled, "The old man cheated me, and he's gonna pay for it. Nobody gets away with cheating Bill McGill."

Chairs crashed to the floor as the other poker players scrambled away when McGill reached for the gun in his pocket.

Before he could even draw it, he found himself looking at the drawn Colt in Garth's hand.

"Don't even think it," Garth warned.

"I was right; you're working with him," McGill accused.

"Wrong again, McGill, but I'm not going to stand by and watch a drunken loser like you shoot down an unarmed man."

"It's not your fight, Fraser," Mo said. "If O'Grady was cheatin', he deserves what he gets."

"I wasn't cheating," Paddy said. "And there's no man here who can ever accuse Paddy O'Grady of cheating at cards."

"He's right, Mo," one of the other players called out. "Paddy was havin' a lucky run of cards, and this fella didn't have the sense to fold when he should of."

Garth slipped his gun back in its holster and turned away to rejoin Rory.

Too drunk to quit while he was ahead, McGill picked up a chair. Rory cried out a warning and Garth turned, too late to ward off the blow that knocked him off his feet. He crashed into the table where Paddy was sitting, and before he could get to his feet, the drunken man leaped on him. The two men wrestled for a long moment before Garth was able to pin McGill's arms to the floor.

"Garth, behind you," Rory cried out.

The warning came too late, and Mo's blackjack smashed him in the head. Garth pitched forward, unconscious.

Attracted by the noise, the sheriff rushed into the bar. "What in hell's going on here?"

In the commotion that followed, nobody noticed Paddy O'Grady use his foot to shove under the table the folded paper that had fallen out of Garth's shirt during the scuffle. He sat back down in his seat, and then bent and picked up the paper and slipped it into his pocket.

"I want you to lock this bum up," Mo said, pointing to Garth lying unconscious on the floor. "He's been trouble ever since he showed up here."

"He didn't start the fight. That man did," Rory declared, pointing to McGill.

"The guy's drunk, and Fraser threw a punch at him," Mo said. "So I whacked him on the head before he could cause any more trouble."

The sheriff bent over Garth. "Ain't this the same guy who claimed a couple guys tried to shanghai him?"

"Yeah, when the two were sitting in here all the time," Mo said. Rory saw him exchange a meaningful glance with the sheriff. "I told you he's trouble."

"Fraser was telling the truth," Rory said. "I was there and saw them."

The sheriff ignored her. "Someone help me tote this guy over to the jail. Maybe a night behind bars will cool him down."

"What about McGill?" Rory demanded. "He was going to shoot my father, and Fraser stopped him. That's how the fight started."

"Can anyone here back up what she's saying?" the sheriff asked.

"I can," Paddy said. "The lad only tried to help me."

Mo snorted. "Don't pay no attention to him."

"Yeah, he cheated in the poker game," McGill accused.

One of the other men spoke up. "That ain't true, Sheriff Buckman. I sat in on that game, and Paddy wasn't cheating."

"Okay, Mr. McGill, get out of here and sleep it off," Buckman said. "Polk, give me a hand with this big fellow."

As soon as the sheriff departed, Mo turned to Rory. "You're through here—you and your father. I don't want either of you steppin' a foot back in here again." He snatched off the velvet pouch Rory had pinned to her gown. "And I'll keep what you made tonight to pay for the chair your boyfriend broke. Now, get going. Both of you."

"Get packing, darlin'," Paddy declared as soon as they returned to their rooms. "We're leaving on the morning stage."

"What's the big rush, Pop? You aren't ready yet to do any traveling. And I want time to say good-bye to the friends I've made here."

"What friends?" Paddy asked. "I'm thinking you mean that Fraser fella."

"I would like to make sure he's okay, Pop. After all, he did save your life. That drunken McGill would have killed you if Garth hadn't intervened."

"Garth, is it! More call for us to be leaving, before you have any more to do with the man. He's a drifter, girl, and once he has his way with you, he'll leave."

"You're a stubborn man, Pop, and once you get a thought in your mind, there's no changing it. I know what Garth's up to, but I'm grateful to him for saving the life of the only man I love." She kissed him on the cheek. "Besides, I think we should stop and consider where we want to go."

Paddy held up a finger and winked. "I've done the considering." He pulled Garth's map out of his pocket and spread it out on the table. "We'll be going right there," he said, pointing to the **X** on the map.

"Why, that's the map Garth showed me." Frowning, she asked, "What are you doing with it?"

"I won it from him in the poker game."

Rory looked doubtful. "Garth wouldn't give up his map, Pop; that gold mine's his dream. You must give it back to him."

"Are you daft, girl? I'll do no such thing. Me heart aches for the lad, but he'd have taken me money if *he'd* won the hand."

"I don't care. Besides, it's crazy to go chasing off after a gold mine that he didn't even know if his uncle had filed a claim on."

He cocked a shaggy brow at her and with a wily smile asked, "What do you really know about the man, darlin'? Could be he has a dozen of these fake maps and is conning poor souls like meself out of our money."

"That's nonsense! Garth's an honest man. Pop, you think up a ridiculous scheme like that, and then start believing it yourself."

"So you say. But gold brings out the worst in people."

Disgusted, she said, "I can see that. Furthermore, if you're so sure it's a fake map, why are you so eager to rush off to it?"

"What have we got to lose, darlin'?"

"For one thing, it takes a grubstake. We don't have much money."

"I won enough to get us started," he said with a cocky smile.

"And what do we do when we run out of money? Oh, Pop, between you and Garth, you don't have the common sense of a gnat! What if the map's genuine? At least we should have the decency to ask him and find out if he wants to come with us."

Paddy shook his head. "Why? So's he can run off with the gold when we're through?"

"But you're convinced it's a fake."

"Me mind's made up, girl. Are you coming with me or not?"

Rory sighed in resignation. "I can't very well let you roam around the mountains alone. Lord knows what might happen to you. And I can't stay here. Sheriff Buckman will see to that. But like it not, we only give it thirty days. If we don't strike gold by then, we leave. Do you agree?"

"Agreed." Padddy grinned widely, then kissed her cheek. "That's me girl."

"I still feel it's not fair to Garth. We're indebted to him for saving your life tonight."

"And you saved his, didn't you? So the score's even."

Whistling, he danced a jig into his room.

Thoughts of Garth troubled her mind as Rory stared at her image in the cracked mirror on the wall. "Maybe it's just as well you don't say good-bye to him. Leaving now will save you a lot of heartache later. As for the money, Pop might as well waste it on mining supplies instead of whiskey."

Desolately, she turned away and pulled out a worn carpetbag from under the bed, packed her few belongings, and went to bed.

But sleep didn't come easy. The last couple of days had been almost magical to her. Garth was very exciting to be around. He was handsome and amusing to talk to. She bet they could talk for hours, and she'd never get bored listening to the deep warmth of his voice.

His kisses thrilled her. A shiver rippled her spine when she thought of the heat of his hand when he clasped hers, and the feel of it on her back, with his warm breath against her ear as he whispered to her when they danced.

She knew his intentions were to get her in bed with him, and there were times when they were talking and dancing that the thought had certainly crossed her mind. Her insides tingled when she was with him. Never having been intimate with a man before, she had no idea what she was feeling. She could only guess that having sex must be a wondrous sensation, since it drove men to spend even their last dollar to have it.

And she thought of how close she had come to succumbing to that sweet seduction today by the coastline. It would have been such a mistake.

Early the following morning, as she climbed on the stagecoach, Rory cast a lingering backward glance at the jailhouse.

Good-bye, Garth Fraser. It was lovely knowing you.

Garth sat up on the cot and looked around. Since his arrival in Buckman three nights ago, he'd awakened every morning in a different bed. How in hell had he ended up in a jail cell?

"So you're finally awake."

Not the best good morning to wake to. It was clear he wasn't going to win any popularity awards in this town.

"Good morning, Sheriff. Why am I locked up in here?"

"Disturbin' the peace."

"You mean that fight in the Grotto?"

"What do you think?"

"I didn't start that fight, Sheriff. McGill was threatening to shoot Paddy O'Grady."

"I've got a witness that says otherwise."

"Who is it?"

"Mo Buckman," the sheriff said.

"Buckman? Isn't that your name, too?"

"Yeah, Mo and me are cousins."

Great. "Sheriff Buckman, there were over a half-dozen people in that bar who must have seen and heard what happened."

"Zat so? Well, Mo was the only one who spoke up."

"I know Rory O'Grady witnessed it all."

Buckman snorted. "I ain't gonna take the word of a saloon whore over the town's mayor."

"Mo's the town's mayor?" Talk about kangaroo courts! He would never get out of this cell.

"Yeah, he founded the town. Put up his saloon, and before we knew it, we had a town. I'm givin' you a break," Buckman said, unlocking the cell door. "You've got a hour to get your ass out of town, Fraser. You've been nothin' but trouble since you showed up here." The sheriff shoved Garth's gun belt and hat at him. "If I see your ugly face around here, I'm shipping you to prison."

"Whatever happened to innocent until proven guilty, Sheriff?"

"Don't push me, Fraser. Ain't that smart-ass mouth of yours got you into enough trouble already? Get going."

"After I say good-bye to the O'Gradys, no one will be happier than I to leave this town."

Buckman smirked. "Them two hightailed it out of here on the morning stage."

"Why did they do that?"

"Maybe because my cousin kicked their asses out of his saloon."

"You mean he fired Rory?"

"Her and her drunken father. Clock's ticking, Fraser."

"Did Rory leave me a note?"

"Does this look like a post office? Get the hell out of here before I change my mind."

Garth headed for the telegraph office. The day he'd arrived, he'd wired Clay his whereabouts. Clay had wired him back and told him that their brother Colt was on the way to California, and had married a woman in New Mexico.

Garth couldn't help grinning as he moved on to the livery. The gal must be some woman, to convince his brother to marry. Colt had always been as much of a free spirit as Garth was.

They'd had some great times together, and Garth realized how much he missed his brother. In addition to which, he sure would like to meet his new sister-in-law. Maybe he should head back to Clay's and wait for their arrival before continuing on.

But it would be stupid to turn back after coming this far. He'd made it up to Sacramento before, and had turned back to help Clay build a house, then sat out the winter with him and Becky.

With the fifty bucks he won last night, this might be the time to get himself set up at the mine, before the cold weather moved in.

At the livery, he paid for boarding his horse Boots, then sat down on a bale of hay to chart his course. He reached into his shirt pocket for the map he'd drawn . . . but it was missing. He always kept the map in that pocket; the sheriff had probably taken it.

Fortunately he had put his poker winnings in the toes of his boots along with his other money, but the few dollars he had kept in his pocket were missing.

He cursed in disgust. The damn sheriff had cleaned him out. It's a wonder the sonofabitch hadn't stolen his Colt, too.

Well he'd drawn that map from memory, and he could do it again. If that crooked sheriff and his cronies had any intention of jumping that claim, he wasn't going to let them get away with it. No claim jumpers were going to cheat him out of Uncle Henry's mine!

Garth saddled Boots and rode out of Buckman.

5

The battered sign on the town's outskirts read HOPE. The stage pulled up in front of a store and the driver jumped down from the box and opened the door. "This is your stop, folks."

"But we want to go to Tierra de Esperanza," Rory said, struggling with the Spanish words.

"Yeah, Land of Hope," the driver said. "This is it. Years ago, folks around these parts dropped all those Mex words and settled on just Hope."

A young boy in the gown of an altar boy ran up and handed the driver a sealed parcel. "Buenos días, Señor Charlie."

"Same to you, Pedro." The driver tossed it up to the man in the box, who shoved it into a canvas bag on the floor.

"¿Ha llegado el correo de hoy?" the boy asked.

"No, Pedro. No mail today." The driver reached into his shirt pocket and pulled out a peppermint stick. "But I've got this for you."

"Gracias, Señor Charlie," he exclaimed with a wide smile. Then he ran back toward a Catholic mission surrounded by a pink stucco wall at the end of the road.

"The assayer's office closed up 'bout ten years ago." The driver pointed to the mission. "You best see Father Chavez. He'll probably know about claims; he keeps all the town records. Good luck, folks."

He climbed back up on the box and the stagecoach rumbled off, leaving Rory and Paddy in the middle of the road.

Rory's gaze swept the town. After three days of being bounced and rocked in hot, dusty stagecoaches, they had finally reached their destination in the heart of the Sierra Nevada Mountains.

Most of the buildings were dilapidated. Caught by a gust of wind, the broken chain that dangled from a sign marked HOTEL, lashed the air like a whip. Rory's gaze halted on a decent appearing structure with a wooden sign that read TIENDA in big, bold letters with GENERAL Y COMESTIBLE painted directly under. Lower and in smaller print, the words *General* and *Vegetable* identified the store in English.

What had Pop gotten them into this time? She had no heart for this latest venture. Why couldn't he have let Garth keep the map? Recalling Garth's excitement and enthusiasm over it, she felt guilty. It had meant so much to him because his uncle had sent it to him.

What they had done was as bad as stealing a Christmas gift from a child.

Sighing, she picked up her carpetbag and headed for the mission. She smiled and nodded when several children who were playing in the dust and mud of the street looked at them with curiosity. They got up and raced ahead of the new arrivals toward the mission.

As Rory walked up the street, she could feel the curious stares from people who were sitting on rickety chairs and porch stoops. Most appeared to be Mexican, with a few Anglo faces among them. They whispered among themselves, but none came forward to greet them.

Upon hearing the sound of voices and strum of a guitar, Paddy's eyes suddenly sparked with pleasure and he paused in front of the building marked CAN-TINA.

"Darlin'," he said, with a grin as Irish as a field of shamrocks, "I've a fierce thirst from the trip. You go on an' I'll just slip in here to ease the parch of it."

"I'm thirsty too, Pop, and you're coming with me. I'm sure the kind father will offer us a cool glass of water to quench our thirsts."

"You've the mercy of yer Grandmother Finn, Rorleen Catherine O'Grady. Black-hearted witch that she was," he grumbled.

"Pop, shame on you. Mum always told me not to speak evil of the dead. And she always said what a good and kindly Christian woman Grandmother was."

"Aye, that she did," Paddy said, with the hint of moistness in his eyes. "Your sainted mother would not speak an evil word about anyone." He rolled his eyes heavenward. "Even one as undeserving as Chloe Finn."

"Then I think you should follow Mum's example." She marched ahead, ignoring the continuous grumbling from her father who followed behind.

The children had carried the word to the aging priest, who was waiting to greet them when they reached the mission.

"Welcome, my children," Father Chavez said. "Come in and rest yourselves."

Father Chavez was a short man with a thick crop of pure white hair and a smile as wide as the Missouri River. Despite his advanced age, he was neither stooped nor slow of step, and from his greeting, he had a better grasp of the English tongue than did Paddy.

"May I offer you a cooling drink to refresh yourselves?"

"That's very kind of you, Father," Rory said.

The priest's brown eyes were warm with friendliness and curiosity. "What brings you to Tierra de Esperanza?"

Before Rory could answer, a woman carried in a tray with a pitcher, glasses, and a small plate of cookies.

"Gracias, Elena. ¿Quiere ir con nosotros?"

With a shy smile, she shook her head and hurried from the room.

"Forgive me. I hope you are not offended. My sister Elena is very shy and declined my offer to join us."

"You mean you are brother and sister by birth?" Rory asked.

"Sí, Señorita O'Grady. Elena was just a young girl when my mother came here to be my housekeeper. When our mother died, Elena remained and took over those responsibilities. What is your purpose for coming here to our town, Señorita O'Grady?"

Rory took the map from her purse. They had invested time and money in this venture, and in fear her father would wager the map in a card game, she had taken it from him to make certain of its safekeeping.

"We want to know if this claim has been filed."

Father Chavez stretched the map out on the table and studied it intently. "Where did you get this, Señor O'Grady?"

"From a friend," Paddy spoke up quickly.

Rory would have preferred he tell the priest how he got it, but since she considered Garth a friend, she decided to hold her tongue.

"These are very old markings on the map. Gold mining in that area has become nonexistent."

"Why is that, Father?" Rory asked.

"The Indians either killed the miners or drove them out. When the Indians moved on, the bandidos arrived. Many have made their homes in these mountains. The few miners up there failed to get enough out of their mines to make the risk they were taking worthwhile. They moved on to—how do you say it?— greener pastures."

"So you're saying there's no longer any mining in the particular area of this map."

"None on that mountain that I know of, Señorita O'Grady."

"The driver of the stage said that you keep the records since the assayer moved out. Would you be able to tell us if anybody has filed a claim on this particular site?"

"I know of no one who has done so, señorita."

"Not even in the past ten years? How can you be sure?"

"Because the last man who intended to file in that area died before he could do so."

"Then we'll be doing it, Father," Paddy said.

"I advise you against such a venture, Mr. O'Grady."

"I'm not one to slight the wishes of a holy father, but Paddy O'Grady is not one to run from a fight, Father Chavez."

"Very well—if I can't persuade you." Chavez went to a cabinet and withdrew a large metal box and began to page through the yellowed records.

"The owner of the claim filed nearest that area has not been seen or heard from since he left here fifteen years ago."

"Maybe we should reconsider this, Pop," Rory said.

"Me mind's made up, Daughter. But I don't want you to come along if there's a chance of you getting hurt."

"We've been through this before, Pop. I won't let you go alone."

The priest extracted a yellow form from the metal file box, sat down at the table, and dipped the nib of the pen into an inkwell. "Your full names, Señor?" he asked.

"Patrick Michael and Rorleen Catherine O'Grady," Paddy said.

"Do you wish both names as owners on the claim?"

Rory smiled. "One for all, and all for one, Father Chavez."

When they finished their business, she asked, "Do you think the general store has the equipment to get us started?"

"There's no doubt of it," the priest replied. "Señor Hastings, the storekeeper, was left with a large stock of mining supplies when the miners stopped coming. No doubt he would welcome the opportunity to sell it cheaply to get some return of his money.

"The mountain is very rocky. Are you a skilled rider, Señorita O'Grady?"

Rory shook her head. "Not in the least."

"Then I suggest you buy a donkey or a mule to ride, and a burro for your supplies. I'm sure Pablo Hernandez can be of help. He raises donkeys and burros. His business, too, has slowed in the past years, and he is having difficulty finding graze to keep them fed."

Mr. Hastings, the storekeeper, was very helpful in recommending what they would need, and he stocked them with a coffeepot, a cast-iron skillet and pot, cooking spoons and a chopping knife, tin plates and cups, and knives, forks, and spoons.

To that he added an ax for chopping firewood, a pickax for mining, shovels for digging, buckets for toting water, canteens, a couple of lanterns and a box of candles, matches and a flint, and a rifle and box of cartridges.

Then there were pillows, blankets, the necessary toilet articles, towels and washcloths, and soap.

Then came the food staples: coffee, flour and baking powder for making sourdough bread or biscuits, onions, beans, carrots, dried peaches and apples, a peck and a half of potatoes, and the necessary condiments of sugar, molasses, cinnamon, and salt and pepper.

"That should last you for a good month, Miz O'Grady," Hastings said.

"What are we having for meat, Mr. Hastings?" Rory asked.

"There's plenty of game and fish in the mountains, ma'am."

"Neither my father nor I are hunters or fishermen, sir."

"Ma'am, if I understand you right, you and your father cannot ride a horse, you don't camp out, don't hunt or fish, and you don't know anything about gold mining. Gold mining is hard, backbreaking, and dangerous work. Why are you doing this?"

"It's my father's idea, Mr. Hastings. Not mine."

Shaking his head, Hastings added hardtack, dried beef, bacon, and chicken jerky to the purchases.

By the time they paid for their supplies, their grubstake had been exhausted.

"I'll pack your purchases into my wagon and bring them up to the mission," Hastings said.

"Thank you, Mr. Hastings."

"Miss O'Grady, I sincerely hope you strike it rich," he said.

"I think I'll stop off for a bit of a nip," Paddy said as they passed the cantina.

"Don't be too long, Pop. Father Chavez has invited us to dinner."

Paddy entered the cantina, and to his delight the saloon was empty except for the bartender. "Amigo," Paddy said, and he slipped an arm around the old man's shoulders. "I'm going off for a time and will be needing some whiskey."

The old man stepped behind the bar and put a shot glass down in front of Paddy and filled it.

"No, amigo, 'tis a full bottle I'm seeking," Paddy said. "But as long as it's poured, I'll have me a nip." He downed the drink, then grinned. "But 'tis an unopened bottle I'm wanting."

The old man looked perplexed, so Paddy pointed to a sealed bottle among the others on the shelf behind the bar. "Like that one."

"Oh, sí, señor," the bartender nodded in understanding. He handed the bottle of tequila to him.

Struggling to conceal his impatience, Paddy said, "No, I want whiskey, my friend."

The old man threw his hands up and nodded. "Oh, sí, señor, whisky." He reached under the bar and pulled out a sealed pint bottle. "*Whisky!*"

"Aye, that's close enough. And a fine man you are, indeed." He held up his hand and counted off his fingers. " 'Tis five of them I'm wanting."

"Cinco!" the old man said excitedly. He opened a cabinet and placed five bottles of whiskey on the bar.

"That's me man," Paddy said, pleased. He dug out the money he'd held back from Rory and laid it on the bar as the man wrapped the bottles in a woven straw pouch. After the bartender extracted the cost, several coins remained.

Paddy's wide grin carried to his eyes. "Well, me friend, there's enough for us to have another wee nip. Will you do me the pleasure of joining me, amigo?"

Grinning, the old man poured them each a drink.

Paddy raised his glass. "May you be in Heaven ten minutes before the devil knows you're dead."

The two old men clinked their glasses together and downed their drinks, then Paddy tipped his hat and picked up the pouch. "Good day, me friend."

He cocked his derby at a jaunty angle and ambled out the door whistling.

That night they stayed in a room at the mission that Father Chavez kept for the use of travelers, and early the following morning he made another attempt to persuade Rory to remain there.

"It is no place for a woman, my child. The bandidos are very bad and ruthless."

"I can't let him go alone, Father. Pop depends on me."

"And you cannot convince him to abandon this search?"

"I've tried, Father, but you can see for yourself; he's a very stubborn man."

They climbed on the two mules, Father Chavez stood at the gate of the mission and watched sadly as they departed.

"Vaya con Dios, hijos mios," he murmured, and made the sign of the cross.

*　　　*　　　*

Dismounting, Garth led Boots behind a large boulder. He pulled a small telescope out of his saddlebag, then grabbed his rifle out of the saddle holster and scaled the boulder, stretched out on it, and waited.

Soon he spied a distant movement and brought the spyglass to his eye. From a distance he had thought it was a wolf that had been trailing him for the past few miles, but as it drew nearer he saw that the animal was a shaggy dog.

Within minutes the dog had come close enough for Garth to see that despite the tongue hanging from its mouth, the animal showed no sign of being rabid. He wasn't going to take any careless chances, though; he cocked the rifle. A wild dog could be as deadly as a wolf, and this dog was following either his or Boots's scent.

On the other hand, the poor dog could just be thirsty and hungry. There was a good way to find out. Garth uncocked his rifle and climbed down.

He pulled a piece of jerky out of a saddlebag and put it on the ground, then poured some water from his canteen onto a tin plate and set it beside the jerky. Garth climbed back on Boots and rode a short distance away, but remained in plain sight.

When the animal appeared, Garth saw that it was limping. The dog halted about thirty yards away from him and neither growled nor snarled, but just stared.

After a long moment, it moved closer. There was nothing threatening about the move, no indication it intended to attack, so Garth cautiously lowered his rifle.

The dog limped to the food and lapped up the water, then devoured the jerky. Returning the rifle to its sling, Garth grabbed the canteen and climbed down. Still cautious, he kept his right hand on the Colt at his hip, and went over to the animal and poured some more water onto the plate. Although the dog didn't make a sound, its gaze remained on Garth's every move. As soon as he stepped back, the dog gulped down the liquid.

Garth had been around domesticated animals his whole life and recognized that this dog was used to being around humans. In all probability, the animal was lost or its owner had perished.

"You lost, fella?" he asked in a gentle tone, and began to stroke him. "And thirsty, aren't you?" He poured a little more water on the plate. "Not too fast, fella," he warned, when the dog quickly lapped it up.

Garth broke off another piece of jerky and the dog immediately chewed it up. When it finished eating, the dog stretched out with its head on its paws and *stared* at him.

Garth fed him another piece of jerky, this time from his hand. "How about letting me take a look at that rear paw, fella?" he asked. When he started to reach for the injured paw, the dog issued a low growl, so Garth got up and walked away to make camp for the night. There was no way he would abandon the injured dog; he could push on to Hope tomorrow.

After unsaddling Boots and feeding him some oats and water, Garth built a fire and filled a small coffeepot, then sat down to wait for it to brew. Rather than use any more of the scarce water preparing a meal, he settled for some hardtack and jerky, which he shared with the dog.

Before bedding down for the night, he decided to try again to examine the dog's paw. This time the injured dog lay quietly and allowed him to do so.

Blood had caked around a splinter embedded deeply in the pad of the paw. There was no end he could grip to try and pull it out; he would have to dig it out.

"You're not going to like this, fella," he warned as he heated his knife. After several attempts he succeeded in removing the splinter; then he poured iodine on the wound and bound it with a bandage.

Throughout the ordeal the dog had twitched at times, but never uttered a whimper or growl. "You did good, fella," Garth said, patting the dog. "It should feel a lot better by tomorrow."

After finishing off the remaining coffee, Garth bedded down for the night.

He awoke at dawn the next morning to discover the dog cuddled against him.

6

Garth had been traveling for a good seven hours when he finally reached his destination. He halted at the outskirts of the town encompassed within the snow-capped peaks of the Sierra Nevada Mountains.

Although the word *Hope* was written on the battered sign, the sheriff in Sonora had assured him it would be the town he was looking for, Tierra de Esperanza.

It was the hottest time of the day, and his shirt clung to him in patches of perspiration. He should have had the good sense to have gotten out of the sun; instead he'd kept pushing on, expecting to reach the town over every rise he'd come to.

This trip recalled the tiring trek to California the previous year when he, Clay, and Becky had crossed another part of this mountain range. It had been the same then: blazing hot during the day and cool at night.

This search had reversed part of that journey. Following the route of the map, upon leaving Sacramento he had traveled through dense forests to the junction of the Sacramento and Joaquin rivers, and from there the Tuolumme River over boulder canyons to Sonora.

Garth untied the bandanna from around his neck and wiped away the sweat, then took off his hat and did the same to his brow. With another swipe of the bandanna around the inside band, he plopped the hat back on his head and then raised himself in the saddle enough to look back at the trail. In the distance he caught sight of the dog, still following behind in a steady trot.

"Maybe its home is here, Boots," he murmured, and rode into the town.

Like so many of the scattered little towns he'd ridden through, this one was in an extreme state of decline. There wasn't a smidgen of shade or a horse trough the whole length of the dusty main street, and being siesta time, it was deserted as well. Garth stopped in front of the general store, one of the few businesses that appeared to still be in operation. Dismounting, he tethered Boots.

A bell tinkled overhead when he entered the store, and the dozing proprietor awoke and got to his feet.

"Howdy," he said.

"Hello," Garth said cordially. "Hot out there, isn't it?"

"Yep. Folks don't try to move around too much this time of day. Best to stay still. You a stranger in these parts?"

"Yes, I am," Garth said.

"Huh. Third stranger to pass through in as many days."

His words struck a chord with Garth. "Is that so? Were they two men?"

The storekeeper eyed him warily. "You a lawman?"

"No. Why, do I look like one? Name's Garth Fraser."

"Can't say you do, Mr. Fraser. But you don't look like no trail bum passing through, either." He extended his hand. "Pleased to meet you, Mr. Fraser. Name's John Hastings." Hastings gave him a quizzical look. "Say, you wouldn't be related to Henry Fraser, would you? He had an accent that sounded like yours."

"I did have an Uncle Henry who lived in these parts before he died."

"Yep, lived right here in this town," Hastings said. "Bought all his supplies from me. Henry was a good man. I felt real bad when he passed on. You here on business, Mr. Fraser, or just passing through?"

"Actually I'm looking for the Misión de La Dueña de Esperanza, Mr. Hastings. Can you tell me where it's located?"

"Right up at the end of the road. You can't miss it. It's got a pink wall around it."

"Thank you, sir."

"Real pleasure talking to you, Mr. Fraser," Hastings called out as Garth left the store. "Any friend of Henry's is a friend of mine."

The dog had caught up to him and was stretched out next to the hitching post.

"So you made it, fella." He gave the dog's head a pat, then mounted and headed for the mission at the other end of the town.

The dog rose to its feet and once again followed them.

The gates of the mission were open, and Garth entered the courtyard. Unlike the floral gardens characteristic of most of the Spanish patios he had seen, this one had nothing more than several benches under four trees that offered some shade. The rest of the courtyard could boast only a vegetable garden and, at the moment, the most important thing—a well. A building that appeared to be the church was connected to the larger one by a roofed passageway.

A priest rose from the shade of a bench and approached him. "Greetings, my friend. I'm Father Chavez. How may I help you?"

"Hello, Father." Garth dismounted and removed his hat. "My name is Garth Fraser, and I've been told this is where to come to find out about previous mine claims."

The priest stared at him with an intensity that seemed to go beyond mere curiosity. Garth shifted uneasily and wondered if he'd become a face on a wanted poster.

"How strange that after all these years, you are the third person who has come this very week with such an inquiry, Señor Fraser. Come inside, and we'll see if I can be of any service to you."

"Do you mind if I water my horse first, Father?"

"Of course not. And your dog as well," the priest said, leading them over to the well.

"Actually the dog is not mine," Garth said, as he poured the bucket of well water into his hat. He held it up to Boots's mouth. "He's been following me since yesterday. I was hoping he belonged to someone here in town."

"He does not look familiar. I see he is favoring a paw."

"Yes, there was a splinter in the pad, so I did the best that I could for him."

"Bless you, my son, for we are all God's creatures." Then Father Chavez's dark eyes lit with merriment. "And I think you have made a friend of this four-legged one for life, señor." The priest ladled water into a bowl and placed it on the ground in front of the dog.

Garth loosened the cinch on Boots, led him over to the shade, and tethered him to a tree. The dog followed and stretched out on the ground.

"Now you must come inside where it is cooler. There you, too, can refresh yourself, Señor Fraser," Father Chavez said. "Then we will get to the business you seek."

The priest was right about the inside being cooler, and Garth sat down and relaxed. As worn as the sofa was, it was a reminder of how long it had been since he had sat and leaned back on something other than a hard chair or armless bench. For a fleeting instant, he felt a heavy sensation of homesickness pressing on his heart at the thought of the home he was raised in and the people he loved and missed.

A woman brought in a pitcher and glasses, and once again Garth felt uncomfortable under her intense stare.

"Where is your home, Señor Fraser?" the priest asked as they drank the refreshing glasses of lemonade.

"Virginia, Father."

"Do you intend to return there?"

"Sometime, sir. I have no definite date in mind, but certainly not before I accomplish what I came to California to do."

"And is that what has brought you to Tierra de Esperanza?"

"Yes, sir."

Father Chavez rose to his feet. "Then what is it you wish to know from me, Señor?"

Garth reached into his pocket and pulled out the new map he had drawn. The priest spread it out on the table and gave it a slight glance. "This is the same map I looked at just days ago."

Damn it! Buckman had gotten here ahead of him.

"Did you get this from the man and woman who filed the claim?" the priest asked.

"Man and woman!" Garth exclaimed, perplexed. "What were their names?"

Father Chavez opened the huge ledger, its pages yellowed from age. "The claim was filed by Patrick Michael and Rorleen Catherine O'Grady. How did you get this map, Señor Fraser? Did you steal it from them?"

"Just the opposite, Father; they stole it from me. That is, they stole the one that I had drawn from memory. I redrew it when I discovered the theft of the first one. The original is still in Virginia. Uncle Henry, my father's younger brother, sent it to us before he died."

The priest nodded. "And your uncle was Henry Fraser."

"Yes. So he did file a claim on his mine?"

"Not to my knowledge. And since your uncle came here often to attend mass, Señor Fraser, I doubt he would have gone elsewhere to file the claim."

"Mass? You mean he converted to Catholicism?"

"Oh, yes. Henry died right here at the mission."

"I didn't know that. Uncle Henry never mentioned his conversion in any of his letters. And a doctor was the one who informed us of his death."

"Yes, Dr. Estaban. The good doctor was leaving for Sacramento and offered to inform you of the sad news. I'm glad to hear he took the time to do so."

He took his time, all right—three years, to be exact. "The doctor said nothing about the mission, so we assumed Uncle Henry died in Sacramento. Did he suffer very long, Father Chavez?"

"I can't speak for the length of his suffering, but he remained with us for about a month before he passed on into the hands of our Blessed Lord."

Still stunned, Garth said, "I can't believe I've actually met someone who was with him at the end. I worshiped my Uncle Henry, and I'm glad to hear that he was with someone who cared when he died."

"We all cared greatly for Henry Fraser, my son. And he spoke often, and with abounding love and pride, of his nephews." The priest's eyes appeared to twinkle with enjoyment. "You were his favorite, you know."

Garth grinned with pleasure. "Really? I had no idea. Sure wish I could have spent more time with him."

"You have an opportunity to do so now, my son, and to say a final good-bye. Your uncle is buried in the cemetery behind the church."

"If you don't mind, I would like to do that, Father, then come back and finish our business."

"I will be glad to. I must leave now and hear confessions; just go out that door at the rear. You will see the cemetery."

As Garth reached the iron fence that enclosed the small cemetery, the dark-haired woman who had served their drinks came hurrying out. Garth tipped his hat and stepped aside. She lowered her head and nodded, then rushed away.

It did not take long to find his uncle's grave. A freshly watered small pine tree stood behind the simple cross carved with the inscription HENRY FRASER, 1811–1847.

"I've thought about you so often, Uncle Henry," Garth said softly. "We didn't get the letter you wrote us until three years after you died. I'm glad I finally found you. You have a peaceful resting place in this quiet spot, with a view of the mountains in the distance. And I make this oath, Uncle Henry: I'll let no one cheat the family of your legacy. I'll get your mine back," Garth vowed.

He spent a short time passing among the grave markers, looking at the dates that reflected almost two centuries of Spanish colonization.

At dusk, when a setting sun had dimmed the light into blue shadows, Garth went for a walk in the town—not that there was much to see.

To Garth, who took an optimistic approach about most things, there was something sad about the dying town. He couldn't help thinking about the people who had once lived there. What had become of the dreams they had brought with them?

A town didn't suddenly appear from nowhere; it had to have begun with people—their hopes, their optimism, their faith. Had they all been for naught? Trampled into dust? Or had some seen their hopes and dreams come to fruition?

And was it truly gold that had lured his uncle to this place, or was it destiny that had drawn Henry Fraser? And now him, as well?

His gaze swung to the nearest mountain peak towering above the town. In the fading light of day it appeared shadowy, ominous.

A sudden burst of wind swept across the rocky specter, leaving in its wake an echo that sounded like the wail of a dying animal. A shiver rippled Garth's spine, and he hurried back to the mission.

Father Chavez was waiting for him when he returned to the rectory.

"Sir, I have been thinking about my uncle's claim. If the O'Gradys are now the legal owners of the mine, it appears I'll have to pursue a different tack. Do you have a detailed plat of the area bordering the claim?"

The priest riffled through a mass of musty-smelling maps and pulled out the one he sought. "This is the quadrant where the mine can be found," Father Chavez said as they leaned over the table. "The horizontal lines represent the latitude and the vertical lines the longitude. These contour lines indicate the altitude. And this," he said, pointing to a marking on the map, "is the exact location of the O'Grady claim."

"You mean my uncle's claim," Garth corrected.

"I can only identify it as what has been legally claimed, Señor Fraser."

"Father, please call me Garth."

"If that is your desire." Father Chavez opened the thick ledger he had showed Garth earlier, and traced the registration.

"The site with the coordinates nearest to the O'Grady one was claimed by a Herbert Forsen fifteen years ago." Deep in recollection, Father Chavez nodded. "Ah, yes, I remember the man. Señor Forsen left here to return to his claim and was never seen or heard from since then."

"Maybe he's still working the claim," Garth suggested.

"I think not. The need for food and supplies would have made him return."

Father Chavez went back to checking coordinates on the quadrant against the registration ledger. "As you can see by the markings, there have been several other claims filed in the area, but they did not yield any gold and have long been abandoned."

"What about here?" Garth asked, pointing to the area on the map directly beyond his uncle's claim.

"No claims have been filed on the rest of the area above it. If anyone attempted to mine there, they have either disappeared or left empty-handed. Señor Forsen was the last one to show any interest in that area."

"Well, I'm not going to let Mr. O'Grady and his daughter get away with stealing my uncle's mine. I intend to follow them."

Father Chavez frowned. "I pray you do not intend to harm them, Garth."

"I'm not a violent man, Father. But I will not step aside and let them get away with this."

"You have no way of knowing if Henry was right. That mine could be worthless."

"Then I'll have to find that out for myself."

Father Chavez shook his head. "Is the desire for gold so great that you people are willing to die for it? The mountain has claimed many before you."

"I've had worse challenges and managed to stay alive, Father. I survived four years of war when those around me were falling in battle, and I came to California from Virginia. I can't imagine anything harder than that trek across the Rocky Mountains." Garth shook his head. "After all that, why should a single mountain present a challenge to me?"

The priest walked to the window and gazed at the distant mountain peak.

"Because, my son, you will not be challenging a single mountain; the mountain will be challenging you. Many have climbed it, never to be seen again. It is called Montaña del Diablo."

He turned around and looked at Garth. "Mountain of the Devil."

7

A single lantern atop the gatepost of the mission glowed like a beacon in the darkness that encompassed the town. Inside the mission, Father Chavez and Elena whispered in the deep shadows of the wall.

"He must be warned, mi hermana," Chavez murmured. "Tell him there can be no delay. He must go at once."

Elena nodded, and after wrapping a shawl around her head and shoulders, she slipped through the gate and was swallowed by the night.

Father Chavez returned to the rectory and stole quietly across the floor. First the O'Grady couple, and now the arrival of Garth Fraser. It could all lead to disaster. He frowned in thought. *Are not we told that what we sow, we reap?* The walls of Jericho had begun to tumble.

*   *   *

"Mountain of the Devil," Garth murmured as he lay with his hands tucked under his head. "What kind of bullshit is that?" Having accepted Father Chavez's offer to spend the night, he was unable to sleep as the priest's ominous warning played on his mind.

Never one to dwell on superstitions, he now found himself at odds with a tenet he'd always lived by: when it was your time to go, it would happen whether you were in your bed or the middle of a battlefield.

If all of this portentous legend was to be believed, then how had his uncle made repeated trips without incident between his mine and the mission? And even though ill with consumption, he had managed to reach the mission unmolested before he died.

More than likely, a few accidental deaths had been magnified into those *mysterious disappearances.*

Now the O'Gradys had ventured onto that mysterious mountain, and he had a score to settle with them—especially Miss Rory O'Grady. She was the only one he had told about the map. What had driven her to steal it? Hadn't he told her that he'd give her half of everything, in gratitude for helping keep him from being shanghaied? Greed was so ugly.

He turned over on his side. He was so disappointed in her. Experienced in the ways of women, he had believed her to be a naïve, even innocent young woman, despite the tough façade she tried to present. He'd thought her the vulnerable victim of a conniving father and the cruel hand that fate had dealt her.

Was he ever mistaken! She was as much of a schemer as her father. Deep in his heart, he had hoped she would have resisted such temptation.

Garth yawned and closed his eyes. When he caught up with her and Paddy, come hell or high water, he would get Uncle Henry's mine back.

After another half hour of restless tossing, Garth got up, pulled on his trousers, and went outside to catch a breath of fresh air. The dog trotted over to him, and Garth patted his head.

"Guess we'll be parting company in the morning, pal," he said.

The night was quiet, and his gaze was drawn to the nearby mountain. Moonlight cast its eerie outline into a shimmering specter, its snow capped peak disappearing into the darkened sky above.

"Looks to me like the mountain is reaching to Heaven, not down to Hell, pal," he said.

How could an educated and holy man believe that an evil force inhabited the mountain? If you believed that, you could say the same about any mountain.

He thought of how many poor souls perished crossing the Rockies when they came west. Or what about the Matterhorn in Europe, or the Himalayas in Asia? The plain truth was, the hazards of scaling a mountain had always been a challenge to man. And when one perished in the attempt, a myth or mystical speculation was often attached to the misadventure.

"Death is as common as birth, pal. People die daily from accidents and illnesses. When one drowns, no one blames the river. If one perishes in a fire, no one puts the forest to blame. But let someone die climbing a mountain, and another myth is born.

"Mountain of the Devil, my ass! A mountain is just an obstacle in one's path—not a breeding ground for evil spirits."

As for the danger of bandits, well, cities were rife with murderers, thieves, rapists, and other two-legged vermin like the two sons of bitches who'd tried to shanghai him.

"Pal, I'd be sitting on some damn ship in the middle of the ocean right now if it hadn't been for . . ."

Damn it. Why did she have to turn out to be no better than them?

Despite the restless night, Garth had awakened early and was saddling Boots when Father Chavez approached leading a burro.

"Since I cannot convince you to forsake this foolish venture, my friend, you will have need of a burro."

Garth chuckled. "No doubt to carry back all of the gold I will find."

"You would probably profit more by selling the burro."

"Oh, ye of little faith, Father. Thanks very much for the offer, but I prefer traveling light."

"You joke, but it is good to hear you are a man of faith, Garth. Even if it isn't Catholic," he added with a merry twinkle in his eyes. "But I think you would find Samuel here to be more surefooted than your horse."

"Don't listen to him, Boots. We know better, don't we?" Garth said, giving a final tug to the cinch.

"Well, I guess I'm all set." The two men shook hands. "I can't thank you enough, Father Chavez. I hope one day I can repay you for all the help you've been."

"You can do so by returning safely, my friend."

Garth mounted. "One more thing, Father. I hate to take advantage of your generosity, but would you find a home for the dog? I feel kind of responsible for him."

Father Chavez glanced at the dog who had now risen, and he grinned. "It would appear the perro believes he has already found a home. I told you that you had made a friend for life. Go with God, Garth Fraser."

Father Chavez sighed deeply as he stood at the gate and watched Garth ride away to whatever destiny the mountain held for him.

Once out of the foothills the climb steepened, and the trail sometimes narrowed to no more than a footpath.

Garth knew he was near his destination, but since dusk had begun to move in, he decided to stop for the night and get an early start in the morning.

The sound of a rifle blast bounced from one granite crag to another like a ricocheting bullet. Automatically he dove for cover. Several more shots followed, and Garth realized he was not under fire; the sound was coming from the trail up ahead. He tethered Boots to a tree, then tied the dog, too.

Grabbing his rifle, he cautiously moved up to where the trail widened into a small, flat, plateaulike area. Overrun with foliage, the site was bordered by the granite wall of the mountain on the inside and some scattered fir trees and huge boulders on the outer edge.

Garth crept close for a better view. Rory and Paddy were pinned down behind a huge boulder. Three armed bandits were closing in on them, and another was untying the O'Gradys' mules and burro. That was the bandit he took out first, but his shot attracted the other three, and they immediately turned their attention in his direction.

At that moment he saw another bandit, who'd been concealed in the shrubbery, sneaking up behind Rory and Paddy. Garth's shot found its mark, and that bandit fell to the ground.

Unfortunately the flash of the shot had revealed his position to the others, and a barrage of bullets smacked around him. He dashed to the cover of a tree, and the three remaining outlaws advanced on him. Garth had another one of them trained in his sights, but when he pulled the trigger, the rifle clicked on an empty chamber.

He drew his pistol and got off a lethal shot, but before he could get off another, one of the bandits leaped at him and sank a knife into his shoulder. The pistol slipped through his fingers and he grabbed his attacker's hand, which was raised to deliver another thrust of the knife.

As they wrestled to gain control of the weapon, Garth could feel his strength waning. Rallying whatever strength remained, he slowly twisted the attacker's hand clutching the knife and succeeded in plunging it into the man's heart. He shoved the dead man aside, only to look up into the wrong end of the rifle pointed at his head.

With a malicious smile, the remaining bandit snarled, "Adiós, amigo."

A shot rang out, and for the breathless length of a heartbeat, the outlaw's stunned expression gazed down at him. Then the rifle slipped through his fingers and he pitched forward.

Garth sat up, rolled the man over, and stared into the lifeless eyes that only seconds before had gleamed with mercilessness.

Too shocked to move, for a few seconds he sat bewildered. He'd had many close shaves during the war, but this was the first time he had actually looked death in the face. Finally, after reclaiming his Colt and empty rifle, he got to his feet. He felt woozy and his knees threatened to buckle as he reloaded the rifle, then made his way over to the two people still huddled behind the rock.

"Garth!" Rory cried out joyously. "Pop, look it's Garth Fraser." Then, seeing the condition he was in, she exclaimed, "Oh, God, you're bleeding!"

He sure as hell was, and he sank down on a nearby log to attempt to stem it with his bandanna.

Rory rushed over to him with saddlebags. "Let's get that shirt off you."

"Fancy meeting you here, Miss O'Grady. Did you choose to come to the mountains for the summer?"

"Actually I was against this whole idea," she said, slipping the shirt off his arm. "But as long as we had the map, Pop was determined to check it out."

"Your frankness is refreshing, Miss O'Grady, considering your previous deceit."

"Deceit?" she asked, perplexed. "Oh, I suppose you mean about the map."

"Got to hand it to you, lady. There's that intuition of yours kicking in again," he said sarcastically. "You had me convinced you weren't interested in gold mines, and I actually thought that crooked sheriff had stolen my map. Instead, it was none other than little Miss Innocent O'Grady."

She gaped at him in surprise, like the actress he knew her to be. "But I didn't . . ." She cut off what she was about to say when Paddy came over and joined them.

"How bad is the lad hurt?" Paddy asked.

"Not too bad. The wound isn't very deep, and the bleeding helps to flush the wound. Lord knows what else that knife's been used for. Shouldn't be a problem unless it becomes infected," Rory said.

"Ouch," Garth yelped when she poured some whiskey into the wound.

Paddy patted him on the shoulder. "We're beholden to you, me boy." Then he moved away and went over to a tree and slumped down against it.

"He doesn't look too good. Was he wounded?" Garth asked.

"No. The climb up here has exhausted him."

"That was a great shot he made. That bastard had my head in the sight of his rifle."

"What are you talking about?" Rory asked.

"When he shot the bandit who was about to kill me."

"Pop didn't shoot him. His rifle was out of bullets." She folded a napkin into a square, and tied it in place with his bandanna. "There, that should do it."

Garth looked confused. "Then who in hell shot him?"

Rory shrugged. "It wasn't one of us."

Garth drew his pistol. "I better check to make sure all of those guys are dead. Maybe one of them is still alive; I counted five altogether."

"You wouldn't harm a wounded man, would you?" she asked.

"No, I'd set him free so he could come back to shoot at us again." Disgusted, he walked away, checked out the bodies, then pulled them into a pile.

"Good-bye, Miss O'Grady. It's been a pleasure, as usual."

She chased after him. "What should we do about the bodies?"

"Elementary, Miss O'Grady. Let them lie, and you and your father get your asses back down that trail."

"You know we can't do that. Pop's too ill right now."

"Then drag them over to the rim and push them over."

"I'm a Christian, Mr. Fraser, and believe every man deserves a decent burial."

"Then start digging."

She hurried to keep up with his long stride. "The least you could do is help. You're the one who shot them."

"Consider this, ma'am: if I hadn't shot them, they'd have shot you, then I'd be burying you and your father. That is, after they all got through with *you*."

"You certainly had me fooled," Rory said, chasing after him when he marched away, disgruntled. "Are you really as coldhearted as you sound?"

"I wasn't until I met you, lady." He walked away, leaving her staring at him with an astonished look on that lovely face that he had once considered so beautiful.

Rory had another problem to resolve. She went over to her father. "You lied to me, didn't you, Pop? You didn't find that map; you stole it from Garth Fraser."

"Now, now, don't go getting all worked up, darlin'. I didn't steal it. The map fell on the floor when he and McGill were fighting. All I did was pick it up. And you know as well as I do, that crooked sheriff would never have given it back to him."

"I don't believe you. Why did you lie to me, Pop?"

"Because just as I suspected, you wouldn't believe the truth."

"I might have believed you back then. I don't believe you now."

"Besides, the man owed it to you for saving his life."

"Garth thinks that I *stole* the map!"

"And did you tell him to the contrary?"

"No. I doubt he'd believe your story any more than I do. I knew he'd never hurt me because I'm a woman, but I was afraid of what he might do to *you*."

Paddy hung his head like a youngster caught with his fingers in the cookie jar. "I'm sorry, darlin'. You're a good daughter, and I don't deserve you."

"That's right; I'm too good to be a party to theft. So you have to tell Garth the truth and give him back his mine."

"Now, why would you want me to do such a fool thing, girl? I've as much right to the mine as he does. The map would have been lost to him, anyway, so we might as well take our chances with it."

"Is that how you justify *stealing* it instead of giving it back to him? I'll never believe another word you say."

" 'Tis the truth, darlin'. I swear on the grave of your sainted mother, may she rest in peace."

"How do you expect her to, when you act like this?"

"You agreed to try it for a month, and if there's no gold by then, we'd leave. Are you going back on your word?"

"I'll not be bound by any promise made to a lie. As soon as you get your strength back, Patrick Michael O'Grady, we're leaving!"

Rory had a pot of coffee and bacon and potatoes frying in a skillet when Garth reappeared, wearing a clean shirt and leading a horse, with a gray shaggy dog following behind.

"I'm about to eat. Do you care to join me?" she asked.

"I don't usually break bread with my enemies." Then he sniffed the freshly brewed coffee. "Guess I could use a cup of coffee, though."

"I figured you could." She handed him a steaming cup and went back to the fire.

"So where's Paddy?" he asked, blowing on the steaming liquid.

"He bedded down."

"Without eating?"

"He was more exhausted than hungry. When did you adopt the dog?"

"Actually, he adopted me on the way to Tierra de Esperanza. I removed a splinter in his paw, and he's been with me since."

"What do you call him?"

"I thought I'd call him Saddle. Boots is my horse and Saddle's my dog. Apropos for an ex-cavalry man, don't you think?"

"The reason why escapes me."

" 'Boots and Saddle' is the bugle call to mount up."

"Really? Glory be, just think: if any more animals adopt you, you can add a Bugle or Guidon to your menagerie."

He finally cracked a smile. "Gotta admit, you've got a good sense of humor. And a man sure has to hold on to his when he meets up with you, Miss O'Grady."

"You can call me Rory. It's acceptable to drop the formality after kissing a woman."

"Now I see your angle; you put me on the defensive and I back off. Won't work, Miss O'Grady."

The hot coffee tasted good, and was a reminder that he hadn't eaten since dawn. Still he made a token protest when she handed him a fork, a plateful of the bacon and potatoes, and a hunk of hardtack.

"Don't be stubborn, Fraser. There's no sense in letting this food go to waste."

Her appealing smile was as persuasive as the smell of the food. "Okay, but just this once."

"Do your animals need to be fed?"

"No, I fed and watered them already."

The food hit the spot and tasted a damn sight better than the cold jerky he had planned on eating.

"Thanks, that was very good," he said when he finished.

Rory refilled his plate, and his eyes followed her as she filled a plate for herself and sat down to eat. What a shrewd little operator she was. After what she did to him, did she think she could buy his trust with a damn plate of bacon and potatoes?

And worse, even though he was still angry with her, he realized he still desired her physically. At least he was smart enough not to trust her again.

"Looks like you know your way around a campfire pretty well."

"I do. Pop and I have seen our share of campfires. After Mum died, there were times we had to sleep under the stars."

"What kind of times?"

"Oh, for instance if we didn't have money to take a stage, or . . ." Her voice trailed off.

"Or what, Rory?"

Her eyes flashed in irritation. "Or we had to sneak out of town without paying for our room. Is that what you wanted to hear?"

"Is that the reason you're up here? You're a fool,

Rory. You're wasting your life. Get away from your father, before he corrupts you any more than he has already."

"What I do with my life is none of your business."

"It became my business when you stole from me. You sure had me fooled, lady. I thought you were decent and honest, when all the time you were setting me up to get your hands on my map."

She jumped to her feet. "The map fell from your pocket when you were fighting with McGill. If I hadn't picked it up, somebody else would have, so you'd have lost it regardless. Do you think the sheriff would have given it back to you? Even if he'd put no stock in a damn map to a gold mine, he would have destroyed it out of sheer nastiness. So why don't you just go ahead and shoot Pop and me, if it will satisfy your need for revenge."

"If I wanted revenge, I wouldn't have risked my life when you were under attack. I'd have let them gun down your father and have their way with you before they killed you. They weren't after your mine. They were after your mules and you, lady! You had to be plain loco to come up here with nothing better than a sick old man to protect you. Father Chavez must have warned you of the danger."

"Yes, and Pop told me to stay behind. He's not as irresponsible as you accuse him of being."

"And you're not the innocent I once believed you to be. No matter what you want me to believe, you're just as bad as he is. The lure of gold brought you up here."

"Believe what you want. I'm not going to try to convince you otherwise. I'm grateful you risked your life to save Pop and me, and regret you were hurt doing it.

"Good night, Captain Fraser. You and your regiment are welcome to share our campfire for the night."

8

Saddle was lying at his feet when Garth awoke. He sat up and stretched, and the dog came up and licked his face.

"Good morning, Saddle," Garth said, scratching him behind the ears. "How long have you been awake?"

Paddy was snoring loudly a short distance away, and Garth glanced around for Rory. Her bedroll was rolled up neatly and tied, but there was no sign of her. Then he heard a scraping sound coming from the nearby trees and got up to investigate. He found her digging a hole.

"Good morning."

She glanced up from the bottom of the hole. "I expected you'd be gone when I woke up."

"Obviously you haven't had your second cup of coffee," he said.

"How's your shoulder?"

"Doing fine. I checked it this morning and changed the bandage, so don't try to change the subject. You don't intend to pay any attention to what I said yesterday, do you?"

"We already had this argument. I told you what I intend to do." She tossed up the shovel. "I think this hole's deep enough."

He reached out a hand and pulled her up. "Why are you digging this hole?"

"I'm sure not going to stay here with dead bodies lying around."

"You should be leaving, not digging."

"I said we would leave as soon as Pop is rested."

"I thought you meant overnight."

"That's your mistake, not mine. I'm not a member of your regiment, Garth, so I don't have to take your orders."

"It was meant as advice, Miss O'Grady. The scent could attract wild animals. If you had told me that last night, I would have disposed of them."

"Yes, *your* way."

"Do me the favor of going back and getting that second cup of coffee down you, will you? I have no desire to stand here and argue. I'll finish up here."

"Four hands are better than two," she said.

Garth dragged the bodies over to the grave and dumped them into the hole, then shoveled the dirt back in. "There. Does that ease your conscience? Now be sure to pray for their rotten souls."

He tossed the shovel aside and stormed away.

Rory watched him ride away with Saddle trotting at his side. Why couldn't he understand she wasn't defying him? As soon as Pop was well enough to travel, they were leaving.

After several anxious hours, Rory was happy to see Garth's return. She waved and shouted excitedly, "Garth, I've found the mine."

"Really?" He dismounted. "Are you sure it's my uncle's?"

"See for yourself."

She had cleared away the foliage that had concealed a boarded-up entrance to a mine. Time and nature had washed away most of the paint from the stakes, but the letters **H** and **F** were distinguishable on one stake and an **F** and part of an **S** followed by an **E** on the other one.

Rory grabbed a sack of supplies and carried it into the mine. Garth picked up one of the heavier pouches and put it down beside several others lined against the wall.

"What's the sense of unpacking all of this, if you're going to leave when he's feeling better?"

She sighed deeply. "Garth, he's too ill right now. So please stop harping about it?"

In a lighter vein, she said, "There's a crude tunnel that appears to be partially manmade. It's only about four or five feet high, so it's too low to stand up in, but in parts, its roof and sides have been shored up with posts."

"How long is the tunnel?"

"Pop figures at least twenty feet. It must have been a tremendous job for someone to do alone."

"That doesn't make sense. Why would Uncle Henry put all this work into a mine he didn't even file a legal claim on?"

"How well did you know your uncle?"

"I adored him. Whenever he'd come back to Fraser Keep, he'd talk about hitting the big strike or finding a pot of gold at the end of the rainbow. I was only six when he left for California in 'forty-five, and that was the last time I saw him. The only reason I came out here was to trace his route and fulfill his dream."

"Do you still feel there's a threat of being attacked again?"

"It's hard to say, but I don't see evidence of any regular bandit activity around here. I'm prone to think those five who attacked you were not part of a larger gang. All that shooting would have brought the rest of the gang here by now. Just the same, I wouldn't push your luck too far; get out as soon as you can. I intend to do the same. I have no desire to die alone here on this mountain, and enough sense to know I probably will, if I remain too long myself."

"From the beginning, I thought it was a mistake to come here," Rory said. "But what were our options? After the incident in the Grotto, we had to get out of Buckman, and as long as we had the map, Pop was determined to come here."

"That doesn't explain why you came with him."

She looked at him, appalled. "I would think that would be obvious. I was concerned about his health, and since I had no better place to go except another saloon in another town, why wouldn't I?

"Furthermore, the thought of camping in the mountains for a while didn't sound too bad. No matter what you think, I'm not consumed with gold fever—though maybe, deep down, I did hope we'd strike gold. It wasn't until Father Chavez's warning that I realized I'd made a big mistake."

"Why didn't you back out then and sit it out at the mission?"

"Pop's the only one I have in this world." Her voice faded in despair. "It's not easy to run out on someone you love, Garth." She turned away and went back outside.

For another long moment Garth remained and glanced around at the mine.

What in hell are you even doing here, Fraser? Is this what you've been wasting your life dreaming about for the past twenty years?

He turned away in disgust and went over to where Rory had made Paddy a bed under the shade of a tree.

"How are you feeling, Paddy?"

"Curse this cough. I feel as helpless as a newborn babe." He winked and grinned. "Knocks the legs out from under a man worse than a pint of straight Irish."

"Well, take it slow, and as soon as you're on your feet again, I'll give Rory a hand in getting you back to the mission."

"Aye, that I will, me boy."

"Are you returning to town?" Rory asked when he climbed back on Boots.

"You're not getting rid of me that easily. More than likely I'll hold off and go back with you." He tipped his hat. "Take care, Miss O'Grady," he said, and he rode away.

A half mile farther, Garth reined up at the site of a narrow waterfall spilling from a rocky crag above. Dismounting, he walked over to the water's edge and cupped a handful. It was refreshing and tasted as pure as spring water. But his uncle had never drawn a waterfall on the map he'd sent. Why not?

Garth moved away to the shade of a tree where he could look at it more from a frontal view. The sun's rays gleamed with the spectrum of the rainbow through the waterfall's misty spray. Something about the sight of it began to tweak at his memory.

"What can it be, boy?" he murmured, stroking Saddle's head. "What's my brain reaching for? A vision? A forgotten dream?"

His thoughts kept going back to the question of why his uncle hadn't indicated the waterfall on the map. It would have been an easy landmark to find.

The longer he stared at the waterfall's spectrum of colors, the harder he thought, going over every detail of the map and his uncle's letter.

Suddenly Garth bolted to his feet. "I've got it!" Saddle leaped to all fours with his ears perked alertly in response.

"In his letter, Uncle Henry called the mine *the pot of gold at the end of the rainbow*! That's the clue, Saddle! The *waterfall's* rainbow! He had the sense to figure that the map might fall into the wrong hands, so he left it off deliberately. I bet that's why he didn't file a claim, too. The mine is right here, not a half mile away. Uncle Henry, I should have known you were too smart to do the obvious."

Due to the moisture from the waterfall, the foliage was thicker and higher here. Garth got down on his knees and began to search until he found what he was looking for—two stakes driven into the ground, marking the claim.

Garth grabbed the pick from the pack tied to the saddle and began to dig and toss away the rubble that had concealed a split in the granite wall of the mountain. He had to duck his head to get through it, but once inside, he let out a loud whistle and stood up.

"This is a natural cave, Saddle," he told the dog, who was already sniffing out the corners of the cavern.

Garth checked out the cave's interior. There were signs of where his Uncle Henry had started to dig on the rear wall. The cave was dry, and with some effort, he could probably enlarge the opening to stable Boots inside at night.

And then he saw the one thing that absolutely convinced him. Garth's heart swelled with emotion as he stared at the H.F. carved on the wall of the cave, then reached out and traced the letters with his fingertips.

"I didn't give up on you, Uncle Henry. I told you I'd find it."

The first thing he did was unload his saddlebags and the rainproof pack tied to his saddle. Along with a blanket, hygiene supplies, and a few changes of clothing, he had brought jerky and coffee, some tin dishes, a coffeepot, frying pan, a couple of crucial mining tools, and ammunition for his rifle and pistol.

Since the waterfall was a source of fresh water, there'd be no need to haul that in. But there was always a need for meat and firewood, so he gathered and stacked plenty of wood in the cave, and as he set a couple of snares, he said a special thanks to the Boxer brothers, two backwoodsmen in his regiment who had taught him how to trap birds and small mammals.

Next, he set to the task of enlarging the opening of the cave. He cut away as little of the foliage as possible to prevent it from being seen by a casual observer.

With only a thin wall of dirt and rock, due to the hollowed cave behind it, enlarging the opening was easier than he had anticipated. By dusk, he had made an opening large enough to accommodate his horse.

"We'll all have a roof over our heads now, Boots."

Satisfied with the results of his labor, Garth realized he hadn't eaten all day. He built a fire, washed up, and then answered the growl of his stomach with hot coffee and jerky.

As he took a bite off the stick of jerky, he thought about the fried bacon and potatoes that Rory had fed him last night. It sure had been more appetizing than jerky.

Satisfied he had done as much as he could for that day, Garth spread out his bedroll under the protective roof of the cave and the watchful eyes and alert ears of Saddle, and closed his eyes.

For a long time he lay thinking about the day's un-expected development. Since he had found his uncle's mine, whose mine had the O'Gradys found?

Father Chavez had told him there weren't any other claims filed in this area, and he couldn't believe his Uncle Henry would have put all that labor into build-ing a tunnel in a fake mine just to throw off the curi-ous—which again raised the question of why his uncle hadn't filed a claim on the proper mine, to protect himself from claim jumpers.

Then he recalled the priest had indicated that there had been another man who had shown interest in this area. What was the miner's name? Harold . . . Hubert? Herbert? Yeah, Herbert. Now think, Fraser, what was it? Herbert . . . ah, Forsen. Herbert Forsen, that was it!

That would explain the initials H.F. on the stakes: Forsen and his uncle had identical initials. The letters in the other cave stood for Herbert Forsen, not Henry Fraser.

Which meant the O'Gradys would have wasted their time and money on a mine that Forsen had prob-ably abandoned. *Which would serve them right: what you sow, you reap.*

Garth doubted Forsen had ever discovered any gold, word always got out about any strike. So most likely the O'Gradys wouldn't strick gold either, if they remained.

But *he* would. He'd dodged Yankees for four years during the war, Indians and everything nature could throw at him on the trek west, and he sure as hell could dodge a few outlaws if any showed up here. He believed too much in his Uncle Henry's judgment to quit now, when he was this close.

As he lay thinking about his good fortune, his thoughts strayed to the O'Gradys again. He sure as hell didn't owe them any consideration, but with Paddy sick and all, he'd help them get back to Hope. Then he'd come back to the mine, and if he found any gold dust, he'd still split it with Rory.

A promise was a promise, no matter whom you made it with.

The next morning, Garth saddled Boots and rode down to see the O'Gradys. Their mules and burro were tethered to a tree, but there was no sign of either of them. There were supplies lined against the wall inside the cave, and he checked the campfire's ashes. They were cold, so they hadn't built a morning campfire.

The cave showed no signs of blood or a struggle. Bandits would have carried off the excess food and supplies, and certainly the mules and burro. And if O'Gradys had given up and left, they would have ridden back to town on the mules.

He was about to go out and check around the area for them, when he heard a faint sound coming from the tunnel.

Stooping down at the entrance, he was relieved to see Rory at the other end scraping the wall with a pick.

"Good morning!" he shouted.

Rory dropped the pick in surprise. "Garth! I didn't hear you coming. What are you doing here?" She crawled out of the tunnel, dragging the pick behind her.

He hurried over and helped her to her feet. "What in hell are you doing with that pick? I thought you were getting out of here."

"I was bored, so I might as well try finding gold while Pop regains his strength."

"Where *is* Paddy?"

"He thought he'd try stretching his legs. He said he'd search for water and some fresh meat."

"If he's well enough for that, why not just leave?"

"Garth, he's so weak, he can barely move. I'm just humoring him."

"I hope he doesn't intend to fire a gun."

"You said there's no further threat of attack."

"I said I doubt it. Don't you two have any sense of survival? If you want fresh meat, you have to trap it. You fire a gun and the shot will be heard for miles. How do you think I found you so quickly when you were under attack?" He shook his head in disgust. "The two of you have no business up here. You're inviting disaster in everything you do."

She slumped down and leaned back against a tree. "I'm getting real tired of your survival lectures, Davy Crockett."

"The truth hurts, doesn't it?" Garth got his canteen and unscrewed the cap. "Here, you look like you could use a cool drink."

Rory took a long draught from the canteen, then handed it back to him. "Thank you. That really tasted good. I used up the last of our drinking water last night. Couldn't even make coffee this morning."

The nag at his conscience grew greater. No matter how angry he'd been toward her, it bothered him to see her going without water—especially when he knew where there was a plentiful supply of it.

"I should have guessed it was too early in the morning to try to beard the lion. Especially when she hasn't had her morning coffee yet."

"Knowing how your interests run, Fraser, *she* wonders if you mean *bed* instead of *beard*?" Rory opened her mouth to say more, then suddenly broke into laughter. "Did I just say that? I really am miserable in the mornings, aren't I?"

He grinned. "You're also very pretty in the mornings—even with dirt on your face. So that makes it tolerable."

Those gorgeous eyes of hers widened in surprise. "A compliment, Fraser! Does that mean you're not angry at me anymore, or is it just that detestable cheerfulness of yours that comes up every morning with the sun?"

"Of course I'm still angry for what you did. I just don't like to start a day with an argument. Unlike someone I know."

He changed his tone. "Honey, is this really worth what you're going through?" he asked gently.

She closed her eyes. "I suppose it would be if we strike gold."

"What if you don't? And what if you get hurt . . . or worse?"

Rory opened her eyes. "Then I guess you can stand over my grave and remind me that you told me so."

She tried to sound flippant, but fatigue had crept into her voice.

"You aren't even certain there is gold in that mine, Rory."

"*You* believe there is. Isn't that why you traveled from one ocean to the other? Crossed plains and mountains?"

"It really isn't, Rory. My brother and I came west in pursuit of our sister. Then I figured as long as I was here, I'd check out Uncle Henry's mine. But I always figured that one day, when I got through stretching my legs, I'd go back to Virginia and settle down."

"And how long do you figure that will take?"

He grinned. "Can't say. My legs still have a lot of stretching yet to do."

He clasped her hand and pulled her to her feet. "Let's get working on that coffee." While she filled the coffeepot from his canteen, Garth knelt down and built a fire.

"Give me your canteen and I'll fill it. I've found a source of fresh water farther up the trail. I can be back by the time your coffee's ready." He mounted Boots and rode away.

Rory smiled as she watched until horse and rider disappeared. With Pop's health so shaky, Garth was a godsend, and it felt good to have someone like him around to lighten the load. He seemed to do everything so effortlessly and solved every problem in the same easy fashion. And from a completely selfish aspect, he was good for her morale.

"You and that morning cheerfulness of yours, Fraser," she murmured. "Thanks to you I feel better already, and I haven't even had my *first* cup of coffee." Grinning, she put the pot on the fire and reached for the slab of bacon to slice.

Returning to his camp, Garth filled Rory's canteen and then checked the snares he'd set. There was a rabbit caught in one of them. He stuck it in a pouch and attached it to the saddle. What the hell, he could eat jerky again tonight. But before leaving, he reset the snares just in case he got lucky again.

Paddy had returned to camp—without water or meat—by the time Garth got back. "Good morning, Paddy."

"Top of the morning, young man," Paddy said.

Garth handed him the pouch with the rabbit in it. "Here's your supper tonight, Paddy. You well enough to skin it?"

"A rabbit!" Paddy's face lit up with that Irish grin of his. "I'll be doing just that, me boy."

"I'm relieved you didn't fire that rifle."

"Just you never give it a mind, me lad." He winked at Garth, and whispered aside, "Me darling daughter's been harping at me about it like a fishwife."

"I heard that! I was just warning you, Pop, like Garth did to me."

"Well, I'm feeling poorly from me walk, so I think I'll take me a wee nap."

"Don't you want something to eat first, Pop?" Rory said worriedly when he handed her the rabbit. "I've fried some bacon and potatoes."

"I'm not hungry, darlin'."

"But you've got to eat something." But he had already disappeared into the cave. She sighed and turned back with a worried frown. "You feel like some bacon and potatoes, Garth? I hate to see good food go to waste."

"Sure, why not?" he said.

His eyes followed her movements as she filled a plate. Even thieves had feelings, too, he reasoned, and despite what she had done to him, Garth could see she was also a daughter struggling with worry over the health of her father. And yet she held her emotions in check. He admired that kind of fortitude.

"He'll be okay, Rory. He's had a bad bout with the illness and just needs some time to rest."

"Do you really think so?" she asked.

"Of course I do, honey. Why, my Grandfather Fraser suffered with consumption starting before I was born and he eventually died from old age. Paddy just needs a good rest. A few decent meals under his belt wouldn't hurt, either. Once you get back to the mission, let him rest and relax for a while. Elena can put some meat on his bones, and Father Chavez is good company and will be the best medicine Paddy could have."

"I hope you're right."

He stood up and handed her his empty plate. "Thanks for breakfast. I've got a couple things to do, so I better get going."

His gaze was drawn to her face. "You know, it wouldn't hurt for you to take a good rest and put on a couple of pounds, too. I've noticed you look a little peaked since you've left Buckman."

She looked distressed and unwittingly raised her hand to her face. "Really?"

Good God, why did I even mention it! "I don't . . . that is . . . I didn't mean to sound ungallant—I only meant—"

The plucky challenge returned to her eyes. "I've noticed you've developed a stutter since you left Buckman, Mr. Fraser. Perhaps you've suffering from foot-in-mouth disease."

"I think you're confusing it with hoof-and-mouth disease, Miss O'Grady. I read recently that it appears to attack only cattle and sheep."

"I stand corrected. And now they can add horses' asses to their list," she said with a saucy shrug as she turned away.

She always managed to get in the last word, Garth conceded in amusement. But he still had some *unfinished* business with her.

Rory came over as he prepared to leave. "Thank you for the rabbit, Garth. Will you join us for supper?"

"Think I'd enjoy that much more than jerky," Garth said as he tightened the cinch.

"I've noticed you always loosen Boots's cinch whenever you stop. Why is that?"

"I only do it when I expect to stay awhile. Do you like to remain trussed up in a corset if you don't have to?"

The question caused her to laugh. "You clearly know a great deal about ladies' corsets. The truth is, I'd rather not be trussed up in a corset at any time. I never wear one if I don't have to."

His gaze swept her body in a slow, bold appraisal. "So I've noticed."

She met the return of his eyes with a brazen smirk. "So *I've* noticed."

Garth's gaze followed her trim figure as she walked away. He folded his arms across his chest and leaned back against Boots. "There goes a whole lot of woman, fellas."

Faded Levi's failed to disguise her long legs, tiny waist, and the best-looking little ass he was itching to get his hands on. "There's no one who wants that luscious body of hers to remain *untrussed* more than I do."

Saddle raised his head and cocked a furry brow.

Garth returned to the task of picking at the wall in search of a vein. Gold mining was a slow and laborious job—and not to his liking. But not because he wearied of the hard labor; he was no stranger to danger and hardship. He'd certainly borne them enough times throughout the war and the trek to California.

But through the years, from the time his uncle had left for California, Garth had dreamed of the search for Uncle Henry's mine—dedicated himself to finding it. It had become a mission to him. But unlike the nobility of an Arthurian knight's quest for the Holy Grail, or the cynicism in Diogenes's search for one honest man, his mission was clear: the luster in *finding* the mine, rather than the sheen of the gold that might be within it.

He hadn't had any luck finding gold in the past two days, and he was considering forgetting about the whole damn thing.

"Hate to admit it, Saddle, but I think Uncle Henry was wrong about this mine. I'll keep at it until the O'Gradys are able to leave, but I don't think I'll come back again," he said as he scraped at the wall.

Suddenly he caught a flash of glitter on the hardened granite. He scraped away at the surface and stared at the thin golden vein that snaked through the rock.

With renewed energy, he worked through the night, laboriously scraping the gold dust into a pouch. Although the yield was small, it was large enough to fire his enthusiasm to keep going, and help to appease the O'Gradys.

9

Dirty, hungry, and exhausted, Rory threw the pick down in disgust and went outside and stretched out on the ground. She glanced at her father, lying in the shade a short distance away. He'd coughed all night, and his feeble attempts at walking were only aggravating his condition. Not that she blamed him for trying: lying on a blanket all day would be far more boring than scraping at that wall inside with a pick.

Why was she even doing it? She hadn't discovered the merest grain of gold in the week she'd been trying.

Greed, that's why, girl. The greatest motivator of the human race.

And where was Garth? He hadn't been around for the past two days. Each day she had hoped he would show up, but no such luck. Things were never dull when he was around: they were either sparring or he was trying to seduce her. One was as exciting as the other. But the best times were when they just sat quietly together and talked.

She sat up and looked at her hands. They were disgusting. Not only were they blistered from the pick handle, but there was black dirt under her fingernails!

She flopped back again. She'd sell her soul right now to sink into a hot, scented bath.

Garth was right; she should have sat it out at the mission until Pop got this out of his system. At least there she would have had the luxury of sitting down and having a decent meal or a tub of hot water to bathe in. Of course, as sick as he is now, what would he have done up here alone? Thank God she had come with him.

But she had no one to blame but herself. Deep down, the thought of finding gold was just as alluring to her as it was to Pop—or she wouldn't be here now.

She picked up her canteen to quench her thirst. After a couple of swallows it was empty. She checked her father's canteen. There was still plenty of water in it, but she hated to drink from it, so she put it aside.

Rory gently put a hand to his brow. He was still running a slight fever, but it didn't feel as bad as yesterday.

He opened his eyes and at the sight of her, he grinned as usual, love gleaming in his blue eyes.

"Pop, my canteen's empty and I'm going to fill it. Garth said he'd found a source of water a short distance above, so I'm going to look for it. Do you need anything before I go?"

"No, I'm doing fine. Stay on the path, darlin', so you don't get lost."

She kissed him on the cheek. "I will, Pop."

Slinging her canteen strap over a shoulder, she grabbed the empty water bucket and started off. The higher she climbed, the hotter it seemed to be, despite the altitude. Hot in the day—cold at night. One would think they were in the middle of the desert.

The dirt from the mine turned to grime as she began to perspire. Suddenly she stopped and gaped in pleasure at the sight of a narrow waterfall dropping straight down from the rocks above. This had to be the water source Garth had mentioned.

She cupped a handful of the cold and refreshing water. It was so delicious, Rory wanted to shout with joy. The spray from the waterfall splattered her head and shoulders as she filled the canteen and bucket, and the cooling mist felt as good as the water had tasted. She took off her battered hat and raised her face to get the full benefit of the spray. As cold as the water was, it was rinsing away the sweat and grime.

After glancing around, she sat down and pulled off her boots and stockings, then stripped down to her camisole and under britches.

Even though there was no way to stand or sit under the water, the spray felt so great that she grew even bolder and slipped off her remaining clothing. If only she'd known about the waterfall, she would have brought along soap to wash her hair, too.

Rory began to sing as she cleansed her body using her camisole as a washcloth.

*   *   *

Garth came out of the tunnel. Just as he picked up the canteen to take a drink, he heard a woman singing. He knew at once it could only be Rory. Parting the foliage that concealed the entrance to the cave, he gasped—not from surprise, but from awe at the sight of Rory's naked backside.

She looked like a wild wood nymph. Bathed in sunlight, her naked skin glistened with rainbow-ladendrops.

Desire swelled his groin with a painful surge of lust. With just a few steps he could touch her, feel that luscious flesh against his own. He restrained himself and instead, like a peeping voyeur, remained concealed.

Having finished washing, Rory proceeded to rinse out her underclothing. She dropped the garment and jumped back in alarm when an animal brushed her leg. Then she recognized it and bent down and patted its head.

"Saddle, you gave me a fright. What are you doing here? Did you come for a drink, too?"

Suddenly she realized that where Saddle was, there was probably Garth. She glanced around quickly, then shrieked when she saw him.

A hot blush swept over her as she tried unsuccessfully to cover her nakedness with her hands. In desperation, she dashed into some nearby foliage.

"How long have you been there?"

"Long enough to admire the view," he answered with a grin.

Rory glanced hopelessly at her shirt and Levi's lying nearby. "Kindly go away so I can dress."

"Rory, I've been watching you for the last five minutes. It's a little late for modesty now."

"How dare you! I thought you were a gentleman, Garth Fraser. How could you do such a thing?"

"I've never been able to ignore a beautiful work of art—and your body, honey, is one beautiful work of art." He started to unbutton his shirt.

"What do you think you're doing?" she cried, when he removed the shirt and approached her. "Don't you dare touch me, Garth! I'm indebted to you for all you've done for us, but I won't let you rape me."

"You're not the first woman I've seen naked, and I've managed to reach twenty-eight years of life without raping any of them. I thought you could use this." He tossed her his shirt and turned away.

She shivered from the cold and her fingers trembled as she put on the shirt and buttoned it. His shirt was warm from the heat of his body, and it covered her to the middle of her thighs when she stepped out of the foliage and sat down in the sunlight. Rory bent her legs and tucked her chin on her knees. His shirt draped over her legs in divine warmth, and she watched Garth wring out her underclothes. His body was proportioned magnificently. Her gaze fixed on the ripple of corded muscle across his broad shoulders and biceps. A delicious shudder went through her. She thought of that day on the hillside overlooking the ocean. They had come so near to making love. It would have been disastrous had she submitted.

Why? she now asked herself.

His voice intruded on her musing. "They should dry quickly in this sunshine."

"Thank you," she murmured. Considering her own thoughts, she felt ashamed of her unjust accusation. She should have known that he was not the kind of man who would resort to forcing any woman. He wouldn't have to. She was certain he had women lined up waiting and willing.

"I'm sorry for what I was thinking earlier."

He turned to her, and his grin melted any remaining chill that might have lingered. "Why? It couldn't have been much different from what I *was* thinking—though I had a more persuasive and enjoyable method in mind." His teeth flashed in a wider grin. "How about your shirt and pants? Do you want them washed, too?"

"Might as well. I've nothing to lose at this point."

A mischievous gleam sparked his dark eyes. "Don't be too sure about that."

An awkward silence fell between them until he asked, "So, how's Paddy feeling?"

"He seems a little better."

"Then why the worried frown?"

"For the last couple of days, I've smelled whiskey on Pop's breath. I've searched his bed and pack but there's none there. I wish I knew where he's hidden it." She looked at him and thrust out her chin spiritedly. "I'll find it, though. He isn't going to outsmart me."

Saddle came over to her, stretched out, and closed his eyes.

"Does this dog do anything but sleep?"

"Occasionally, but sleep seems to be his strong point. He's like a companionable friend, who will listen to what you have to say and never remind you that you're wrong."

Rory began to gently stroke the dog. "Does he ever bark?"

"Never. A growl escaped him a time or two, but I don't remember ever hearing a bark out of him."

"Do you suppose something could be wrong with his throat that prevents him from barking?" she asked with a worried frown.

"I don't think so." Having finished her laundry and strung it out to dry, he sat down beside her. "I think he was just well trained. More than likely by some miner or trapper who knew a barking dog might reveal a position at the wrong time."

"If that's true, he won't be much of a watchdog."

"Let's hope he's never put to the test. I have to say he's a pretty good hunter. He usually tracks down his own food, so I rarely have to feed him. He must have found a mountain stream somewhere, too, because this morning he returned toting a mountain trout between his jaws."

Garth reached for her hand and she winced when he grasped it. He looked in shock at her red and blistered palm. "Rory, what happened to your hand?"

"Oh, it's just a little sore."

He turned over her other palm. "How did you do this?" he asked grimly.

"It's from the pick handle. I don't have any gloves, and—"

"My God, Rory, your hands can get infected. All that dirt and those open sores!"

He strode to his saddlebags and pulled out a tin of unguent and a roll of white gauze. Tenderly he spread some of the balm on her palms, then wrapped them in gauze. "Don't you dare go near that pick again. If Paddy wants gold, he can damn well wait until he's well enough to dig for it himself."

"It wasn't his idea; it was mine." She looked at her hands swathed in bandages. "Thank you. They feel better already, Doctor."

"How long are you going to keep it up, Rory?"

She laughed lightly. "I was thinking the same thing earlier. I really hate it here." She gave him a guarded glance and swallowed hard. "Ah, Garth, I've been thinking a great deal about this problem. I know I have no right to ask, but until Pop is able to travel, I wonder if you might consider teaming up with us? If we find any gold, I'll give you half of whatever we find."

He gave an exasperated sigh. "Rory, you could have had that without stealing the map. I told you back in Buckman I'd split whatever I found with you, for saving me from being shanghaied. My word is my bond. If you'd believed me, you wouldn't be going through all this now."

She had just confessed how much she needed him and knew that nothing would be gained by telling him the truth about the map now. It would only sound like an alibi because she wanted his help.

"Your uncle's belief might be just another wasted dream, Garth, but as long as we have to stick around here, why not try? At least he died convinced he'd found the big strike—that pot of gold at the end of the rainbow, like so many others like him were seeking."

Garth was tempted to tell her that it hadn't been a pipe dream, that he had succeeded in finding gold and had every intention of dividing it with them. But in truth, they owned the mine, and Paddy O'Grady wouldn't hesitate to claim all of what legally belonged to them, no matter how illegally he'd obtained it. So it might be wiser to hold off, in the hope he could convince them to leave. No matter what Rory had done to him, he couldn't carry a grudge big enough to want to see her harmed. If Paddy wasn't so sick, though he'd kick the old man's ass all the way back to the mission for even bringing her here.

If he could persuade Rory to go back and wait at the mission, he'd give her the gold dust he'd discovered, then come back alone and continue to mine.

"Why stay on, Rory? We could leave now. When Paddy gets tired, we'll stop as often as necessary. Even if it takes a week to get back, that's no worse than sitting around here waiting for him to get better. Then I'll come back and work the claim. I swear before God that I'll give you half of whatever I find."

He pulled her into his arms. "Honey, there's no . . ."

The feel of her in his arms stoked the coals of his desire for her, and words fled. He lowered his head and covered her lips.

Surprisingly, she parted her lips. And Lord, she tasted so good, felt so good. So soft, warm—and so desirable. He broke the kiss long enough for a much-needed breath, then reclaimed her lips.

Her response was as heated as his. He lowered her to her back and kissed her again and again. He drove his tongue through her parted lips as he slipped a hand under the shirt and filled his hand with one of her breasts. Her gasp of shock was a weak deterrent as the feel of the rounded globe sent his lust soaring.

She broke the kiss and turned her head away. "No, I won't let you do this," she said breathlessly when he pushed up her shirt.

"You know you want it as much as I do," he whispered, and dipped his head and laved her nipples. When she sucked in a breath, he raised his head, "You liked that, didn't you?"

The aroused passion in her eyes told him everything he wanted to know. He lowered his head again and began to suckle one of her breasts. The taste of her was like heaven, and her warm body beneath him an aphrodisiac. Dragging his mouth away, he raised his head again and looked deeply into her eyes that had darkened with lust. "You really don't want me to stop, do you?"

"I...I..."

He felt on the verge of imploding and knew he couldn't hold on to his control much longer. "Say it, Rory. For God's sake, say it!"

She arched against him and cried, "I don't want you to stop."

His lips reclaimed hers. Too hot and hard for more foreplay, he went for the jugular.

Her eyes were closed, and her breath quickened to gasping breaths when he slid his hand along her naked warmth to the junction of her legs as he reached for his fly.

"Rory!" Paddy called.

The shout was like a bucket of ice water poured on his genitals. "Oh, God, no," he groaned.

Garth sat up and pulled her to a sitting position just as Paddy O'Grady came hobbling along the trail using a shaved limb as a staff.

"So here you be. You had me worrying, darlin'."

"What are you doing up, Pop? You should stay in bed. I was on the verge of leaving when Garth joined me," Rory said.

Paddy's gaze swept Garth's bare chest and then the shirt she was wearing. "And just what would he be joining you in, daughter?" he asked. Suspicion glittered in his eyes.

"In doing her laundry, sir," Garth said and stood up. "If you'd care for me to do yours, we'll be glad to leave and give you privacy."

"Yes, Pop, the water's cold, but refreshing," she encouraged as Garth held out a hand and helped her to her feet.

"I don't want a bath now."

"Well then, sit down and rest, Paddy. Rory and I have been considering leaving the mountain, and we'd like to hear what you think of the idea."

"I don't think I could do it," Paddy said.

"Pop, we could stop as frequently as you want. It wouldn't matter to us how long it would take us to get back."

" 'Tis a good idea, darlin', but I know me strength, and I'm ashamed to say I've not much of it. I'm feeling better by the day, so 'twould be better to wait for a couple days."

Rory sighed. "I suppose so." She stood up. "I doubt all my clothes are dry yet, but I'll put them back on still damp." She gathered them up and disappeared out of sight. When she emerged from the foliage, she handed Garth his shirt.

Their lingering gazes locked. "Thanks for the loan of it."

"The pleasure was all mine."

Paddy spun around and eyed him suspiciously. "Pleasure? What do you mean by that?"

"I mean what a pleasure it was to sit and have a quiet chat with your daughter, Paddy."

For an instant the old man gave him a belligerent glare, then broke out suddenly into a grin.

"Tell me, lad, do you play chess?"

"Most of my life, Paddy."

"Would you be doing me the pleasure of joining me in a game?"

"You're on, Paddy. Look for me tomorrow."

"That I will, me boy. That I will. Coming, darlin'?" Leaning heavily on his staff, he started back down the trail.

"Garth," Rory said, "will you think over my proposition?"

"I will, if you'll think over mine. I'm still for packing up and heading out right now."

Before she could guess his intent, he lowered his head and kissed her again. It was a kiss to sink into, reheating the coals he had just been forced to bank. But that moment had passed, and common sense now prevailed. He broke the kiss and stepped back.

"We still have some unfinished business to settle, but thank you for a most pleasant afternoon, Miss O'Grady."

For a brief moment, her startled look met the warmth in his brown eyes. Then she hurried after her father.

Garth returned to the cave, and for the next few hours collected more gold dust. The day had passed into night when he stopped and made a pot of coffee, fed and watered his four-legged companions, then sat down and chewed a stick of jerky. Deep in thought, his mind remained on the memory of the look in Rory's eyes when he'd kissed her good-bye.

"She drives me loco with those expressions of startled innocence of hers," he told the dog beside him.

"Good God, Saddle, the woman makes her living in saloons, stole my uncle's map from me, and God only knows how many times she's lied to me before and since."

He was still feeling the frustration of the abrupt and unfulfilled ending of their lovemaking.

"Then she has the nerve to act like a blushing virgin because I saw her naked. If she's so damn modest, what the hell was she doing bathing nude in the open to begin with?"

He bit off another bite of the jerky. "Then she actually accused me of intending to rape her—just because I peeked at her through a bush! Do you believe that, Saddle?"

He snatched up his cup, and then wiped some spilled coffee off his shirt. "I noticed she didn't cry rape when she was enjoying it. If she's a virgin, I'm the frigging Marquis de Sade! And I can get sworn affidavits of what a tender lover I am. Confidentially, that's just between you and me, boy," he said, aside.

"Saddle, the woman belongs in the theater. I'd bet every grain of gold in that pouch that there isn't a role she couldn't master if she had to play the part. Especially that of a quivering virgin on her wedding night, like she did today."

Saddle got up and started to move away. "Hey, hold up there. Did I say I was through?" The dog came back and stretched out again.

"Sure, she's a spunky little trooper and I admire that. But she's dishonest, so how can I ever trust her? My brother Colt always warned me about women like Rory. But I never believed that some women are just born out and out no good, and believed that if you treated any woman with kindness and respect, she'd return that compliment. Miss O'Grady sure taught me different!

"So keep that in mind with the next bitch you meet up with, boy," he said as he patted Saddle on the head. "Love them, but leave them.

"That's why I'm letting Rory get away with what she

did to me. I know all these weaknesses about her, but I still can't help liking her ... or stay angry with her. And the Lord knows I burn every time I look at her, but it's not her fault that she's so beautiful. I just have to keep reminding myself not to trust anything she says—because as well as I know women, I can't tell when she's working me or being truthful."

Saddle got up again. "Okay, you're right. It's about time to leave."

Garth dumped the coffee grounds onto a tin plate so they would be dry for his morning coffee, then saddled up Boots. Man, horse, and dog left the site to perform their nightly vigil.

The moon cast enough light on the crude trail for Garth to see well enough to ride slowly through the night. After a short distance, the light from the campfire became a beacon in the darkness.

Nearing the campfire, he dismounted and tethered Boots to a tree, and then moved into the concealment of the trees that rimmed the mountain's edge like rows of sentinels.

He had been coming every night for the past week to make sure the O'Gradys were all right. Neither one of them seemed to grasp the danger that could befall them at any time.

In truth, he felt somewhat responsible for them. If he hadn't told Rory about the map, she and Paddy wouldn't even be here.

Maybe he should think seriously about Rory's suggestion of joining up with them for the next couple days. That would make keeping a watchful eye on her a lot easier. He smiled. And being able to keep a watchful eye on him and Rory might make Paddy more cooperative. But it wouldn't do that wily old man any good; the ball had been put in motion between him and Rory. And right now he'd bet the damn gold mine that little Miss Rory O'Grady would soon be lying in bed thinking about that "unfinished business," too.

For about thirty minutes he watched the two move about their campfire, before Paddy disappeared inside their mine and remained there.

Rory had wisely built the campfire at the entrance to the mine. She went inside and built it up so that it extended fully across the entrance in the hope that the fire would keep any animal away, or any human from trying to enter the mine while they slept. She then disappeared herself, apparently retiring for the night. Garth figured he'd remain for another hour, and then return to his own mine.

Suddenly Saddle raised his head and let out a growl so low it was barely audible. Garth knelt down. The dog's fixed stare was on the trees ahead of them. "What is it, boy?" he whispered. "What do you hear?"

Drawing the pistol on his hip, Garth moved toward the trees ahead. He trod very carefully to avoid any misstep that would reveal his position or alert whoever or whatever had caught Saddle's attention.

For the length of a heartbeat he sensed, rather than saw, a movement in the trees. He expected at any second to face an adversary, human or animal. But whoever or whatever had been there had slipped away in the darkness.

Garth sat down and settled back against the trunk of a tree for the night, until the faint rays of a rising sun turned the darkness into a hazy gray.

Then he mounted Boots and returned to his mine.

10

Rory had spent a restless night thinking about not only the situation she was in, but even more about Garth Fraser. The more she saw of the man, the more she was attracted to him. And those moments in his arms at the waterfall were the most exciting she'd ever known. Were his parting words a promise or a warning?

He was truly about the nicest man she had ever met. Not only that; she doubted he had a mean or dishonest bone in that handsome body of his. She had often seen pathetic excuses for men like Mo Buckman hit a woman for accidentally spilling a drink or speaking up to them.

She'd watched men cheat and even kill each other over a card game. Even her own father, whom she loved dearly, hadn't hesitated to steal a map just because the opportunity presented itself. Most of the men she'd met would have killed Pop, if they'd caught up with them like Garth had.

Granted, one met the dregs in saloons, but Garth Fraser was a far cry from any of them. He not only wasn't a violent man, but he had integrity and was a gentleman. He even treated prostitutes like ladies. Why, Shelia had told her Garth had even thanked her for her service, when most men considered the two dollars thanks enough.

Rory had no doubt he would have stopped his en-flaming caresses earlier, had she told him to, but his kisses and touch thrilled her. That was the one thing she feared about Garth Fraser: no man she'd ever known had ever thrilled her like him. He was the kind of man she had always hoped to meet one day, marry, and have his children.

Garth had all the qualities that she had hoped and dreamed for in a husband. But even if they'd met under different circumstances, he had no desire or in-tention of settling down. His dreams lay beyond that horizon he was looking toward. He had places to see, mountains to climb, rivers to cross—and that pot of gold at the end of a rainbow yet to discover.

The wisest thing she could do would be to take his advice and get out of there now. Because as sure as the sun comes up in the morning, if she hung around him much longer, she wouldn't be a virgin on her wedding night.

As she was gathering wood to make a fire, Saddle came trotting up to her. "Hey, what are you doing here, fella?" she asked, hugging him as he licked her cheek. Her heartbeat quickened when Garth appeared seconds later.

"Good morning," she said, hiding her feelings behind a casual smile.

"Here, let me help you with that," he said, dismounting quickly when she turned away to pick up the stack of wood she'd been gathering.

"That's not necessary, Garth. I can do it myself," she snapped. Driven by a feeling of guilt over the hopeless thoughts she harbored about him, she now released it in anger. Why did he always succeed in making her feel like some fragile china doll that would smash into pieces if dropped? No matter what he said to the contrary, or his belief that she was dishonest, it was beyond his capability to treat her unkindly.

"Uh-oh! What do you think, Saddle? Sounds like the lady hasn't had that second cup of coffee yet."

"Just once, Garth Fraser," she lashed out, "I wish you'd do the same."

"What is that supposed to mean? Are you angry because I tried to make love to you yesterday? You didn't try to stop me."

"Thank you for reminding me of that; it's a good excuse to be angry. But that's not my reason."

"Then what is? Paddy get you riled up this morning?"

"No, he's still asleep. You're the one who's got me riled."

He opened his arms in astonished innocence. "What did I do?"

"Just one morning, can't you get up grouchy and irritable like the rest of us? How can you wake up every day of your life with a smile? Even an innocent baby wakes up crying, hungry, and wet. But not you."

"Crying, hungry, and wet? I should hope not."

"No, indeed. Not Mr. Sunshine himself."

He burst into laughter. "Is that all that's bothering you? I thought there was a serious problem."

She threw her hands up in a hopeless gesture. "That's what I mean! Can't you get angry, or tell me you don't give a damn whether I like it or not?"

"But I do care," he said. "I'm just glad to hear there's nothing seriously wrong. Besides, you're real cute when you're riled enough to cuss."

Rory glanced heavenward. "Lord, I can't take much more of this." She spun on her heel and stormed away.

Garth picked up the wood she had dropped and chased after her. "You have to admit you enjoyed it."

"Enjoyed what?"

"My making love to you."

She stopped short and glared at him. "In my lexicon, groping a woman is not considered *making love*."

"And in my lexicon, Miss O'Grady, staring at a woman bathing nude in public is not considered *rape*," he countered with an overbearing grin. "Furthermore, I do not grope or rape. I always love the women I'm with—at the time."

"What a shame the feeling isn't mutual."

"Ah, but you're wrong."

She gaped at him in disbelief. "You're serious?"

"Certainly," he said smugly.

Rory shook her head sadly. "And what do these women reward you with in return, Mr. Fraser: swinging hips or agitated twitters?" She walked away.

He started after her again, and tripped. He and the wood went flying.

Rory turned around. "Oops, tripped over your tongue, did you?"

He raised his arms in the air. "Okay, I'll cry uncle. You've got the last word." He stood up and brushed himself off. Then, laughing together, they gathered up the wood.

"You're welcome to stay for breakfast," she offered as she stacked the wood in his arms. "The pickings are poor, but you're welcome to share what we have."

"I actually have a different thought in mind. How would you like to take a little ride? I'm hoping Saddle will lead me to that trout stream he visits every morning. It can't be too far, because he's never gone for a long time."

He cocked a brow. "And think of how good a cup of hot coffee would taste with a piece of fried trout. So I packed up the makings for coffee and a couple of biscuits."

"You baked biscuits?"

"Lady, you have no idea how talented I am."

The prospect of fresh fish did sound appealing. "Did you remember a skillet?"

"Sure did, honey."

"Then let's get going!"

"That's better."

"Fish and biscuits do sound much better than fried potatoes."

"Actually, I was referring to that lovely smile on your face now, instead of that scowl you were wearing. Good morning, Miz Sunshine." He climbed into the saddle, then swung her up behind him.

How was a person to stay angry with the man!

"I thought you said this would be a short ride," Rory complained an hour later. "We must have ridden at least three miles already."

"We can't stop now," Garth said. "Besides, it can't be much farther."

Garth no sooner had gotten the words out of his mouth when he spotted the stream they sought. High above them, the snow-capped peaks of the Sierra Nevada mountain range stretched out before them farther than the eye could see. The source of the stream appeared to come from the nearest towering peak.

The stream abounded with silvery silhouettes flashing through the water. Garth waded in, and for several minutes tried to catch one of the fish barehanded. He abandoned that method and returned to the riverbank, cut off a slim limb from a tree, then shaved off the leaves and whittled one of the ends into a sharp point. Within minutes he succeeded in spearing a fish.

Rory cut a strong vine from the foliage and strung the fish on it, then gathered wood for a fire. By the time she had a pot of coffee brewing, Garth had succeeded in adding five additional fish to the makeshift line.

"I think this is enough to get us started," he said, pulling off three of them.

"That's wonderful. We can take the other two back for Pop."

As quickly as Garth scaled and gutted the fish, Rory filleted and fried them. Saddle trotted over to the fire. He'd been unsuccessful with his leaps and bounds to catch one of the slippery trout, so she tossed him several pieces of the savory catch.

"This was a wonderful idea," Rory said later, when they finished the last bite of fish and last crumb of biscuit. "I can't remember when I enjoyed fish so much."

"I'll catch a couple more for dinner. I imagine Paddy would enjoy them."

"That's very thoughtful of you, Garth. Where did you learn to spear fish? That sounds like what an Indian would do."

"You learn a lot in the army that doesn't have anything to do with fighting. If we were lucky enough to be near a fish stream between battles, we didn't always have the time to sit with a pole and fish, so it came in handy to learn the art of using a spear."

"You said your home is in Virginia."

"Yes, Fraser Keep is located between the James and York rivers in southeast Virginia, near Williamsburg. It's been my family's home for eleven generations."

"I can't imagine being able to trace your roots that far back and know your family has lived under the same roof. I've only known my own parents and a maternal grandmother. I'm told I have an aunt and uncle in Ireland on my father's side, but I've never met them. Are your parents still alive?"

"No, they died from cholera during the war. My brother Will's six-month-old son died from it, too. There was no medicine available to help them."

"I'm so sorry, Garth," she said sadly. "The little I know about that war makes it all sound so tragic."

"Everything about that war was tragic. It began in sixty-one, supposedly to preserve the union when the issue of states' rights arose. Then in sixty-three, when Lincoln declared the Emancipation Proclamation, it suddenly changed and became a war cry to free the slaves."

"At least some good came out of the war. I don't believe that anyone should ever be sold into slavery."

"You're missing my point, Rory. The war was started over typical rotten Washington political jockeying. The issue of slavery could and should have been fought on the floor of Congress. Isn't that why we elect politicians? And if abolishing slavery was the original intent for fighting the war, why wasn't slavery abolished immediately in sixty-one when the war began? With the South having seceded, there would have been no opposition to vote against it, and it would have been pushed through immediately. So why did Lincoln wait two more years to declare slavery abolished?"

"What do you think was the reason?" she asked, surprised by his bitter intensity.

"Those Washington hypocrites were scared stiff to take such a measure sooner, in fear the Confederacy would win and they'd be drummed out of office. For despite the fact that the South didn't have the money, manpower, industry, railroads, or navy that the North had, the Confederacy was winning the goddamn war.

"What the North didn't have then was leadership. The Yankees couldn't even find a decent military commander to lead them after General Lee turned down their offer, until they finally put Grant in command after a couple of years.

"There'd been a few minor wins by the Yankees, but General Lee and our other Southern generals outsmarted them and outfought them constantly, despite having only half the manpower and supplies. So the people in the North were beginning to doubt the wisdom of the war, and it wasn't until Sharpsburg—the Yankees called it Antietam—in September of 'sixty-two that the war began to shift as the Confederacy's manpower and supplies dwindled. It must have convinced those politicians they had a chance of winning, so they came out with the Emancipation Proclamation a few months later to rally morale with a new war cry."

"Why did that battle make such a difference?" she asked.

"Because it was the first major battle that General Lee lost. It became known as 'the bloodiest single day of the war.' The Confederacy suffered the loss of almost fourteen thousand men killed or wounded, and the Yankees over twelve thousand. Think of it, Rory, twenty-six thousand men killed or wounded in one single day!"

Rory shook her head at the thought of the mammoth tragedy of it.

"And among those killed was a young private named Joseph Fraser, my brother's sixteen-year-old son."

"Oh, dear God," she murmured. Rory reached for his hand and grasped it. "Your poor family. They lost so many loved ones."

"Ours wasn't the only family, Rory. There wasn't a home in the South that didn't suffer such losses. The following year in July, my youngest brother Andy died at Gettysburg, along with nearly sixty thousand others who were killed and wounded during that campaign—Reb and Yankee alike. They were all Americans. I recently read in the newspaper that it's estimated that close to eight hundred thousand men died or were maimed or wounded before the war ended.

"When I let myself think about it, sometimes I feel a sense of guilt for surviving." Anguish had replaced the warmth that she'd become accustomed to seeing in his eyes. "So no matter what you think, Miss O'Grady, I don't wake up with a smile *every* morning."

Then, as if wanting to change the mood, he leaned over and grinned. "Of course I might be able to if you were lying next to me when I woke up."

Determined to keep him from slipping back into the dark mood, she answered pertly, "Unless that proposal relates to marriage, Mr. Fraser, I'll decline the offer."

"You've got a cold heart, lady."

"No, I'm just saving myself for the man I love. Besides, I want to hear more about your life."

"Such as?"

"You've told me the bad part of your life; now tell me the good part. Your childhood. What it was like before the war?"

"Hmmm." He stretched out and tucked his hands under his head. "It seems so long ago. My parents, my sister and brothers. Life at Fraser Keep. The ancestor who built Fraser Keep came from Scotland and was one of the original Virginia colonists. My parents were born and bred Virginians. I grew up with five brothers and one sister. Will's the eldest of us; he's thirty-six." He grinned broadly. "The old married man of the family. None of us would have had a home to come back to after the war if it weren't for him. Then there's Clay, he's thirty-two. He's the one I came to California with. Married a Yankee on the way."

Once again his mouth widened in a grin, and Rory couldn't help thinking how much younger it made him look.

"That's a story in itself. Then there's Colt, who's twenty-six now, two years younger than me. Understand he married a Yankee on his way out here, too. I haven't had the pleasure of meeting her yet, but I'm sure eager to. Jedediah is the next one; he'd be twenty-five now. Last I heard, he was still at home. Then there was Andy. He was twenty-two when he was killed at Gettysburg. Last is Lissy, our only sister. Dad and Mom swore to keep having children until they got a girl."

He shook his head. "What a handful! She wrapped all of us around her little finger. We all adored her and spoiled her rotten. From the time she budded out, we all guarded her like soldiers. Wouldn't let any local boys near her. And what did she do? While we were off fighting the war, the little minx fell in love with a Yankee soldier who had been quartered at Fraser Keep, and they eloped as soon as the war ended. Clay and I chased after her to bring her back, and that's how we ended up in California."

"And did you catch up with her?"

"Finally." The welcome warmth had returned to his eyes. "But that, too, is another story."

"So now you're all here in California, except your brother Will—"

"And Jed. He always fancied the sea. If the Confederacy had had a navy, Jed probably would be an admiral by now. As for Will, I suspect nothing will ever get him out of Virginia."

"And you intend to go back one day yourself."

"Probably, when I've done and seen all I want to. I don't tie myself down to any permanent plans."

"I envy you; it must be wonderful to grow up with brothers and sisters. War, death, or no matter what follows can never erase those memories."

"Yeah, looking back, those were great times."

"What did you do before the war?"

"It was kind of traditional for a young man to spend some time in the military. Clay went to West Point. He ended up fighting half of his classmates during the war. Colt and I preferred the Virginia Military

Academy, so we went there together. We're pretty much alike."

"In what way?" Rory asked.

"Kiss and run, if you know what I mean. No commitments. We went to Europe together to see the world, but never got farther than Paris when Virginia seceded and we had to change our plans. Now that he's married, I guess we'll never make the Grand Tour together. I can't believe that bounder up and married on me."

"Which now makes *you* the remaining bounder."

He sat up with a good-natured grin. "Enough about me. Tell me about your life."

"There's not much to tell. My folks were born in Ireland and arrived in California right before I was born. I can barely remember what it was like to live in a house; a canvas tent was usually what I called 'home.' We moved around from one gold-mining town to another until my mother died when I was eight. A few years later, Pop gave up gold mining for cardplaying." She glanced up at him with a sardonic smile. "Unfortunately he never gave up whiskey."

"Why didn't you leave him when you were old enough, Rory?"

She looked at him, astonished. "Why would I do that? I love him, Garth. He's my father. And besides, before she died, I promised my mom I'd take care of him."

"Paddy O'Grady is a likable old rascal, honey, but he can't offer you the kind of love you deserve."

"How can you say that, Garth? I know he loves me. So he has a weakness for drinking. I certainly wish he didn't, but it doesn't make me love him less."

"He has more than one weakness, Rory. He's content to be a dreamer and drifter without any consideration for the two women who loved him—his wife and daughter. He was content to let you come here where there are all sorts of ways for you to be harmed, for the sake of finding gold—the same thing he failed to accomplish when his wife was still alive."

"I had the impression you understood what family means," she declared indignantly. "Would you love your parents or siblings any less if one of them had a drinking problem, Garth? Or maybe a gambling one? Or, God forbid, if they hadn't fought to defend your precious Virginia?

"I saw how much Mum loved Pop; and how much he loved her. How can you presume to pass judgment on their relationship any more than you can on his relationship with me? Right now, whiskey and consumption have a hold on him. But I would never give up on him because he has a weakness for whiskey, any more than I would because he's ill."

She turned her back to him in disgust. "I suppose you see that as just another one of *my* weaknesses."

Garth spun her back to face him. "Then consider what would happen to him if you weren't around. Who will he have to take care of him if you're harmed or killed? Can't you see, Rory, how he's depending on your strength and not his own?"

"Not any more than I've depended on his in the past. Regardless, it's not your problem."

"It's become my problem, because I'm worried what will happen to you." Tears glistened in her eyes and he pulled her into his arms. "Ah, honey, I'm sorry. I didn't mean to hurt you."

He gently brushed aside a tear rolling down her cheek, then pressed a light kiss to her lips. "I'm sorry, baby. So sorry."

He had intended the kiss to be consoling, not sensual, but his body reacted to it with a surge of hot passion that clouded his brain. He deepened the kiss.

11

The instant Garth's lips touched hers, sensation exploded through her with a power that she couldn't control. Instinctively her body arched to his and she slipped her arms around his neck, parting her lips in a moan of pleasure.

He pressed her to the ground and his fingers freed the buttons of her shirt. When the heat of his palm cupped her breast through the thin fabric of her chemise, her body responded to it with a surge of hot passion that clouded her brain.

She knew it was a repeat of the previous day—just as she knew coming here alone with him would be. And she'd been so wrong in believing she'd been prepared to resist him this time.

Men who had tried to grope her or force a kiss on her had only angered and disgusted her, but that wasn't the case when Garth did; the passion enveloping her now was just the opposite as his mouth consumed her in another kiss. His tongue invaded her mouth with erotic strokes, and she moaned again when he shifted his mouth to her breast.

She gasped in sweet agony when he closed around the nipple with a moist warmth. Within seconds, the thin fabric became too much of a barrier. She ached for the touch of his mouth on her flesh. To feel his hands, his mouth, the length of his hard body on hers—flesh against flesh.

As she groped for his shirt buttons he raised up and she stared, stunned, and dropped her hands.

"Garth, something's wrong. Look at Saddle."

He turned his head and saw what had disturbed her: the dog was standing stiff-legged with his ears perked, staring at a nearby copse of trees.

"No," he moaned pitifully. "Not again!"

"Don't say anything. Just sit up and button your shirt," he whispered. Then he rose to his feet and said loudly, "You ready to leave, honey? I think it's time we get back to the mine."

She couldn't have said anything if she wanted to; her throat was too dry to speak. So she did what he told her to.

Garth walked casually over to the fire. He poured the remaining coffee and grounds over the ashes, and rather than take the time to wash the dishes and frying pan, he slipped them into the saddlebags. Then he got the fish from the stream and wrapped them up in a couple of large leaves and put them in a saddlebag.

Rory found it amazing how he managed to sound so casual and not even glance in the direction of the trees as he kicked dirt over the remaining ashes. When he was satisfied they were completely out, he mounted Boots and hoisted her up. The he whistled for Saddle as they rode away.

After a short distance, he reined up behind the concealment of a boulder. "Do you think you can handle Boots well enough to ride back to your mine alone? I'll send Saddle with you. He knows the trail."

"I'm not going without you, Garth. If you're planning to go back there to check out those trees, I'm going with you. Besides, it could have been just a rabbit or squirrel."

"If that were so, Saddle would have gone after it. Whatever was in those trees was big enough to spook him."

"Maybe a bear? That fish would attract one."

"That's a good point, but I haven't seen a bear track since I've been here."

"That doesn't mean there's none around, Davy Crockett."

Last night Garth had thought he'd glimpsed a shadow of something or someone stalking her camp. If this incident was related, there was no sense in alarming her until he had some positive evidence.

"I went through four years of war, and I could always sniff out Yankee scouts and patrols when they were around."

"So you think it could be a Yankee scout or patrol?" she asked, tongue-in-cheek.

Rory wasn't taking the situation as seriously as she should have. "You're beginning to irritate me, Rory."

"And you could sniff them out, you say," she said. "Must have a bit of a dog in you, Captain Fraser."

He had too much on his mind to appreciate her humor. "I hate to sound ungallant, Miss O'Grady, but it wasn't more than a short time ago that you appeared to be very eager to have a 'bit of a dog' in you."

That wiped the smile from her face. "You surprise me, Captain Fraser; that *was* ungallant, even in jest."

"You're right, I apologize. Guess I'm just a sore loser. We'll have to try it again sometime."

"Over my dead body," she declared. "And no matter what you say, if you're going back there, I'm going with you."

"Then don't utter another word, and do exactly what I tell you to do."

She nodded.

Upon returning to the stream, he dismounted and handed her the reins. "Don't get down, and don't fire this unless it's absolutely necessary." He handed her his Colt. Then he pulled his rifle out of the sling. "If there's any trouble, get out of here as fast as you can."

Everything appeared to be exactly as they had left it. Even the spear lay where he had dropped it. The dead ashes had not been disturbed, and there were no prints other than their own at the riverbank.

Perhaps Rory was right. It was probably nothing more than a small wood creature. He went into the copse of trees to investigate, only to return within minutes. "Okay, let's get out of here."

"Did you find what you were looking for?" Rory asked, handing the pistol back to him. She shifted out of the saddle to make room for him.

"I'm not sure." Garth returned the rifle to the sling and the Colt to the holster on his hip. Then he mounted Boots.

She clasped her arms around his waist and leaned her cheek against his back. "So what did you discover: a pile of rabbit turds, or the hole where a squirrel buried nuts for the winter?"

He could see it was going to be a long ride back; she wasn't going to let the matter drop. But since she was in such good spirits now, nothing would be gained by alarming her at the moment.

"If you don't stop making fun of Saddle's attempts to guard us, you're going to hurt his feelings," Garth warned in a light tone.

"I wouldn't want to do that, now would I, fella?" she told the dog trotting beside them. "And even if you can't bark, I'd rather have you as a watchdog than any other." Then she poked Garth in the ribs. "Well, maybe other than that 'bit of the dog' in your master, Saddle. That one has a powerful bark, but it's not as cute as you."

"There you go insulting his manhood again, Miz O'Grady. Who calls a dog as big and shaggy as Saddle 'cute'?"

"So what would you call him?"

"I guess 'manly.' Yeah, a man's dog, so to speak."

"Don't you mean a dog's dog?"

He cocked a brow. "Guess you could say that if the other dog was female."

"I think you have a dirty mind, Garth."

"So why don't we put my dirty mind to good use and pick up where we left off when we were so rudely interrupted?"

"Don't you wish, Fraser." She slipped off the rear of Boots and ran ahead and began to pick a bouquet of yellow and red poppies.

Garth didn't try to stop her. He dismounted, and, leading Boots by the reins, he walked slowly along, casting an occasional glance behind him.

As long as she remained in his view, it gave him time to think. He'd discovered part of a print that appeared to have been made by a boot heel, but it was too muddy to tell for certain.

A grim line had replaced Paddy's Irish grin, and a glower the puckish twinkle in his eyes when they returned to camp.

"Good morning, Paddy," Garth said.

Ignoring Garth's greeting, Paddy scowled at Rory. "You had me worried again, daughter. Where have you been?"

"Garth and I went for a morning ride, Pop."

Paddy spun and turned the full measure of his irritation on Garth. "A morning ride, is it? And I'm thinking it's not riding the horse you had in mind, Mr. Fraser."

Rory gasped. "Pop, that remark is disgraceful! We had breakfast."

"And where would that be, daughter? At the queen's palace or the fancy restaurant down the road?"

She put her hands on her hips. Rebelliousness flashed in those baby-blue eyes of hers and the return of the brogue on her tongue.

"Garth was knowing of a stream of fish. And need I be reminding you, Mr. Paddy O'Grady, that I be twenty-four years of age? And daughter or not, what I do is me business alone and none of your own."

Paddy turned to Garth again. "What you're up to *is* me business."

Garth snorted. "You O'Gradys are a real pair! Your daughter has repeatedly informed me that *your* business is none of *mine*; now you tell me that what *I do* is *your* business. Need I remind you, sir, that if my map had not been stolen, the three of us wouldn't be here together at all."

"You're not fooling me, Garth Fraser. Coming around here with your fancy ways, sniffing at me daughter's skirt the way you've been doing."

"Frankly, sir, I'm unaware your daughter has a skirt. She's been wearing those jeans for the past week. And since she's a grown woman, what she and I do is *our* business and not *yours*."

He went over to Boots and retrieved the fish, then handed them to Paddy. "Enjoy your breakfast, sir."

Paddy looked abashed, but still stubborn. "Well, it naught can be said that Paddy O'Grady is one to ignore a man's generosity, so I'm thanking you for it."

"You're welcome."

"Now I'll be thanking you to be on your way, Mr. Fraser. We have no need of you here."

"And I'll believe that when I hear it from your daughter, sir." Garth tipped his hat to Rory. "Thank you for a most pleasant morning, Rory."

"I'm sorry, Garth."

"Don't give it a thought."

He mounted Boots and rode away.

As Garth rode along, his anger rose with every clop of Boots's hooves. He'd had it with the thievery, lies, blushing so-called virgins, and drunken old men. He was through playing their games. Paddy could stay here and rot, as far as he was concerned. And Rory with him, if she didn't have the gumption to make a stand.

Tomorrow he'd offer to help them back to the mission as he said he would, but if Paddy refused to go, he'd wash his hands of them once and for all.

He wheeled Boots to ride back to tell them.

As soon as Garth rode away, Paddy handed the fish to Rory, then went back to his bedroll with a fit of violent coughing. Her eyes misted as she built a fire. How could her father have embarrassed her the way he did? She knew it was the whiskey talking, and when it wore off he'd be his usual lovable self. But never before had he spewed such nastiness. She feared the coughing, the lack of eating, and the whiskey had begun to work on his nerves, to change him. She had to get him out of here.

As she prepared the fish, Rory thought about how wonderful the morning with Garth had been, and those incredible moments in his arms again.

Still, it frightened her to think how close she had come once again to surrendering her virginity. It had always been so easy to reject other men's advances, but Garth's kiss and touch made her forget her vow to remain chaste. It was as if she had no will of her own. Just being with him made her happy to be alive. And despite how dangerous his kiss or touch was, she couldn't wait for the next one.

She sighed. He thinks I'm nothing better than a lying tramp, so why try to convince him it isn't true, she pondered wistfully.

Paddy got to his feet and started to stagger away.

"Where are you going, Pop? Your fish is ready."

"I'm not hungry, darlin'."

"But Pop, it's fresh fish. And it's delicious."

"I'll not be eating a bite from the likes of that man. I want none of his charity."

"That's nonsense, Pop. Garth is a good man."

"Good indeed! What did you have to give him for it? You think I don't know what the two of you are up to when you go off in the woods? I'll not be filling me belly with any food me daughter's earned on her back."

Rory was too stunned to respond. She couldn't believe her father would make such an accusation. Over the pain of his words, she struggled with logic. "That's the whiskey in you talking, Pop. I can smell it on your breath."

"Whiskey, is it?" Paddy lashed out. "I'm thanking God I have whiskey to ease the shame of this."

"If that's what you believe, maybe we should pack up and leave here right now."

"Your fine Mr. Fraser would like that, wouldn't he? Then he could be stealing the gold that belongs to us. Well, I can't stop you from letting him have his way with you, but it's not gonna drive me away."

"Oh, Pop, we can't go on like this. Don't you see what's happening to us? This mountain is driving us apart. You're ill, not eating, and you're drinking too heavily. The whiskey is affecting your thinking."

"The only thing affecting me thinking is the thought of what is happening to me own daughter."

Rory's heart wrenched at the look of anguish in his eyes. "Ah, darlin'," he said tenderly in a sudden shift of moods, "hasn't your Pop always looked after you? I love you, and nothing on God's green earth will ever change that."

Normally he was not one to eavesdrop on other people's conversations, but Garth couldn't help overhearing the argument between Rory and her father.

Paddy's accusations to Rory were hateful. He was being stubborn and selfish, treating her like chattel rather than the loving and loyal daughter she was. And if anyone was corrupting Rory, it was Paddy himself in attempting to keep her under his thumb.

Rory was a kind, generous, and compassionate woman. She had a good sense of humor, and was loyal to a fault—which was the hold on her that Paddy abused so badly.

She was spunky and had the grit to back up her intrepid qualities, yet there was a vulnerability about her that made him want to protect her.

And the icing on the cake was her beauty and sensuousness. She'd make some lucky man a wonderful wife someday, if she only got out from under the disturbing influence of her father. The last person she deserved a tongue lashing from was Paddy O'Grady.

He figured Rory had had enough embarrassment for one day, so he left silently.

12

Devastated, Rory watched her father stagger off into the trees.

It wasn't even noon yet and he'd already had too much to drink. And nothing to eat.

He never would have said those nasty things to her if he wasn't drunk. He was alone too much. At least in a town, he was able to play cards or talk to others. Here there was no one but her, and she'd spent all her time in the mine until Garth had convinced her to give it up. Maybe Pop was right; maybe Garth wanted them out of there so he could have it for himself.

If only Pop would turn to Garth for companionship. Garth had a positive attitude about everything, and it would do her father good to be with him. Instead, he rejected Garth.

It was clear he suspected the attraction between her

and Garth, and was probably jealous—or downright afraid—that he no longer would be the only man in her life.

I'm wise to you, Pop. But don't worry. No man could ever take the place in my heart that you hold.

And because of her love for him, she no longer could sit by and watch him destroy himself. Somehow she had to find where he hid the whiskey. She'd search the mine, and if she was lucky, she'd find it before Pop came back.

Rory hurried inside. Even in daylight, it was too dark to see beyond a few feet. She lit a lantern and carefully went through every one of their packs of clothing and supplies again. When she finished with that, on hands and knees she checked the hollowed-out corners of the mine to see if he might have dug a hole and buried the bottles. That, too, resulted in no success.

The only other area to be checked was the tunnel that Henry Fraser had dug and fortified.

Hunched down, Rory ran her hands along each side of the wall and up the posts he'd erected to shore up the ceiling. They all appeared to be undisturbed since their arrival.

After a tedious inch-by-inch inspection, she reached the last post. A few feet beyond it lay the pick she'd been using, and the few feet of dirt she had managed to dig through.

The lantern started to flicker and would probably burn out in minutes, so she would have to abandon her search. Frustrated, she grabbed the pick and gave the ground a solid whack.

Rory cried out as the ground gave way beneath her. The pick and lantern dropped out of her hands and she fell into a deep hole.

Fortunately she landed on the pile of soft, unpacked earth that had collapsed, but the fall knocked the breath out of her and she lay gasping, unable to move.

When she finally had enough breath to sit up, she groped for the lantern lying on its side. There was hardly enough candle wax remaining to keep it lit, and she held it up and looked around.

The hole was at least twenty feet deep, and she could barely make out the rim above, much less climb up to reach it. It was about six feet across.

Then something in the far corner caught her attention. Careful not to spill one drop of the precious wax, she crawled over to what appeared to be a pile of clothing. When she reached it, she saw that it was the skeletal remains of a man dressed in a plaid shirt and gray trousers.

Rory screamed, dropped the lamp, and lurched and stumbled back through the dirt into the opposite corner as the scattered drops of remaining wax wavered into extinction. She clawed at the wall, trying to do the impossible and scale it, then fell back. Frightened and sobbing, she huddled in the darkness and tried to hang on to her sanity.

"Garth," she sobbed. "Please help me, Garth. Please help me!"

After returning to his camp, Garth realized that he should have had it out with the old man once and for all. If that was part of a human footprint in the trees this morning, it could mean that he was correct last night: someone had been lurking in the shadows at the O'Grady mine. Obviously someone without a weapon, because there had been plenty of opportunities to use one in the past week. Neither Paddy nor Rory carried a handgun, so it would be easy to overpower either one of them. So was there really a threat?

"But one thing I know for certain, Saddle," Garth said later as he bedded down for the night. "Before I leave this mountain, I'm going to face down that wily old man and tell him what I really think of him for what he's done to his daughter."

Throughout the night, Garth's struggle with his conscience made sleep impossible. He would not let Rory continue to go on like this. He had hoped for their sake that Paddy would have been well enough to travel by now. But no such luck. So he made up his mind to tell her the truth about the real mine at once.

Garth got up at dawn, built a fire, and put on a pot of coffee. After a quick breakfast, he saddled Boots and rode to the O'Grady mine.

Arriving at the camp, Garth was surprised not to see a campfire. Rory was an early riser.

He called out her name several times but there was no answer. He didn't like it. His instincts told him something had to be wrong. He went over and felt the campfire ashes. They were cold, and from the looks of them, at least a day old. That would mean she hadn't even built a fire last night. His fears increased when he saw Saddle sniffing at a frying pan lying nearby. The pan was dirty and the dog was eating the remains of some fried fish. Rory would never have left food lying outside overnight, for fear it would attract animals.

Now he was certain something serious had happened to her—and he feared the worst. That fear increased further when he saw the flowers she had picked the previous morning lying in a wilted heap on the ground. Whatever had happened, she hadn't had time to even put them in water, so it would have to have been shortly after he left.

All kinds of fears began to whirl through his head. Bandits had snatched her. A wild animal had carried her away. He even had an image of an angry and drunken Paddy harming her. The most hopeful thing he could think of, as dangerous as it might be, was that she might have taken off and gone back to the mission.

But no matter how angry she was, she wouldn't desert her father. If the camp had been attacked by bandits, there would be more destruction—and their two donkeys and the burro were there. As for a wild animal? There wasn't a sign of blood anywhere, so it was unlikely an animal was the culprit.

That left one possibility: Paddy. Even in his weakened state, had the man been so drunk and out of control that he had harmed her? Where was he, anyway? His shouting for Rory surely would have wakened Paddy. Could both of them . . . His glance swung to the mine. Dreading what he might find, he walked slowly to the entrance and went in.

Loud snoring led him to Paddy, asleep in one of the dim corners. There was no sign of Rory. Garth went over and awakened him.

Snorting, the man sat up. "What—"

"Paddy, where's Rory?" he bit out.

"Did I not tell you to leave us alone, Mr. Fraser."

"Where is she? What have you done to her?"

"If me daughter's not outside, then she's in the tunnel."

Garth released him and went over and glanced in. "It's pitch dark in there."

"Then she must be out gathering wood."

Garth went back outside. There was still no sign of Rory, and the pile of wood stacked neatly near the entrance made it unlikely she was gathering more.

Paddy came outside yawning and scratching at his belly. He smelled like a brewery.

Disgusted, Garth asked, "When was the last time you saw her?"

"Don't remember. Where's the coffee? I need me coffee in the morning."

Garth studied the ground for prints, but saw nothing that reflected a struggle. "Damn it, Paddy, think! When was the last time you saw her?"

Paddy went over, sat down on a huge rock, and buried his head in his hands. "How's a man to think when me head's aching something fierce?"

"And drowning in whiskey. Paddy, I swear—sick or not—if you've harmed one hair on her head, I'll drown you in something other than whiskey."

Paddy dropped his hands and glared at him. "I'd no more lay a hand on me darling girl than I would a babe in arms. I'll not listen to another of your accusing words, Garth Fraser."

"Come on, Saddle, let's check out the trees. You'll be more helpful than he will be." Paddy got up and followed him anyway.

For the next thirty minutes, they searched the whole area for what Garth feared would be her body. When they returned to camp, Paddy was near to collapsing and both men were near their wit's end.

"For God's sake, Paddy, you've got to try and think back. When was the last time you saw her?"

"I can remember coming back here."

"What time was that?"

"I don't know. I'd fallen asleep in the woods and it was dark, and there was no campfire. I thought it was strange 'cause Rory always set one on the entrance at night. Then I figured she was still mad over a fight we had."

"Well, did you speak to her?"

"No. It was too dark to see anything, and I thought she was sleeping."

"After being gone all day, it didn't occur to you to check to make sure?"

"I thought of it, but I was feeling poorly. I couldn't find the lantern where she always put it when she was through in the tunnel, so I laid down and went to sleep."

Garth jerked up his head. "Where is it?"

"What?"

"The lantern. Where is the lantern?" Garth quickly stood. "Give me some candles. I'm going to look in that tunnel."

Paddy got a packet of candles from the mine, then Garth lit one and stuck the others in his pocket.

"You're too big for the tunnel. You'll have to stoop to get through it," Paddy warned.

But Garth was already on his way.

Rory opened her eyes. How long had it been? Minutes? Hours? Days? From the time she had begun dropping in and out of sleep, she had lost all sense of time, alone down here in the darkness.

She buried her head in her hands. Surely by now Pop would have noticed she was gone. Could she have been down here for only a few hours? No, it had been longer than that. It had been hours before she had even fallen asleep the first time.

What if Pop was too drunk to even notice she was gone? Still worse, what if something had happened to him when he'd stomped off? He might have encountered a bear or mountain lion. Or bandits may have returned and killed him. He could be lying dead up there even now! Oh God, what if their last moments together had ended in a quarrel? And how long would it be before Garth came looking for her?

She held back a sob.

She was cold and her legs felt cramped, so she stood and stamped her feet to get the circulation going.

"All right, Rory, get a hold on yourself and think of what you can do. You've been in worse situations than this and managed to get out of them. So start using the common sense you were born with.

"First off: as gruesome as it is, you know that thing over in that corner cannot harm you.

"Secondly: it takes a very long time to die of hunger, so it's a pretty good guess that Garth or Pop will discover you long before that can happen.

"Third, think of what would make matters worse, and don't do those things." She continued to stamp and shake her feet. "If you move around too much, the dirt might give way again and you'd drop deeper, or even get buried alive. So try to remain as still as possible." She stopped stamping and quickly sat down.

"Just be patient and wait for Garth to show up. Take your mind off your situation until he does. Try singing; that always helps to take away your troubles."

Rory started off with "Oh! Susanna," then followed it up with "The Old Gray Mare" and "The Yellow Rose of Texas."

When she got through those, she turned to some more Stephen Foster songs, but by the time she finished "My Old Kentucky Home" and "Beautiful Dreamer," her optimistic mood had sunk to depression, and she found herself wiping away tears as she sang "Abide With Me," and followed it up with "Nearer My God to Thee."

She felt as if she were singing her own dirge.

She tried to swallow, but her throat was too dry from singing.

"Another thing, Rory, is that you could die of thirst before anyone found you, and *that* is your worst problem at this time."

Well, you just can't sit here doing nothing and wait for someone to come along, like your poor friend over in that corner must have done."

Every detail of his remains was vivid in her memory. His boots, a plaid shirt, gray trousers. The horrific-looking empty sockets that had once housed his eyes. In those terrifying seconds she recalled seeing his hat, which must have been dislodged during the fall, lying next to his head. And the . . .

"My God! Why didn't I think of this before?"

Did she dare attempt it in the darkness, or should she wait for help?

The Lord helps those who help themselves.

Before she lost her courage, she crawled over to the opposite corner and began to grope for her objective.

Reflexively, she jerked her hand away when it made contact with something. Then she forced herself to reach out again and felt a boot. Her hand trembled as she traced the trouser leg up a skeletal leg until her fingers touched the object she had remembered—a gun belt. Where there was a gun belt, there was surely a gun.

Rory groped for the handle and gingerly pulled a gun out of the holster, then she crawled back cautiously to her corner.

Drawing on the little knowledge she had about guns, Rory cocked the gun, raised her arm above her head, and pulled the trigger.

13

Garth was nearing the end of the tunnel with no sign of Rory or a cave-in, when suddenly there was a blast so loud it shook the timbers, and he was afraid the ceiling would come down on him. When the dust settled, he realized it had not been an explosion, but a pistol shot that had come from somewhere ahead. With renewed hope, he crawled forward.

He could see only a few feet ahead, but there was no missing the gaping hole.

"Rory," he shouted. "Rory, are you down there?"

She jerked up her head. "Garth! Garth, is that really you?" she cried joyously.

"Honey, are you hurt?" he yelled.

"No, I don't think so. I'm able to move, but I'm very thirsty."

"Hang on." Garth pulled the package of candles out of his pocket, sank them into the dirt around the rim as far as he could reach, then lit them. Now he was able to see her below, and she was no longer alone in the darkness.

"Honey, just stay still. I have to go back and get some rope."

"Please hurry, Garth. There's a dead man down here, too."

"A dead man?"

"His remains. Just hurry and get me out of here."

"I'll be back as quickly as I can." He skimmed back down the tunnel. The short distance seemed like miles.

"I've found her, Paddy," he shouted when he emerged. "She's unhurt but fell down in a deep hole. I need some rope to get her up."

He'd never seen the old man move so fast.

He shook his head when Paddy handed him a cut-off piece of rope. "This isn't long enough. The pit's about about twenty feet deep."

"That's the longest piece we've got. What if you lower me down, and I jump the rest of the way? Rory could stand on me shoulders then," Paddy said.

"It's too risky to tie pieces together. And there's no telling how firm that ground is down there, and your additional weight could start another cave-in when you jump. Besides, you're not in condition right now for that kind of activity. There has to be some way . . . I've got it! The mule reins are even stronger than a rope. Quick, let's get them."

Within minutes, Garth had crawled back into the

tunnel. He tied a canteen to the end of one rein and lowered it down to her.

"Drink it slowly, honey," he warned when she reached for it greedily.

When she finished drinking, she slung the straps of the canteen over her shoulder. "What do you want me to do?"

"Are you wearing a belt?"

"No."

"Damm! It would have been something to tie the reins to. I guess you'll have to tie them around your waist, and that's going to hurt you."

Rory drew a shuddering sigh. "I know where I can get a belt." She crawled over the dirt and tried not to look as she unbuckled the belt and pulled it through the loops of the deflated trousers.

"I need a knife," she said when she put the belt around her waist.

"What for, Rory?"

"To punch another hole in this belt. It's too big for my waist."

He tossed down his knife, and she quickly worked a hole through the leather, then stuck the knife in her pocket.

"Are you ready now?" he asked.

"I guess so."

Garth stretched the middle of the rein across his back and under his arms, then dropped the loose ends of the rein down to her. "I want you to firmly tie those ends to the belt—not the buckle, since the leather will be much stronger."

When she did what he told her, the rein was tautly looped under his arms and the two ends to her belt.

She gave a shaky laugh. "Garth, which one of us is the head of the horse and the other the rear end?"

"I think we're both horses's rear ends, or we wouldn't be here to begin with. Now this is where it gets harder, hon."

"You think taking a belt off a skeleton is easy, Fraser?"

"If you don't stop being so feisty, I'm going to leave you down there and throw you a piece of raw meat every now and then," he teased.

Garth admired her courage and grit. The woman had taken a bad fall, spent most of a day and a half in total darkness with a skeleton lying a few feet away, and still had the spirit to make light of it.

"This is going to be very physical. Are you sure you didn't injure your legs?"

"Do knees knocking together count?"

"It could help. Have you ever climbed a rope?"

"No, but I've climbed trees when I was younger," she called up.

"That's good news, because you have to climb this wall."

"Garth, trees have branches to hoist yourself up on."

"The hoisting's my part. But I have no way to get any leverage, so you're going to have to use those gorgeous legs of yours."

"How would you know what my legs look like?"

"Are you forgetting I had a full view of them when you were bathing at the waterfall?"

"I'm glad to hear it was only my legs you were look-ing at," she said drolly.

"How could you have doubted it?"

The light banter seemed to have worked. The earlier fright and hysteria were gone from her voice, so it was time to attempt getting her out of there.

"You're doing great, honey. Now, there's no head-room for me to stand up and pull you, but I can sit down and back up—and as I do, you'll have to walk up that wall. I want you to grasp both of those reins to-gether now, and after I get you several feet off the ground, start climbing stiff-legged, just as if you were walking. It's hard, but it can be done. When you get close enough for me to reach you, I'll pull you up the rest of the way by hand."

"Now I really know which of us is the rear end, Captain Fraser."

Garth sat down, took the two reins firmly in hand, and began to pull. He had to raise her off the ground high enough so she could start climbing. The effort was strenuous without leverage, and the progress measured in inches, not feet.

The muscles in his shoulders and arms were al-ready feeling the exertion when he felt the change on the reins as she began to use her legs. With every few feet of progress, he shortened the rein. He peered over the top and saw she was about three-quarters of the way up, but his muscles had begun to feel like putty.

"Time out," he yelled. With one hand firmly grasp-ing the reins, he brushed aside the middle candles, then reached down and grasped her by the wrist and hauled her over the top.

It drained his remaining strength, and he collapsed on his back with Rory on top of him. They were both too breathless and exhausted to move, but continued to lie there gasping for breath.

And that's when all the strength and bravado she had been struggling to maintain completely gave out. She began to sob, clutching him as if she were drowning. He tightened his arms around her, and as much as he wanted to hold her and rock her in his arms, the area was too confined to allow it.

"Come on, baby," he said gently. "Let's get out of here before the whole damn tunnel collapses. You think you can make it?" She nodded, and he could see how she was struggling to regain her control. "When we get out of this rat hole, you can sit down and have a good cry. So slip past me, and you go first." He wiped the tears off her cheeks and grinned. "Only don't move too fast, because we're still harnessed together."

She managed a game smile, and between sniffles she teased, "So this time *you'll* be the rear end." Then she squeezed past him and started to crawl her way out on her hands and knees.

Garth followed on his hands and knees, enjoying the view every inch of the way.

Once they were out of the tunnel, he freed himself to enable Paddy to kiss and hug his daughter.

Her hair and clothes were covered with dirt and grime, her face streaked and muddied where her tears had blended with the dirt.

After the O'Gradys' tearful reunion was over, Garth said, "Let's get you back to the waterfall, where you can get rid of that dirt."

"If you're going, I'll be coming with you," Paddy declared.

Garth shook his head, unable to believe the man was still on that theme when his daughter was still shaking from her brush with death. He lifted Rory onto the front of the saddle, then climbed up, put his arms around her, and pulled her back against him. He held her in the circle of his arms all the way to the waterfall.

When they reached his camp, Garth sat her down and got down on his knees and removed her boots and stockings.

"Oh, how I wish I could sink into a nice hot bath right now," she said wistfully.

"I wish I could think of a way for you to do it, honey. We don't have a large enough kettle to boil the water, or a tub or barrel for you. But I have thought of a way to at least give you some privacy. I'll sink poles on each side of the trail, stretch a rope between them, and then drape a blanket on it."

"I guess that would be better than nothing," she said.

"Depends on who you ask," he said with a wink.

Garth went off to find a couple of saplings that would serve his purpose. By the time he got back, Paddy had arrived on his mule.

"Will you build a fire, Paddy, so we can cook some grub while Rory bathes? She must be damned hungry."

Paddy set to the task while Garth trimmed off the sapling's leaves.

When he finished, he drove the poles into the ground, tied on the rope, and draped the blanket over it.

"Voilà, mademoiselle," he said, with a courtly bow and dramatic flourish of his arm. "Your bath awaits." Then he whispered aside to her, "Could you use some help scrubbing your back?"

"I can handle it, thank you," she said with a saucy backward glance. Rory scooted behind the blanket and shed her clothes.

Once she got used to the cold spray, it was a relief to rinse away the dirt. She took the opportunity to launder her clothing as well. The hot sunshine quickly evaporated most of the moisture off her skin, and she donned dry clothing and rejoined Garth, who was kneeling at the fire.

"I feel about ten pounds lighter."

Garth looked up at her and grinned. "You looked real cute with those muddy streaks on your face."

"Where's Pop?" she asked.

He nodded toward the trees. "Sleeping like a baby. He was done in. Here's your boots; I cleaned them for you."

"Thank you, Garth. You didn't have to do that."

"And I heated a pan of water to soap that dirt out of your hair."

"You're going to spoil me. I'm not used to being waited on."

"You deserve to be, honey. Sit down on that rock over there. I'll wash your hair, but you better take off that clean shirt or it'll get wet."

Rory hesitated for a moment, then unbuttoned the shirt and slipped out of it. She grabbed her towel and wrapped it around her shoulders like a shawl.

Garth poured warm water over her head and began to massage her scalp as he worked the soap into suds. It felt wonderful. His hands felt so strong, yet so gentle. She thought of how frightened she had been in the mine, until she'd felt his hand grip her wrist in a firm hold. Only then had she been certain she was safe, she'd known he'd never let go. And even now, as comforting as his touch felt, it was equally exciting. And she yearned for both. Rory closed her eyes as the feel of his fingers sent currents of desire spiraling through her.

He poured more of the heated water over her head to rinse out the suds, then pulled the towel off her shoulders and dried her hair vigorously.

"There, it's all clean and shiny again."

Their gazes locked as he reached out a hand and helped her to her feet. His eyes were filled with desire; hers with yearning.

If only she could let him make love to her. She had waited so long for someone like him. If it was wrong, why else would they have been brought together on this mountain? It had to be right.

Kiss me, Garth, her eyes conveyed in an unspoken message. *Please kiss me.*

A thousand pinpoints of pleasure sparked through her body as he slid his hands up her bare arms. "Rory, I—"

"So I close me eyes for a moment, Fraser, and you're up to your tricks again," Paddy accused, jolting her back to the world.

"I can't *believe* this!" Garth mumbled. "I washed her hair, Paddy. That should be obvious, even to you."

"And if it weren't for me watchful eye, what would have been next?"

"Where was that *watchful* eye yesterday, when Rory needed you?" Garth turned away, whistled for Saddle, and disappeared into the trees.

"Pop, why do you deliberately antagonize him?" Rory asked. "We're indebted to him. He's saved your life, and this is the second time he's saved mine."

"So in payment, you're willing to let him have his way with you?"

"If that *ever* happens, it will be because I *want* it to happen. I'm a woman, Pop, not a child! It never bothered you when I worked in the Grotto. What do you think those men I danced with there were saying to me? They weren't discussing the weather. If I do let Garth make love to me, it will be *my* decision."

"I'll not hear of it, Rorleen Catherine."

"You have nothing to say about it, Pop." She snatched the blanket off the line and wrung out her wet clothes, then stretched them out on the foliage to dry.

Two hours later, Garth returned leading their other mule and the burro.

"Garth, what are you doing?" Rory asked.

"I packed up your camp and sealed up that mine. It's not safe. The whole place could cave in."

Paddy snorted. "And you're hoping we'll leave, I'm sure."

"I've made no secret of that."

"And you're staying; is that it?"

"I've only stayed here to give Rory a hand getting you back to the mission. My God, man, she could have been killed in that cave-in! Doesn't that mean anything to you?"

"She can go, but I'm staying," Paddy said adamantly.

"Stay and break your fool neck, if that's what you want, but I'm taking Rory out of here."

"Will both of you stop this!" Rory cried. "I've had all the squabbling I can take. Pop, I want to leave, and you're too sick to remain. That mine isn't safe, and I will never go back in there again. Isn't this all hard enough, without the two of you snarling at each other like a couple of dogs over a bone? You both could take a lesson from Saddle. He never makes a sound."

She stormed away and began to fold her clothing.

Garth came over to her. "Rory, let's sit down and discuss this calmly and quietly. I have something I have to tell you."

"It's settled, Garth; you know how I feel."

"It's not settled. Can't you see that stubborn old man has no intention of leaving? You know your father better than I do. Is there any way we can convince him to leave?"

"Not in the mood he's in now. I'll try to talk some sense to him in the morning."

"Can he be bribed?"

She laughed. "I think Pop could be bribed to do just about anything except commit murder." Rory looked askance at him. "Although he might make an exception in your case."

He expelled an audible sigh. "No doubt. Why does he dislike me so much? I usually get along with anyone. I'm beginning to take it personally."

"You intimidate him. He doesn't make friends easily, and we move around so often that he couldn't, even if he wanted to. The other thing is, he's convinced . . . I mean, he feels your intentions toward me are . . . Well, you know how fathers are when it comes to their little girls."

"I can't fault him for that, but it would be easier on all of us if his protectiveness wasn't so selective. Just the same, what I have to tell you concerns him, as well. It will soon be dusk, so let's eat and get you settled in here properly for tonight at least."

While Garth skinned and cut up the rabbit he had trapped, Rory dug beans, an onion, and salt and pepper out of her pack and got them cooking on the fire.

Paddy quieted down, content for the moment to drink from the whiskey bottle he mysteriously produced. By the time they ate their meal and cleaned up the dishes, it had turned dark.

14

Before we bed down, I want to bring up what's on my mind," Garth said. "Rory's accident proved to me that I should have told you the truth earlier. That fall could have been fatal, and it would have been my fault. I've been dishonest with you. I knew that mine wasn't Uncle Henry's."

"I don't understand what you mean."

"Pay him no mind, daughter," Paddy said. "The man's trying to get rid of us so he can mine it himself."

"Pop, I'd like to hear what he has to say, so be quiet and let him finish. Why do you think it's not your uncle's mine, Garth? His initials were on the stakes."

"I believe those are the initials of Herbert Forsen, not Henry Fraser."

"Who's Herbert Forsen?" Rory asked.

"According to Father Chavez, the nearest claim to

Uncle Henry's mine was filed by a Herbert Forsen fifteen years ago. No one has seen or heard from the man since then. I think you might have spent last night with him, Rory. He must have had the same kind of accident you did, and probably broke his neck in the fall—or died of thirst in that pit."

Paddy scoffed. "And just how would you be knowing that, Mr. Fraser?"

"I have no way of knowing, or if you would have found gold there, but I *do* know it wasn't my uncle's mine. I'm no geologist, but I think that perhaps for hundreds of years dirt kept washing down from above and started to pile up there. If you remember, there was no solid rock base or rock formations. The mine had just a lot of dirt piled on top of itself. That could explain the soft pit holes, and why you weren't seriously injured when you fell, Rory. Forsen may have had a previous minor fall, which would explain why he shored up the walls and ceilings. It didn't help the floor though, did it?"

"This is all becoming clearer to me by the moment," Rory said. "I've been wasting my time trying to find gold there."

Paddy started chuckling. "You see, darlin'? Didn't I warn you? The man's trying to convince us the mine's dangerous and worthless."

"Pop, what he's saying makes sense. But, Garth, then the same could be true of your uncle's mine," Rory said.

Garth shook his head. "No, it's not."

"How can you be so sure?"

Garth pointed to the thick foliage. "My uncle's mine is right there. It wasn't until I saw this waterfall that I figured this out. It was never on the map Uncle Henry drew, which made me wonder why. He deliberately left it off, in the event the map fell into the hands of a scoundrel like you, Paddy."

"But where's the opening to it?" Rory asked.

"Come with me; I'll show you. This high foliage conceals the crack in the wall. The waterfall is such a distraction that apparently no one pays close attention to what's nearby."

Once inside, Rory looked around in awe at the size of the cavern. "I can't believe it. You can stand up straight without even having to bend your head."

"That's right. I even bring Boots in here at night. You'll be sleeping under a roof tonight, Rory. And I want to show you something else." He took her hand and led her to the two initials carved on the wall.

"Garth, this is proof that this mine really belonged to your uncle. Do you think he was right about the gold?"

"I know he was. I've already found some."

Paddy started laughing. "Then if that other mine really belonged to that Forsen fella, than *this* is the mine we filed our claim on. We're the owners."

Grinning like a banshee, he shook a finger at Garth. "You outsmarted yourself, Mr. Fraser. The mine and the gold belongs to me and me daughter. And you'll not get a speck of that gold, no matter what you've done for us."

"Yes, he will, Pop. I promised him my half," Rory said.

Paddy glared at Garth. "Have you no shame, man, that you'd take the yield after me daughter's hard-earned efforts?"

"If it doesn't bother *you* to take it, Paddy, why should you expect it to bother me?"

"Hear that, daughter? Are you just gonna stand there and allow him to speak such disrespect to your father?"

"You can't expect his respect from the way you've been acting. This isn't like you, Pop. Garth earned this gold and you know it. You're beginning to sound crazy and vindictive."

"The greed for gold can do that to a man," Garth said.

"I've no need for the likes of you to be defending me, Garth Fraser. 'Tis bad enough you turned me daughter against me."

"You're drunk, Paddy. I think you better sleep it off, and we'll discuss this in the morning."

" 'Tis the very thing I was fixing to do, Mr. Fraser." Bottle in hand, Paddy went over and lay down. "But I'll be keeping me eye open if you're thinking of any more of your hanky-panky."

"You do that," Garth said, amused, allowing Paddy to have the last word.

"I'm sorry, Garth, Pop hasn't been himself lately," Rory said quietly when they moved outside. She sat down at the fire and hugged her knees to her chin. "I'm getting very worried about him. Before we came here, he was fine most of the time, but now—"

"He's bored, Rory; he's got too much time on his hands. And too much whiskey in his stomach."

"I know. That's what worries me the most. In his mind he always figured that he looked after me, and that I enjoyed wandering as much as he did."

"And do you?"

"I guess I did for a while, but I've grown weary of it and would like to settle down. Now he's facing the reality that his health is failing and he's getting too old for the footloose life he enjoys. Do you think he's not ashamed of how much he has to depend on me now? It's not only the whiskey that causes him to lash out in these nasty tantrums. He's really not angry at you or me, Garth; he's angry at himself."

"Unfortunately, whiskey isn't the answer, honey. Sad to say, if he keeps drinking at the rate he's doing now, he'll soon be entirely worthless."

She nodded sorrowfully. "I know, but it eases the pain of it, doesn't it?"

"Once we're out of here, it's not too late to get him back where he'd be comfortable. Paddy's right about one thing, though," he said in a lighter vein. "I do have some hanky-panky on my mind." Garth went over to the waterfall and pulled out a bottle.

"What is it?" she asked when he held it up like a trophy.

"Wine. Father Chavez put it in my pack when I was leaving. He said not to open it until the time was right. And that I'd know when that time came," he added with a wry grin.

He came over to the fire with the bottle and his tin cup. After pulling the cork out of the bottle, he filled his cup and handed it to her. "This may not be imported French wine, but at least it's been blessed. I really like that old man."

Garth stretched out on his side, propped up an elbow, and cradled his head in his hand.

"What?" she asked when he lay there staring at her.

"I'm trying to decide which flatters you the most: moonlight, firelight, or sunlight. Moonlight brings out a silver glow to your hair, firelight turns it into shimmering copper, and sunlight . . . well, sunlight turns it to gold. You're the loveliest and most desirable woman I've ever seen."

"At least on this mountain," she said lightly.

Though Rory tried to sound flippant, she cherished this moment and delighted in his every word.

Firelight played on his dark hair and handsome profile, and as they talked, they continued to pass the cup between them until it was empty, then he refilled it again.

The combination of the warm fire and the wine had mellowed her into relaxing. Rory stretched out opposite him and, assumed the same position as Garth, only inches separating their heads.

"This is such a lovely night. When I think of last night, it's hard to believe I'm lying here now under these stars. They're so beautiful."

He reached over and squeezed her hand. "Honey, last night was just a bad dream. Tell me what's your best dream."

"My best dream? That's easy; I've dreamed it so often. One day a knight will come riding up on a white charger and snatch me from the clutches of a Mo Buckman, or some such dragon who is plaguing my life. He'll carry me off to a little house surrounded by a white picket fence."

"Wouldn't that dream call for a huge castle surrounded by a moat?"

Her light laughter carried on the evening air like the distant tinkle of a wind chime kissed by a gentle breeze.

"This is *my* dream, Fraser. No castle or moat for me, simply a little house with a white picket fence. And it wouldn't matter to my knight that I worked in a saloon or my father was a drunk, because he'll love me and we'll look forward to the future, not back to the past. And together, we'll watch our children grow up without ever wanting for what they didn't have, but thankful for what they *did* have: being loved and giving love."

"And how would that knight on the white charger afford to build that little house and fence, and feed his devoted wife and loving children?"

"It won't matter what he does for a living, as long as it's an honest job. The important thing is that he's content to settle down and do so."

"I wonder if you would really be contented, Rory. Dreaming and actually living that dream can be very different. Dreams are an escape from reality. The best favor we can do ourselves is to recognize the reality of who and what we are, and change our life if we don't like it. Not just dream how we'd like it to be."

"That's easier said than done. Especially when there's no way or opportunity to achieve whatever that dream may be."

"Yet sometimes, when you've achieved it, you may find that it isn't what you hoped it would be. For instance, I think you would be bored living the life of your dream."

"Bored! Why would I be bored? I've thought about this dream over and over again since I've been a child. And at no time did I ever imagine it would bore me."

"Then why are you still single, Rory? You're a beautiful woman, and there are at least a dozen men in the West for every woman. Surely there's a decent man among them who's more than willing to marry you and settle down."

"I guess none of *my* dozen are interested in marrying me," she said, reaching for the cup.

"I think it's just the opposite—*you're* not interested in marrying any of them. I can't visualize you churning butter or setting dough for bread. No matter what you say, you're adventuresome, Rory. You like your freedom and independence as much as your father does, and the only commitment you're willing to make to any man, is to him."

Rory fought back the rise of anger. She would not let anything he said spoil this evening. They were both adults and were capable of having a discussion without her stomping off like a spoiled child. But why couldn't he see it all narrowed down to her just wanting a sense of security, and feeling her life was worth something to someone?

"I believe you can't visualize me that way, Garth, because you think of me as just a saloon girl. Isn't that the real reason?"

"Just the opposite. I've been trying to get you into bed from the time I met you, and I've learned a lot about you since we've been here. You would no more prostitute yourself for a wedding ring and picket fence, than you would for two dollars from a drunk in a saloon.

"Look at you now: lying here gazing at the stars as if you haven't a care in the world, when last night you were fighting like hell to hold on to your sanity in a dark pit you were sharing with a skeleton.

"Honey," he said gently, "you're a fighter, a survivor. Not one who's willing to sit back in a rocking chair and settle for a white picket fence to keep out her troubles. The only thing you're *really* looking for is a man who loves you regardless of your past, and whom you love regardless of his."

"Do you think I'll ever find that man?" she asked wistfully.

"Of course you will. And you'll know it when you do. Only don't be disappointed if he's just a trail bum or a drifter. Our dreams don't always play out according to the scripts we write for ourselves."

"What's *your* dream, Garth?"

"I don't have one anymore. I used to dream of finding Uncle Henry's gold mine."

"You don't sound like you're too happy to have found it. From what you've told me, even with only half of the gold you found, you'll be a rich man and can do anything you want."

"I pretty much do that now without being rich," he said. "It doesn't take too much to make me happy."

"Surely discovering the gold can't make you un-happy."

"No, but like my uncle, my dream had nothing to do with acquiring riches. It was about keeping the dream alive."

"So now that your dream's fulfilled, you no longer have a dream," she said softly. "That's what you've been trying to tell me all along." Her eyes were misty as she looked into his. "I'm so sorry for you, Garth."

He chuckled. "Hey, listen to us. Feeling sorry for our-selves because we struck gold." He emptied the remains of the wine bottle into the cup. "I propose a toast."

She smiled and sat up. "So what are we toasting?"

"Here's to keeping our dreams alive." He handed her the cup.

Rory raised it in the air. "To dreams. Long may they wave." She took a swallow of the wine and passed it on to him.

"O'er the land of the free and the home of the brave." Garth downed the remaining wine, and then they broke into laughter.

They settled in their former positions, stretched out again opposite each other eye to eye with their chins cradled in their hands.

"That wine was delicious," she said. "I must be sure to thank Father Chavez when we get back to the mis-sion."

"Did I ever tell you that my brother Clay has be-come a vintner in the Napa Valley?"

"You told me he raised grapes. What's a vintner?"

"He makes wine from those grapes."

"Was it your brother's dream to grow grapes?"

"Well, when our grandfather was alive he made his own wine at Fraser Keep. Clay used to trail after Granddad like a disciple."

His words touched her heart. She could tell from his smile that he had slipped back into that fond memory.

"Fraser Keep." Rory sighed in contentment and laid her head on her arms. "Garth, tell me more about your life before the war. I want to hear about the cotillions and fancy balls. The kind of gowns the women wore, the music, the fragrance of honeysuckle and magnolias. Oh, it all sounds so romantic to me. I've heard the women wore beautiful gowns of satin and lace, frilled petticoats, and satin slippers."

"I never really noticed what they were wearing. I had my eyes on . . . other things." He winked.

"What kinds of dances did you do?"

"Waltzes, some hoedowns, sometimes a quadrille—and of course, it wouldn't be a ball without a Virginia reel."

"And what was your favorite choice?"

"None of them. My favorite dance ever was a slow waltz with a beautiful blond woman with the most incredible blue eyes I've ever seen. It cost me twenty-five cents."

She must have drunk too much wine, because suddenly she felt very warm under the intensity of his stare.

"Were you ever in love with one of the ladies, Garth?"

"I loved all of them," he said, grinning.

"No, I mean really *in* love."

"Yes. Just one. Until I was five. That's when I found out she was married to another man—my father. Funny thing, though, I never got over that childhood crush. And she and I always remained good friends."

"Darn you, Garth. Can't you ever be serious about anything?"

Undaunted, Rory closed her eyes and began to move to a melody floating through her head. "I can just see them swaying to and fro to a lovely Viennese waltz."

"Is that before or after they had their mint juleps on the veranda, while a slave knelt before them massaging their aching feet for them?"

She opened her eyes in surprise. "Are you angry with me?"

"Not with you, Rory. Every now and then it gets my dander up when I think of how the Yankee propaganda maligned the women of the South. It made them all out to be indolent and witless, with not a care in the world except for what they'd wear to the next ball. In truth, they were the most indomitable army in the Confederacy. Someday history will have to recognize their courage and fortitude during the war and give them the respect they deserve."

"I'm sure it will, Garth. But I've never thought of them as being lazy or stupid like you said. I always just . . . envied them."

Garth reached for her. "Paddy's right about one thing, honey. I do have some hanky-panky on my mind. Rory, I—"

She stood up to avoid the contact. She knew he intended to kiss her, and she was beyond resisting him. She wanted him to make love to her, but knew it would be disastrous if he did. It would create a bond between them that would only make parting from him even harder.

Soon they would head back to the mission and go their separate ways, so it was wisest she didn't get any more involved with a man who openly said he wasn't interested in settling down.

"Since we drank all the wine, I guess we should get to bed. Sunrise comes sooner than we think."

"Yeah, you're right. You go ahead. I'm going to bed down out here."

Pop was snoring away, having passed out for the night. He'd left a lantern burning, and she went over, removed his boots, and covered him. Then she blew out the lantern and crawled into her bedroll.

15

It was past noon and Rory had just finished cutting up dough for biscuits when Garth came out of the cave to fill his canteen.

"Paddy gone?" he asked.

"Yes. You don't think he'd go back to that other mine, do you?"

"It wouldn't do him any good, because I sealed it up tighter than a drum."

He took off his shirt and went over to the waterfall and stuck his head into the spray. Then he came back, shaking the water off his hair like a wet dog.

"I'd appreciate your not parading around here half-naked."

"What?"

"You're not fooling me one bit. I know what you're up to."

He started to laugh. "All I've done is take off my shirt." He arched a brow. "Does that bother you, Miz Rory?"

"It sure does—and wipe that smirk off your face. Besides, it's very improper. I'm sure a gentleman like you would never parade around in front of one of your fine ladies in Virginia."

"Well, Miz Rory, I really can't say, because I've never been on a mountain mining gold in the heat with one of those fine ladies in Virginia."

He came over and pulled her back against him. She sucked in a breath and closed her eyes when he trailed light kisses along her neck.

Shrugging out of his arms, Rory began to put biscuits into a pan to bake later for dinner. "Get away from me, Fraser. Can't you see the cook is occupied? So stop distracting her."

"Hey, Irish, you've got some flour on the end of your nose."

She turned around, then started to laugh. "I can't look any worse than you do, Fraser. You should see your chin."

They were both laughing by the time she wiped the flour off her nose and his chin.

"I've had enough of chipping at that wall for the day," he said. "I thought I'd go back to the fish stream and catch a few for dinner. Would you like to come along?"

"Yes, I would, thanks."

"Good. I'll saddle Boots."

Rory had cleaned up her cooking supplies by the time Garth rejoined her. He leaned down, hooked an arm around her waist, and pulled her up behind him.

"I'd like to fish, too," Rory said when they reached the stream.

Garth chuckled. "Have you ever tried to spear a fish before? They're pretty fast, you know."

"No, but I figure if a big, clumsy bear is fast enough to do it, so am I."

"Okay." Garth found her a strong limb, shaved it, and carved one end into a point. "Good luck."

"You sound like you think I can't do it."

"Not at all. I've learned better than to underestimate your capabilities, Miz Rory."

Rory took off her boots and stockings, rolled her pants up to her knees, and waded into the water. She discovered spearing a fish wasn't as easy as she thought it would be.

After a lengthy time, she finally succeeded in spearing a trout, and in her excitement she dropped her spear. Garth splashed after it as the current started carrying fish and spear away.

Laughing, he brought them back. "We shouldn't eat this; we should have it mounted to hang on the wall of that little house you hope to have one day." He strung it on the vine he had started.

"Hush up, Fraser, or I'll have you mounted right next to it." Laughing, she picked up her spear and returned to the task, proud of herself.

Rory managed to spear another fish before Garth quit for the day, but she was enjoying the fishing too much to stop—and he was enjoying watching her too much to want to stop her.

How many women would find enjoyment in standing barefoot in cold water trying to spear a fish? Rory was willing to take on any task that faced her.

He hoped they'd get enough gold out of this venture so she could have an easier life than what she'd been used to. And he sure hoped that one day she'd meet that knight in armor she dreamed of marrying.

Right now she was having such a good time he didn't want to disturb her, so he pulled the book he'd been reading out of a saddlebag and sat down to read, his gaze, more often than not, rising above the top of the book to watch her.

A short time later Rory came over and plopped down beside him, and he put the book aside. "I caught two more, so along with yours that gives us ten fish. We can eat five tonight for supper, and keep the other ones in water for breakfast tomorrow."

"Sounds good, honey."

Rory picked up the book he had put aside. "What are you reading?"

"It's Robert Browning's *The Ring and the Book*, and some famous lines from a few of his plays and poems."

"Poems?"

"His poems aren't romantic ones like his wife Elizabeth wrote to him. Her *Sonnets from the Portuguese* are said to be beautiful."

"I can't picture you as enjoying romantic poetry, Garth."

"I confess I've never read any. Some epic poetry yes, but romantic, no. I mainly enjoy the wisdom and optimism Browning expresses in his works.

"*The Ring and the Book* is a story of a Roman murder case. It's anticipated to take at least twelve books, because each novel will be written from the viewpoint of an individual character in the trial. It's fascinating, so far. Probably the finest thing Browning's ever done."

"This is a side of you I never suspected existed, Garth. You're really impressed with him, aren't you?"

He stretched out on his back and tucked his hands under his head. "Honey, do you remember when we were discussing our dreams, and I told you that if we attain them, they don't always live up to what we anticipated? Robert Browning warned, 'A man's reach should exceed his grasp.' That's the point I was trying to make."

"Well, whether you and Mr. Browning agree with me or not, I'm not giving up my dream. Besides, I am reaching way beyond my grasp."

"No, you aren't. That dream will come true for you someday. But suppose it doesn't, which one thing would you want the most? The knight in armor? The house? The picket fence? There must be one thing more important than any of the others."

Rory gazed deeply into the mahogany eyes of this man who had come to mean so much to her. He was the image of that knight in armor, yet she could never hope to attain anything greater than these stolen moments with him.

"I want to look up into the eyes of the man I love, and then down into those same eyes in my son as I hold him in my arms."

She broke her gaze and returned to paging through the book. " 'Grow old along with me/The best is yet to be.' What a wonderful thought, Garth. Do you believe the best is yet to be?"

"I keep trying to prove that to you, but we always get interrupted."

She closed the book and bopped him lightly on the head with it. "You ninny, can't you ever be serious?"

"Okay, I *seriously* hope that I haven't yet experienced the best thing that will ever happen to me. And I *know* you haven't."

Her eyes flashed with devilment. "Oh, is that so? I once believed you were the smartest man I'd ever known, Garth Fraser. Now I know better."

"What made you change your mind?"

"You don't recognize the best thing that could ever happen to you even when it looks you right in the eye."

"Let me guess. That would be you?"

She smiled coquettishly. "Of course."

He reached up and dug his fingers into her hair. His eyes glowed with the flame of arousal. "Honey, when you flirt, you're lethal."

No one knew better than she that she was reaching far beyond her grasp, but if this was all she had to hold on to, she would seize the moment. Spurred to boldness by the urgency of her feelings, Rory lowered her head and kissed him.

The feel of his lips was a tantalizing sensation and she kissed him with a hunger that one day would be just a memory.

He pulled her across him, and she stretched out against his long, muscular length, abandoning herself to the sensations that swirled within her as his hands roamed her back and the curve of her hips and waist.

With a muffled moan, he rolled over, and his ragged breaths feathered her cheek as he unbuttoned her shirt. Burying her face against his neck, she breathed in the intoxicating scent of him.

The sudden chill of the air on her naked breasts dueled with the surge of heat that burned through her when his tongue caressed her taut nipples. She matched his urgency and unbuttoned his shirt, and reveled in the sweet tantalization of her breasts against the crisp hair of his chest. The driving need for his touch became unbearable as he slipped her Levi's past her hips. She melted against him. He kissed her with a passion that flooded her soul as it did her body.

"You're so precious, sweetheart. So very precious," he murmured between kisses.

She savored every lingering kiss, every heated touch, and every whispered endearment, then groaned with ecstasy when he slid his hand to the core of her sex to prepare her for his entry.

"Oh, my God!" He sat up in shock. "No, no, no!" he cried out in anguish and slammed his balled fists on the ground. "You're a virgin!"

In the throes of passion, Rory opened her eyes and looked up, dazed. "Yes, I told you I was."

He quickly pulled up her Levi's.

"What are you doing?" she cried, when he began to fumble at the buttons of her shirt in an effort to close them.

"You don't understand; I've never deflowered a virgin."

"You mean you're not . . . we're not—"

"Not right now. I've got to adjust to this."

Laughing hilariously, she cried, "I can't believe this. Garth Fraser, the relentless womanizer!" She slapped his hands away and rebuttoned her shirt properly.

"How do you think *I* feel? I've been trying to make love to you from the time I met you. It's a plot. An evil torture, devised by Satan himself. And I'm sure your father had a hand in it too."

He stormed down to the river and into the cold water.

After both had recovered from the shock, neither was yet ready to return to the mine. Rory lay contentedly gazing at the water and the fish darting through it, while Garth lay at her side, half dozing.

"Garth, what are you planning on doing with your gold?"

"I haven't thought about it."

"You certainly must have a need for it, or are you wealthy already?"

"No, my family lost everything except the plantation in the war. My brother Will had all he could do to hold on to Fraser Keep. My brother Clay's got a good start here in California with his winery, but it will take several years of good crops before he'll get out from under the debt. I'd like to help him out now, if he'll take it, but he's pretty proud and might not take money from me. I sure hope Will doesn't hold any such thoughts. Even though they've brought in a couple of crops since the war ended, plenty of money is still needed to restore parts of Fraser Keep."

"Would Clay let you buy into his business?"

"Probably, but I'm not ready to become a business-man, Rory. There's a lot more of this country that I'd like to visit, like the Northwest Territory, even Alaska and Canada. And I want to see more of the Southwest, especially Texas. I've been reading a lot about those amazing cattle drives that are starting to come out of Dallas and Fort Worth. Wouldn't mind going on one to see what it's like.

"I've spent most of the past ten years in a military academy or fighting a war. It's time I sow a few wild oats."

Rory smiled in amusement. "Why do I suspect there's *never* been a time in your twenty-eight years that you didn't sow some wild oats?"

Garth sat up. "What about you, Rory? What do you intend to do with your gold?"

She shrugged. "I've never been able to plan my life that far ahead. I hope that I won't have to go back to working saloons, but I'm not skilled to do anything else. Pop claims he's going to build a big mansion in

San Francisco. Maybe I'll just sit on the porch and wait for that knight in armor to ride up."

"So you intend to remain with Paddy?"

"Of course. All we've got is each other."

"Why don't you go east? There are some grand cities, like New York, Chicago, and St. Louis."

"And what can they offer me that San Francisco doesn't? I'm not seeking the adventure and excitement that you are, Garth."

"I only meant there may be better opportunities for you in one of those larger cities."

"Is that why people are coming to California by the wagonload? Is that why, when you speak of all the rivers you have yet to cross, you don't ever speak of returning to Virginia? Practice what you preach, Garth Fraser."

He gently caressed her cheek. "I only want you to be happy, honey. I don't want to ever think of you as needing something, or being at the mercy of a Mo Buckman ever again." He lowered his head and gently kissed her.

"Well, I don't want to think of what my life will be like in the future. For now, I'm happy right here with you," Rory said. She stood up and brushed herself off. "We better be getting back to camp before we run out of light."

Later that evening, Garth and Paddy sat down after dinner for a game of chess. Garth's mind was on the possibility of being alone with Rory later that night. His gaze continually strayed to her as she sat at the fire brushing her hair. His fingers itched to dig into it.

He stared, transfixed, as the glow of the fire rippled along the long strands of her hair and his groin knotted with every stroke of the brush.

She was so beautiful. But not the hardened comeliness of women who depended on their looks. Rory had an intangible radiance that bordered on ethereal—and an innocence that belied the profession she'd chosen.

"I'm thinking you should've figured it out by now," Paddy said.

"Chess is a thinking man's game, Paddy."

Paddy snorted. "You know what I mean. She didn't take the map, son. I did."

"Why?"

"Because she's a dear and loving daughter, who figured you'd be angry with me if you knew I did it. 'Tis no wonder I love her."

"I mean, why did you take the map, Paddy?"

"I've no excuse for the foul deed," he said sadly. " 'Twas that devil Satan whispering in me ear. All me life, I've yearned for something better than I had. When I was younger, it was always hoping to hit that big strike; when I grew older, it was winning the big pot. Always something that seemed at me fingertips. And there were times I could almost touch it. All I'd have to do was reach for it."

He shook his head. "But when I did, all I ever drew back was me pint of whiskey."

Garth waited patiently as Paddy picked up the pint beside him and took a deep swallow.

Paddy swiped the back of his hand across his mouth and then continued. "When I saw that map on the floor, something told me this was me final chance. 'Take it, Paddy,' Satan whispered in me ear. 'Tis your last chance.' And in those few seconds, I sold me soul to the devil. And I'm thinking the day will be coming soon when I'll have to face me maker, and he'll be asking me the same question as you did." Paddy glanced up sorrowfully. "And I've no excuse for the deed."

"What do you expect me to say, Paddy? It was a wrong thing to do."

"But you know the saddest part of it all, son?" He glanced at Rory. "All that time I was hoping for something better, I was richer than anyone I knew, and never gave it a thought. I'm ashamed of what I did, and know I'm not deserving of it, son—but I'm asking ye to forgive me."

"It's over, Paddy. I'd only be harming myself more than you, if I didn't put it behind me."

"You're a good man, Garth Fraser, just like Rory keeps saying. I only wish I'd paid her more mind."

Rory looked up and saw the two men staring at her.

"What is it? What's wrong?" she asked, alarmed.

"We're just admiring your beauty, Rory. It stands out like a fresh blossom in the midst of a weed patch."

"From the looks on your faces I'd say it's more like you're thinking this bloom looks a little wilted."

Her infectious laughter spread to Paddy and Garth, and all three of them were soon engulfed in unexpected merriment and peace.

16

Garth was an early riser, and when Rory opened her eyes, she saw he was up and around. For several days things had been going well, with the exception of Paddy's behavior. He made no effort to help with the workload, and disappeared every day only to return smelling of whiskey—but at least not drunk.

At the sight of the blanket slung over the rope, Rory saw that Garth had bathed. Figuring she might as well take advantage of it while he was gone, she gathered up what she needed and hurried to the falls.

The water was icy cold, but it opened her eyes. By the time she finished, she felt refreshed and wide awake. When she went back to the fire, she discovered Garth had returned with a load of wood.

"We used up most of the wood I had accumulated, so I thought I'd go and gather up some more," he said.

"Do you want company?" she asked.

"If it's yours, I'm up for it."

"You're always *up* for it, Fraser," she said, trying to keep a straight face, knowing he was still sensitive about their last disastrous encounter.

"You understand, Miss O'Grady, that bawdy innuendos from a woman can often entice a man to *bigger* and *better* things."

"I figure I don't have to worry; I'm a virgin."

He hugged her to his side. "Keep it up, lady, and that won't be for much longer."

For the next thirty minutes they accumulated a stack of wood, and before carrying it back to camp, they sat down to rest.

"So, how did you sleep last night?" he asked.

"Like a baby, after Pop's snoring drove me out of the cave. What about you?"

"Great. I always sleep better with a bed partner."

"We were not bed partners, Garth."

"How would you know? You didn't blink an eye all night."

"You mean—"

"Well, I couldn't very well let you lie there shivering after the campfire burned out."

"You didn't . . . I mean, did you . . ."

"After you rolled over and cuddled against me, what did you expect me to do? I put my arms around you and kissed you. I didn't realize you were sleeping."

"I don't believe you. I would have wakened if you kissed me."

"That explains it," he said, drawing her into his arms.

"Explains what?"

"Why you didn't kiss me back. I hope I have better luck this morning."

His kiss sent shivers of delight spiraling through her, and whatever time they had left together, she wasn't going to waste it by playing coy. She slipped her arms around his neck.

Feeling unsteady from the alcoholic stupor that sleep had failed to dissipate, Paddy opened his eyes and smacked his lips together several times. His mouth felt like it was stuffed with cotton. He needed a hot cup of coffee to cut through the thick of it.

There was no sign of Rory or Garth outside, and no campfire, either. Why had they left without building a fire or brewing a pot of coffee? Paddy piled up some wood and tried to set a match to it.

After several failed attempts, he got a fire started and then stumbled back inside to get the coffee and pot.

Paddy went back outside, and after a great deal of fumbling and spilled coffee grounds, he set the coffee to brewing. A man needed a cup of coffee in the morning, the same way he needed a bit of a nip. A reminder he intended to see to at once.

He rooted around in the folds of his bedroll in search of his bottle, but couldn't find it. Still clutching his pillow in his arm, like a child with a stuffed toy, he went back outside.

"She took it! Me only pleasure, and she took me bottle away. Treating me like a babe, she is. Me own flesh and blood!" He clutched his hands to his chest dramatically. "Och, 'How sharper than a serpent's tooth it is to have a thankless child,'" Paddy quoted, in the finest tenor worthy of a Shakespearean thespian.

Sizzling and spitting, the coffee started to boil over and he threw the pillow aside and tried to grab the coffeepot from the fire, knocking it over in the attempt. Frustrated, he kicked away the pot and the splattered log.

"Well, I've got me another pint."

Unmindful that the log he had kicked away had landed on the pillow he'd tossed aside, Paddy shuffled down the trail.

"You have the most beautiful blue eyes I've ever seen," Garth said, his head cradled in his hand as he lay on his side gazing at Rory. He played with some blond strands that clung to her cheek.

"I feel the same about your brown eyes."

Garth chuckled and lay back. "Honey, men do not have beautiful eyes."

Rory rolled over and cuddled against him with her head resting on his chest. "Who says so?"

"Me. But handsome's good."

"Very well, you have the handsomest brown eyes I've ever seen."

He scrunched up his nose in disapproval. "That doesn't sound too great, either. Forget my eyes, and let's get back to yours. What color of eyes did your mother have?"

"Blue. Same as Pop's."

"Then where did that slight mingling of green come from?"

"Must be the Irish in me coming out. And speaking of the Irish, I better get back. Pop's probably awake and looking for his coffee." Rory sat up.

"Paddy told me the truth about the map. Why did you lie to me, Rory?"

"At the time, I believed you might have harmed him."

"Good God! Do you think I'm some kind of savage who would harm a sick old man?"

"Will you please not shout?"

"Well, why did you let me go on all this time believing you were a thief?"

"I thought of telling you, but I had nothing to gain if I did. Besides, you wouldn't have believed me anyway."

"You don't know that."

She looked him boldly in the eyes. "So now that you know differently, does it actually make a difference to you?"

"Certainly. I can respect you a lot more than I did before."

"Hip, hip, hooray! But in the end, it doesn't change anything."

"No, because the theft of the map is no longer an issue with me. As I told Paddy, I put that behind me some time ago."

"Well, it matters to me," she declared. "And while we're on the subject, Garth Fraser, I want to make something very clear. I've only told you *one* lie—and that was only to help my father. I've never cheated anyone in my life, but *you* act as if it's a way of life with me. I've never come near being as intimate with any other man as I have with you, even though you believe I'm a cheap saloon girl. So that speaks more poorly of your actions, than it does mine—because you're the one who's trying to take my virginity, knowing how you really feel about me.

"Well, I'm through with waiting for your pats of approval. Save them for Saddle." She started to walk away, then spun on her heel.

"Furthermore, as long as we're talking about honesty, I don't trust anyone who's as cheerful as you are in the morning."

She left him with a bewildered look on his face.

Garth caught up with her and slipped an arm around her shoulders.

"You are one feisty little female, Miz Rory. But I like it. Must be why I'm so attracted to you."

"Or maybe because I'm the only female around." Rory stopped abruptly. "Is that smoke?" she asked, pointing ahead.

"Sure is, and looks like it's coming from where the mine is located."

"Bandits?" she asked, alarmed.

"Stay here while I check it out. Saddle, stay with her," he ordered, and took off on a run.

The burro was lying on the ground and the air was filled with the loud neighs and whinnies of the other panic-driven animals as they reared and yanked at the bonds that tethered them to the nearby trees. The scrub around the base of the mine was in flames and had spread to the foliage that concealed the entrance. Crawling flames and thick smoke prevented Garth from entering the mine.

"Paddy, are you in there?" he shouted. When there was no answer, he repeated his call several times.

"Pop," Rory cried, appearing suddenly at Garth's side.

"I told you to stay back," he yelled. "If he's in there, he's okay, the fire can't burn through rock."

"But the smoke?"

"The cavern's large, Rory," he yelled, and raced over to the animals. Boots fought the reins, but Garth managed to untie him and get him over to a tree upwind from the fire.

"Be careful, the smoke's got them spooked," Garth warned, when Rory started to do the same for one of the mules. A flying hoof came down on her foot, and she winced with pain but managed to hold on to the reins.

As soon as Garth moved the other mule to safety, he knelt over the suffering burro lying on the ground. One of its legs was broken.

Unable to watch, Rory turned her head away when he drew his Colt, held it against the animal's head to muffle the sound, and pulled the trigger.

While Garth beat at the fire with a horse blanket, Rory poured buckets of water along the edges of the flames until the fire was isolated near the entrance of the cave, where they were able to finally squelch the last of the flames.

"Stay here," Garth ordered, and he went inside to check out the mine. There was no sign of Paddy, and even though his bedroll had been pulled apart, everything else in the cave appeared untouched.

After checking the rear of the cavern, Garth rejoined Rory. "No sign of him." Spying an object on the ground, he bent down and picked up the blackened coffeepot.

"From the looks of this, I'd say that Paddy started to make coffee and got interrupted."

"Do you think he was attacked by a wild animal?"

"I don't know, Rory. My common sense tells me that an animal big enough to drag off a human would have gone for Boots or one of the mules. He probably just took off the way he always does, and left the fire unattended."

"Why must you always suspect the worst of my father?" she snapped.

"I *was* giving him the benefit of the doubt," he said, exasperated. "I could have suggested he got careless and started a fire, then ran away leaving the animals behind to perish in the flames."

"That's what you're really thinking, isn't it?"

"Rory, I'm not going to argue about it. It's just another example of his carelessness and irresponsibility. Probably every bandit within a hundred miles has seen the smoke, and now the foliage that concealed the entrance to the mine is gone. The mine can be spotted easily now by man or beast."

"The mine! Is that all you think about? You're as bad as Pop." She limped away in anger.

"Rory, come on back. I don't want you alone, and . . . why are you limping?" He plopped down on the ground. "Oh, hell!" He was fed up with the whole damn situation. "Go with her, Saddle. I have to clean up this mess."

Her foot was aching so badly that Rory didn't get far. After a short distance, she was forced to sit down and lean back against a tree.

Saddle came up and stretched out with his head in her lap. "He's right, you know, Saddle. It's just that he makes me so angry. Everything he does seems to be the right thing to do, and he doesn't realize how irritating it is to people who aren't as perfect as he.

"But you know what's the most frustrating? He doesn't intentionally try to be right about everything. He just always is. How *could* Pop have been so careless? This whole area could have gone up in flames if we hadn't caught it in time."

And stupidity must run in the family, because she was sitting here pouting, when Garth was right and there was work to do. She'd rest her foot just a few more minutes, then she'd go back and help.

"I surely hope Garth will be over his anger by then, Saddle, and we won't have any more cross words between us. He never stays angry for too long." She closed her eyes and leaned her head back against the tree.

"Rory, wake up."

She opened her eyes to discover Garth bending over her. "Are you okay?"

"Oh . . . yes, I'm fine. I must have dozed off." Rory got to her feet. She yelped with pain when she put her weight on her left foot, and she started to collapse. Garth caught her just before she went down.

"What's wrong?"

"The mule stepped on my foot."

He picked her up in his arms and carried her back to camp.

Garth set her down on an upturned keg and got down on his knees. She winced with pain when he tried to remove her boot.

"Honey, your foot's so swollen I can't get your boot off. Why didn't you tell me sooner?"

"We had our hands full at the time, remember?"

He gingerly tried to remove the boot again, and she sucked in a breath from the pain.

"It looks like I'm going to have to slice the boot to get it off you."

"No, these are the only boots I have."

"Honey, it'll be too painful to pull it off."

"I'll need the boot, Garth."

"All right—if that's what you want. There's no gentle way to do it, though."

"Just get it over with."

He curled his fingers around her leg, and grasped the heel of her boot. "You understand if it's broken, I might have to shoot you," he said, in an attempt to take her mind off the pain.

"Very funny, Garth, but it's my foot, not my leg." Then she cried out when he began to work the boot off her foot. Her breath came in short gasps as she fought the urge to scream. If only she could black out until he finished—but she'd never fainted in her life.

"Let it out, baby. Swear, scream, do what you have to. Don't try to hold it in."

"When I . . . get off . . . this moun . . . tain. I'm . . . never going . . . to put . . . on a . . . high boot . . . again!" she managed to cry out between gasps of pain.

"There, it's off," he finally said, sliding the top of the boot past her toes.

Garth gingerly peeled off her stocking and cradled her foot in the palm of one hand as he gently examined her foot with his other.

"Nothing feels broken, honey, but that doesn't mean it's not. It's badly bruised, and will probably look even worse by tomorrow. You want to lie down while I get a bucket of cold water? Soaking it will help bring the swelling down."

"Do you mind bringing my bedroll out here? I'd rather be in the sunshine than the cave."

As she waited, Rory glanced around at the campsite. There was quite a change in it from the time she'd left. Fortunately none of the flames had reached the trees. Garth had pulled out all the remnants of the burned foliage and cleaned up the area. Now that it was barren, she was surprised to see that the thick, high foliage had concealed not only the crevice in the rock, but several huge boulders and rocks around the base of the cave. Boots and the mules were tethered in their regular spot, and other than the faint smell of the smoke that still remained, one would never have guessed the chaos that had reigned earlier.

"How long was I sleeping?" she asked as he carried her over to the blanket he had set at the base of one of the boulders.

"A couple of hours."

"You sure were busy in that time."

"Yeah. That's why I got worried, when I realized how long you'd been gone."

"What did you do with the remains of the burro?"

"I buried it."

"Poor little thing. Too bad it had to suffer."

"No one gets a free pass when Paddy's around."

"Are you trying to start another argument?"

"I'm merely pointing out how an innocent life can be carelessly destroyed by him. There's an analogy there, in case you missed it."

"You're wrong, Garth. Pop hasn't destroyed my life."

He turned his head and looked at her. "Yet."

He went over to the waterfall and filled a bucket with cold water, then came back and submerged her foot in it.

"I suspect that by morning most of the swelling should be down, and we can get a better look at it. Until then, you stay off it. Understand?"

"Yes, Captain Fraser. Forgive me if I don't stand and salute."

Then he examined the palms of her hands. "At least they're healing nicely."

Her mouth twitched as she failed to suppress a smile.

He stood up. "All right, let's hear it. What's so funny?"

"You *do* fall in love with whatever woman you make

love to. And right now, I'm the chosen one. That's why you resent Pop so much. You feel he takes advantage of me—an irritation to your nobleness, my mighty knight in armor. I think you're even a little mad at yourself because you can't do anything about it."

He started to laugh. "You figure you've got all the answers, don't you, Miss Smarty?"

"Yes, I do. Right now I've got you squirming."

"Is that so? You know, lady, if you weren't hurting right now, I'd make you eat those words."

"And how would you do that?"

"By proving to you who's the one that does all the *squirming* in my subverted attempts to make love to you."

"Are you sure you don't mean *perverted* attempts, Fraser?"

"One of these times, you're going to find out what you've been missing."

"Really? So that's what's on your ... mind," she said, glancing at the bulge that had begun to form in his pants.

"And you know I'm right. So why that Mona Lisa smile?"

"Because right now I can *see* that I'm right. But as you said, 'by morning the swelling should be down.' " She tapped a finger on her lips, as if in deep thought. "Hmmm, I believe there's an analogy in there, in case you missed it."

Garth's warm laughter carried to his eyes. "No one could ever accuse you of being dull, honey," he said, and got down on his knees to inspect her foot again.

Rory fought the urge to tangle her fingers into the dark hair of the head bent attentively over her foot.

"So what do you think?"

"It's going to be pretty sore for a few days." He raised his head and smiled. "Maybe Paddy will share some of his whiskey with you to ease the pain. Or I could try to kiss it better," he said hopefully.

"You wouldn't take advantage of a helpless female, would you, Fraser?"

He slid his hands up her arms, and drew her nearer until their mouths were mere inches apart. "It's an old remedy. When I was young, my mother always kissed my hurts to make them feel better."

"Sure sounds better than sharing Pop's whiskey," she whispered.

She closed her eyes when his arms wrapped around her. Spats were forgotten, the fire, and her aching foot. The heady sensation of his mouth on hers was all the medicine she needed.

Rory was asleep when Paddy returned to camp. His step was livelier, and his derby was cocked at a jaunty angle.

"Top of the evening to you, me boy." Then he looked around in surprise. "What happened?"

"A fire," Garth said. "When you left camp this morning, did you leave the campfire unattended?"

"There was no wind, or even a breeze, to be doing it harm."

"Never underestimate the capability of even a spark, Paddy. This whole place could have gone up in flames;

Rory was hurt when we were putting it out, and the burro was injured. I had to shoot it."

"Rory's hurt?" Paddy said, alarmed.

"One of the mules stepped on her foot. She was fortunate not to end up with a broken foot, but she'll be in pain for a few days."

"And 'tis all me fault." For the first time since Garth had met him, Paddy appeared to show remorse.

"It makes us vulnerable now, Paddy," Garth tried to explain patiently. "Other people will have seen the smoke. We were concealed before, but now we're more exposed."

"And the burro's dead," Paddy said sorrowfully.

"Unfortunately."

"And 'tis all me fault," Paddy said gravely. He pulled off the bandanna from around his neck and dabbed at his eyes.

The old man seemed genuinely sorry. In an attack of tenderheartedness, Garth said, "Accidents happen, Paddy."

Maybe he should try a different tack with the man. Why not appeal to his manhood? The old guy *did* love his daughter, even if he had a damn poor way of showing it.

"With Rory laid up for the next few days, we can't leave her alone, so I'm going to need your help more than ever around here. You'll have to remain with her when I go to catch fish, for instance."

" 'Tis the least I can do," Paddy said, blowing his nose.

"You know how she's used to staying busy. Maybe you could keep her occupied playing cards or something."

"That I can do," Paddy said eagerly. "But I'm not much for cooking."

"I can do the cooking for a few days. And I'll stay close to camp as much as possible myself. Of course, when I'm at the back of the cavern there's no way I can look out for her. I suppose I could forget mining until she's back on her feet."

"You don't want to do that, me boy," Paddy said quickly. "She's me daughter, and she needs me. I'll not fail her," he declared resolutely.

"Good," Garth said, patting him on the shoulder. He was so pleased with the reults of his conniving, he wished he could do the same to himself. "I'll get back to work first thing in the morning, and why don't you gather some more wood for tomorrow morning's campfire? You'll find a big pile of it in those trees about a quarter mile south of here."

17

For the next couple of days everything ran smoothly again. Paddy would go out and gather wood diligently for the campfire, and Rory would pretend that she didn't notice the smell of whiskey on his breath when he returned. She and Paddy would play cards or chess, or she would read Garth's book while he worked in the mine or caught fish for their meals.

By the third day, Paddy began to spend less time playing games and more time "gathering wood." He was gone all afternoon the following day, and came back in an alcoholic stupor, then stumbled into the mine for a "nap."

"I thought it was too good to last," Garth said later as he knelt and examined her foot by the campfire. "Old habits die hard. Rory, Paddy's fully able to travel now, so let's get the hell out of here in the morning."

"That's fine with me."

Garth cupped her foot in the warm palm of his hand. "It looks good. Even the bruise has started to fade, so you can walk on it now."

She felt the tantalizing rise of passion as he slid his hand to the calf of her leg.

"Are you sure it feels better?" he asked.

"Very sure," she said.

"Maybe, I should check it closer to make sure," he added as his hand moved to the buttons on her Levi's.

She lifted his hand away and slid her arms around his neck. "Yes, maybe you should," she murmured, just before his mouth claimed hers.

They both knew it was a dangerous game they were playing, they were pushing each other to the limit. But neither of them was willing to call off the exciting challenge of it.

Rory had just finished frying the fish for dinner when Paddy came out of the mine, looking the worse for wear. As soon as he finished, Paddy put aside his plate.

" 'Twas as good as usual, darlin'. Now I think I'll be taking meself back to bed."

"Pop, Garth and I decided that since my foot's fine and you're well enough to travel, we'll leave in the morning."

"Have you now? Well, Rorleen Catherine, I think I'll be the judge of that. Good night, darlin'."

"He seemed to take that well," Garth said.

"You don't know him as well as I do," Rory said, with a worried glance at the entrance to the mine.

By the time she and Garth finished cleaning up the dishes, his loud snores carried to the outside.

"I suppose I should go to bed now, too," Rory said.

"How are you going to fall asleep with that snoring in there?"

"I've grown used to it."

Garth went inside and came back with his bedroll, spread it out, and then he laid back and gazed up at the stars.

"One of these days I'm going to forget what a bed ever felt like," he said. "I can count the times on one hand that I've slept in an actual bed in the last seven years."

"Better get used to it, since you intend to spend the next few years roaming. You can't fold a bed up into your saddlebags."

"Hey, let's make a vow that before we split up, we make love together in a bed."

"I thought you had an aversion to deflowering virgins," she said.

"After considerable thought, combined with a considerably greater pain in my groin, I've decided to make an exception in your case. Good night, honey."

"Good night, Garth," she said with a smile.

Rory blew out the lantern and removed her shirt and Levi's. Then she lay in the dark thinking about Garth.

Her desire for him was becoming stronger each time they were together. She could no longer fight this attraction. Awake or asleep, she thought of him constantly.

And what was she proving to herself, or anyone, by denying herself the one thing—the one person—she wanted more than anything on earth?

Saving herself for her wedding night now seemed naïve and ludicrous. She couldn't imagine wanting any man as much as she wanted Garth.

Until now she'd had few choices in her life; anything she wanted from the heart was always pretty much beyond her reach.

For the first time, she'd discovered that love and marriage did not always go hand in hand. Maybe living happily ever after meant accepting a compromise, if you couldn't have what you really wanted.

The night when she had lain in that pit, only one man had been foremost in her mind. One man.

Driven by an irresistible urge, Rory got up and went outside; drawn to the figure on the ground like a moth to a flame—and the outcome could only be just as self-destructive.

Garth sat up as she approached, but didn't ask what she wanted. He knew her reason for coming as well as she did.

Hot blood coursed through her, fueled by the glowing desire in his stare that never wavered from her own. She paused before him and their gazes locked with a heat far greater than the burning embers of the campfire.

Still, neither spoke. Her mouth felt too dry for words, and what would she say even if she tried? She could feel her courage begin to falter, but her legs were trembling too much to try to bolt.

As if sensing her waning courage, he grasped her hand, pulled her down, and cradled her in his arms.

"No last-minute reprieve this time, Rory."

Then he claimed her lips in a consuming kiss. As the kiss deepened her mind spun helplessly, drawing her deeper into swirling erotic sensation. Dear God, it felt so incredible! Why had she fought it for so long? She closed her eyes in pure ecstasy.

Garth's gaze clung hungrily to the sight of her dark lashes against her cheeks. Did she have any idea how beautiful she was? How much he wanted her?

He was hard and hot already. Helpless to resist the temptation, he placed a light kiss on each closed lid, then reclaimed her lips with drugging, intimate kisses that drained the breath from both of them. Tracing her swollen lips with his tongue, he plunged it into the parted moistness that opened in invitation.

When he slipped his hand under her camisole, her gasp heightened his arousal. Cupping one of her breasts, he began to gently stroke the taut peak with his thumb.

He had lusted for this woman for weeks, and his control was slipping fast. This time there'd be no stopping after a few hot kisses and petting. And she wanted him as much as he wanted her, or she wouldn't have come to him.

He pulled the garment over her head and laid her on her back, where his mouth and hands could have freer access.

Lowering his head, he licked the tips of her nipples, toying with the hardened peaks until his name became a sensuous sigh on her lips.

Her sighs changed to gasps when he closed his mouth around one of her breasts in an erotic suckling that wrenched a groan from her throat. She squirmed beneath it, dug her hands into his hair, and pressed his head to the other quivering mound. He went willingly.

Sliding his hands down the smooth plane of her stomach, he pushed her drawers past the curve of her hips and pulled them off. Then he leaned back and let his eyes devour her nakedness.

If he thought her face beautiful, her naked body robbed him of his breath. He yanked off his shirt impatiently and stripped off his remaining clothing, then stretched out on the inviting flesh that beckoned to him.

Rory was swept along in a torrent of long-suppressed passion as Garth lightly traced the outline of her mouth with his tongue. The heady masculine smell of him permeated her senses, and overpowered by the arousing scent she reached out and caressed the corded column of his neck. She could feel the tautness that held his body in check, and she slid her hand into the dark thickness of his hair. Its texture tantalized her fingertips.

Her hunger for him was becoming unbearable. When he reclaimed her lips in a hot, wet kiss, her tongue danced erotically across the roof of his mouth, dueled with his until he pulled away, muffling a groan into her hair. Sliding her arms around his neck, she hugged the muscular strength of him into her own rounded curves as he rained light kisses on her lips, her jaw, and the hollow of her neck. When he reached her breasts, he returned to that delicious suckling that sent exquisite sensation spiraling throughout her body.

She traced his heated flesh—the muscular slope of his shoulders, the hard length of his spine, the warmth of his skin. When he drew her tighter against the intimate proof of his arousal, the sensation became ecstasy. She wished he would never stop. And she sensed the best was yet to come.

Garth smothered his groan against her mouth in a passionate kiss when her groping hand found the inside of his thigh and began to trace a trail to his throbbing organ. Raising his head, he stared down at her and lightly glazed her cheek with his fingertips, then slid his fingers to her chin and tipped her face to his. Her golden hair was spread out on the blanket and her passion-laden eyes inflamed his lust even more.

He had waited so long for this moment, and despite the pressure in his groin that threatened to explode, he forced himself to exercise control. He never wanted to forget this moment—and he was going to make certain she would never forget it, either.

He lowered his head to her naked flesh, and what had been arousing foreplay before erupted into an erotic exploration.

Driven to the brink of madness, she cried out for mercy to gain release from the exquisite torture. "No more, Garth. Please, no more," she pleaded when he began to nibble the flesh of her inner thigh.

Garth raised himself and thrust into her, rupturing the thin membrane. She cried out and writhed beneath him in an effort to dislodge him.

"Don't struggle, honey. It'll just hurt worse," he cautioned, and began to move slowly in and out. Sweet sensation replaced the initial pain. The blinding, breathtaking, mindless ecstasy continued to build as the tempo and force of his thrusts increased, and his name slipped past her lips in a blissful cry as their bodies shuddered with the rapturous tremors of climax.

As Rory's breath returned to a normal rhythm, her chest ached from the throbbing of her heart.

Garth smiled tenderly as he toyed with some errant strands of her hair. "I knew it would be like this."

Her eyes misted as she gazed at him. "I had no idea. Does making love always feel like that?"

Garth smiled and rolled over, pinning her to the ground with his weight. "Not always. It often depends on who you're making love with."

He lowered his head and gently kissed her swollen lips, then lay back again and cradled her head against his chest.

Within minutes, his steady breathing revealed that he had dropped off to sleep.

Rory lay awake in his arms. What just passed between them was the most incredible sensation she had ever experienced. Had he felt the same, or was she just another conquest to him? The sexual attraction between them had been building from the time they met. Would this end it, or would Garth want to do this again? And if he did, having now experienced the thrill of it, would she be capable of refusing?

Rory rose and quickly donned her clothing, then slipped away and returned to her bed in the cave.

Garth opened his eyes when she got up but didn't try to stop her from leaving.

God knows he wanted her again, was ready for her again. He'd made love to a goodly number of women, but none came near to matching Rory. She'd been incredible. Even the most skilled prostitutes in Virginia or France hadn't stirred his blood as much as she had tonight.

That, and the fact that she'd been honest about her virginity, had come as a big surprise to him. He had believed that her story of saving herself for the man she married had all been a part of her act. She'd sure fooled the hell out of him.

Count your blessings, Fraser, because this was the first of many more such times if we remain on this mountain.

And that would be a big mistake. The more often they made love, the more involved they'd become. And he wasn't about to let a few nights of hot passion make him forget his dreams.

So keep your pistol in its holster where it belongs, Fraser.

Troubled, he tucked his hands under his head and gazed up at the stars. They didn't look any different than they had before, even though his world had just been turned upside down.

Perhaps it was lucky that he was taking her back soon—because he couldn't help wonder about how else he'd been mistaken about Rory O'Grady.

18

Rory woke up to the sound of Garth whistling outside. She quickly pulled on her stockings and boots and went out to join him. Bright sunshine indicated the start of another hot day, and she paused in the entrance of the cave to watch Garth.

He was shirtless and had already worked up a sweat chopping wood for the campfire he had built. He had such a beautifully proportioned body. Broad shoulders, a powerful chest, and slim hips. Fascinated, she watched the corded muscle ripple across his tanned shoulders and biceps with every swing of the ax.

Closing her eyes, she recalled the strength in those arms, the feel of them around her, and knew that after last night, she could never deny that man anything he asked of her—especially her body.

The day suddenly became much *warmer*.

Rory noticed he had restrung the blanket over the rope, so she went to her pack and got what she needed.

Garth put aside the ax and smiled at her when she came over to the fire. "Good morning. How are you, this bright and cheery morning?"

"Fine. I thought I'd like to ah . . . clean myself up after last night."

"I figured you would, so I put the blanket back up. As soon as you finish, I'm going to wash up, too."

She ducked behind the blanket and shed her clothing, then quickly washed away the remnants of their lovemaking, brushed her teeth, and washed out her underclothes.

By the time she was through, Rory felt ready to face whatever lay ahead of her today.

Garth had brewed a pot of coffee and she poured herself a cup. After several sips of hot coffee, watching his flexing muscles, and his shirtless chest, she felt like racing over to the waterfall to cool off again.

"This is a luxury for me," she said. "I'm used to having to build a fire and make the coffee in the morning."

"It might be a good idea to wake Paddy. The sooner we eat and finish packing up, the sooner we can head back." At her look of despair, he leaned down and kissed her lightly. "Hey, why so glum this morning?"

"You heard Pop last night. He's a stubborn man. What if he refuses to leave?"

"I think I would like to hear the answer to that from you, Rory."

"I think he's too ill to travel."

"You need your eyes opened. If he'd run out of whiskey, you'd see him tearing down this mountain like the hounds of hell were yapping at his feet. He's perfectly capable of traveling; he's only playing on your sympathy. The best thing you can do for the both of you is call his bluff and leave. You'll see him come running."

"I'm staying, Garth. I'm not leaving him," she declared flatly.

"Damn it, Rory, that's just what he wants. And he knows exactly what he can get from you."

"And last night, didn't *you* get what you wanted from me?"

"So *that's* what this is all about—morning-after guilt? Sorry, I'm not buying it. You came to me, remember? And all of this outburst because you know your father is too stubborn to leave. Rory, I won't try to deny that in the beginning I believed you playing the blushing virgin was just some more of this act to bamboozle me; and I'm sorry, I misjudged that; I was wrong. But when we made love last night you were into it as much as I was, so don't imply now that it was against your conscience."

She couldn't believe her ears. Was this the same man who had made such tender love to her? "Last night meant nothing to you, did it?"

"Of course it did. Last night was wonderful. *You're* wonderful. It was the best sex I've ever had. What are you asking? If you want me to say it was the most emotional moment I've ever known, the answer is no. But physically, nothing can compare to it."

"Last night I came to you with the only thing I had to give—my virginity. The one thing I was saving for the man I hoped to marry one day. And now I find out it didn't mean anything to you other than *the best sex you ever had.*" She couldn't bear to even look at him, and turned away.

"Rory, what did you expect from me? Surely not marriage; You know my thinking on that subject. And when that wedding day you dream of finally comes, you won't be less of a woman, love him less, just because you're no longer a virgin. Surely you don't believe he'll be coming to that wedding bed a virgin himself?

"Frankly, I've never understood why a man should expect a woman to deny herself the same bodily pleasures that he enjoys, any more than I can understand a woman who doesn't enjoy that pleasure."

He came over and tried to take her in his arms. "Honey, I'm sorry if—"

"Don't touch me!" she cried, and shoved him away. "Don't you dare touch me!"

A glint of anger flared in his eyes. "Considering last night, it's a little late for that now, isn't it? We both know we can't keep our hands off one another. But we'll discuss this later when you're in a better frame of mind. In the meantime, I'll assume we're not leaving."

"There's nothing keeping you here. Go with my blessing," she snapped.

"Right now you're not only battling Paddy and me, Rory, but your conscience as well. Why you feel any guilt is beyond my comprehension, so I'll leave you to that labor." He went back to chopping wood.

Rory worked off her anger by continuing to vent as she started to unpack the mule. The physical work also helped calm her down. Within minutes she regretted her outburst.

She walked over and put a hand on Garth's arm. He looked down at it, then swung his gaze up to hers.

"I'm sorry, Garth. Please forgive me."

He put his arms around her in a bear hug. "I understand, honey. You just haven't had that second cup of coffee this morning."

"Top of the morning," Paddy greeted, suddenly appearing at the entrance of the cave.

"Good morning!" Rory exclaimed. She and Garth exchanged astonished looks. "You must be feeling better this morning, Pop."

"That I am, darlin'. That I am. Fit as a fiddle." He kissed her on the cheek.

Rory felt his forehead. "And you don't feel feverish—but you sure are acting that way."

He gave Garth a pat on the shoulder. "And how be you this fine morning, me boy?"

"Fine, Paddy. Glad to see you're feeling better."

Paddy rubbed his stomach. "Better, and hungry enough to eat a horse." He grinned at Rory. "Darlin', what's holding up breakfast?"

"Pop, you haven't eaten breakfast in days," Rory said.

"All the more reason why I'm hungry for one now."

"Well, we want to get started back to the mission, so we planned to eat only jerky this morning."

"Ah, yes, leaving. 'Tis the very thing I want to discuss."

Rory shook her head. "I'm not taking no for an answer, Pop. You're coming with us, so I don't want to hear another argument on the subject."

"Will you listen to the girl?" Paddy said to Garth. "Ah, it would bring a tear to her sainted mother's eye to hear her. Put your hands over your ears, Katie love," he yelled skyward.

Arms akimbo, Rory declared, "You keep my sainted mother out of this, Pop. I don't want to hear any of your schemes, so save your breath—because we're not staying."

"Garth, me boy, you're an intelligent, level-headed young fella, with a fine head on your shoulders."

"Well, thank you, Paddy."

"Will you sit down and listen to what I have to say?"

"I'll listen, sir, but I have to tell you, I agree one hundred percent with Rory. And there's no better time to leave than now, while you're feeling well enough to travel."

"And that's me very question, me boy: if I'm feeling well again, why *are* we leaving? Didn't we all come here to find a gold mine? Well, we've found the mine, and we've found the gold.

"So why leave now?" he continued. "Did you not say we don't have to fear any further bandit attacks?"

"That's only an opinion, Paddy. I said I think it's unlikely, because if there were any others around, they would have discovered us by now. Although there have been a couple times when I suspected we were being watched."

"But nothing's come of it, has it?"

"Well, no," Garth said.

"So there you go, me boy. Just what I said. Now, I agree to us being partners. 'Tis a grand idea. We'll work together and split it down the middle."

"What I found is no big bonanza. It's a narrow vein, Paddy."

Paddy's eyes widened hopefully. " 'Tis big enough to make us rich, isn't it?"

"Certainly big enough for us to live comfortably the rest of our lives."

Paddy exuberantly rubbed his hands together. "So why leave it behind?"

"Pop, Garth said that once we get back down to the mission, he'll come back here and finish mining."

"But we're here now, the mine's here, the gold's here—so why all the coming and going?"

"I can see the logic to what you're saying, Paddy, but there are other kinds of dangers up here. Wild animals. Accidents. Landslides. As well as another attack of your illness. I don't want to be responsible for your lives."

"Garth, me boy, life's a risk no matter where we're at, but it doesn't stop us from eating and drinking to stay alive, now does it?" He winked at Rory. "So what do you think, darlin'? Stay or go?"

"If you don't mind, Pop, I'd like to talk to Garth privately," Rory said.

"Sit down and drink your coffee while we're gone," Garth suggested. He took her hand and led her over to the privacy of the trees.

"Does what he said make any sense to you, Garth?" Rory asked.

"It's logical, but not sensible when putting your life at risk is the issue. If sense was involved, we'd get out of here without giving it a second thought."

"Well, how much longer do you figure it will take you to finish off that vein?"

He shrugged. "With not having to cook or gather wood, I could probably finish it in about a week."

"Do you think you could put up with Pop and me for another week?"

He slipped his hands around her waist. "I figure I can. Besides, we still have a lot more unfinished business to complete, don't we?" His lips grazed her earlobe, her cheek, and then took her lips with a demanding mastery that left her wanting more. "So keep that kiss on your mind, sweetheart, because I'll be doing the same for the rest of the day."

They went back to the campfire, where Paddy waited anxiously.

"Okay, partner. You've got a deal," Garth said.

A monumental weight had been lifted from Rory's shoulders, and she smiled from ear to ear as the two men shook hands.

As for her feeling of guilt, well . . . Didn't Garth's words make sense? Why *should* she feel guilty? And he'd said it was the best sex he ever had. So as far as the unfinished business between them was concerned . . . Her eyes sparked with devilment and she started to giggle. "I think I can handle that, too."

Throughout the day, the feel of Garth's kiss remained on her lips. And that evening, as soon as Paddy passed out in a drunken stupor, the outcome was inevitable. They made love throughout the night, long glorious explorations of one another, and quick couplings when they'd awake from dozing with flared passions that demanded instant satisfaction.

By the time the first rays of a rising sun appeared on the horizon, Rory knew she was in love.

19

She sighed and shook her head when she heard Pop exchanging cross words with Garth for disturbing his sleep so early.

"Liquor and anger make for an explosive combination, Saddle," she said as she prepared breakfast. "I've seen plenty of that in the saloons I've worked in.

""You understand, boy, Pop has always been as endearing as you are when he's sober. But whiskey's always had a bad effect on him. I have to find where he's stashed it!"

Saddle wagged his tail and she tossed him a bite of bacon. "I'm sure going to miss you when we leave—both you and that big galoot you adopted."

Garth stopped working long enough to eat breakfast, and Saddle trailed after him when he went back inside the mine. As soon as her father walked away,

Rory followed him to find out exactly where he went when he disappeared—which, no doubt, was where he had his whiskey hidden.

She stayed a safe distance behind him, following the route back to Herbert Forsen's mine. He continued on a little farther and stopped in a copse of trees. She remembered the area well. It was where they had buried those four bandits who had attacked them when they first arrived. She had purposely avoided that area after they had buried the dead bandits.

Rory watched as he retrieved a flat stone from the bushes and scraped away a corner of topsoil from one of the graves. He pulled out a bottle of whiskey.

So that's where he's hiding it! The sly old fox. To her further surprise he also pulled out a flat pan, then refilled the hole and walked away. She rushed over to the hole, scraped the dirt away quickly, and pulled out two remaining whiskey bottles. Then, curious to know where he was going with the pan, she hurried after him.

As she followed, she opened the bottles one after the other and dumped them out. "Thank goodness that's the end of that," she said with satisfaction, after she tossed the last bottle away.

Rory had never been on this part of the mountain before. Well off the beaten trail, it was lined with many crags and bluffs.

She followed Paddy up the rocky slope. The incline was steep and she couldn't imagine how her father did this daily.

When she crested the slope to the plateau above, she saw that her father had knelt by a narrow stream.

When he dipped the pan into the stream and shifted it back and forth, it became clear to her.

He's panning for gold!

Rory couldn't believe that was what he'd secretly been up to. The question was: was he having any success?

She made her way back down the slope toward camp. She wanted to hold off telling Garth until after she'd spoken to Pop. Not knowing what he intended to do with the gold he panned, it would be wiser to hear the full story first. *Oh, Pop, the fur's really going to fly on this one.*

As she neared the Forsen mine, Rory paused to admire a wildflower growing among the scrub. The colorful little floret was a comforting reminder that there was still some beauty in the world.

As Rory rose to her feet, she heard a loud rustling in the tall foliage nearby.

"Pop, is that you?" she called out.

When there was no answer, she began to back away, her gaze riveted on the area where she had heard the noise. The sound came again, this time louder, as if something or someone was thrashing around in the brush.

"Pop?" she called out.

The brush parted, and two little bear cubs about the size of Saddle broke through.

"Oh, you darlings, you gave me such a fright." She froze at the sound of a chilling growl, and screamed when a huge grizzly bear lumbered out of the brush. The bear rose up on its hind legs and growled again, its mammoth jaw opened to reveal sharp, yellowed teeth.

She had never seen anything so tall and frightening, and she screamed again, then turned and bolted. The bear thumped after her on all fours with long, loping strides.

Rory headed for a pile of boulders that led to a bluff above, in the hope of scaling them before the animal caught up with her.

Panic-stricken, she scrambled up the rocks, but her foot slipped and became wedged between two of them.

She still wasn't high enough to escape the bear, and she frantically struggled to free her boot, but her foot was held too securely. Horrified, she screamed again as the animal reared up and approached, prepared to attack.

Garth tossed aside his pick and came out of the mine. The vein had finally run out. There was no sense in trying to squeeze another grain out of it.

Seeing no sign of Rory, he stuck his head into the waterfall spray to rinse off the grit. Saddle came trotting up with a fish between his jaws and dropped it at his feet.

"Don't tell me you and Rory went fishing." He picked up the fish and tossed it into a nearby bucket of water. "Thank you, oh mighty hunter, but we've had enough fish for a while. How about some meat? Since the fire, we don't have any little critters coming around to trap," he said, shaking the water out of his hair. "And where's Rory? You're supposed to be looking after her."

Saddle suddenly stiffened and perked up his ears. "What is it, boy?"

Suddenly a scream rent the air.

Saddle raced off in the direction of the scream, and Garth followed, crashing through the brush. When Rory screamed again, raw terror in the sound, he was petrified that he wouldn't reach her in time.

He could barely keep Saddle in sight as the dog sped ahead of him.

Saddle charged directly into the path of the bear advancing on Rory. His sudden appearance distracted the huge beast, and with a low growl, Saddle leaped at it. The bear swiped at him with deadly claws that would have ripped him open, but Saddle dodged them and crouched to spring again, just as two rifle shots kicked up dust at the feet of the bear.

When Garth reached the scene, he drew his Colt and was about to shoot when two more rifle shots hit the ground on each side of the animal. The bear plopped down on all fours, raised its head, and emitted an angry roar as it backed away. Several more shots kicked up the dirt around it again. Nuzzling and shoving the cubs ahead of her, the bear disappeared into the brush.

Damn, this was one time he was glad Paddy hadn't listened to him about not firing a rifle!

Garth ran to Rory and she flung her arms around him and began to sob. He kissed her and held her in a tight hug until her trembling ceased, then stepped back slightly.

"Oh, my God, baby, are you hurt?"

"No, just scared," she managed to say. "My foot's stuck and I can't get it out."

"Let me look." He knelt to examine her foot. After several useless minutes of trying to free it, he stood up and carefully lowered her to a sitting position.

"I can't budge it, either. Honey, I'm going to have to go back to get Boots and some rope. We'll have to move that rock away enough for you to slide your foot out. Tell Paddy I'm going to need his help."

Fear filled her eyes, and he drew her into his arms again. "I'll be back in a few minutes," he said tenderly.

"What if the bear—"

"The bear won't come back," he assured her. "She's got her cubs to protect."

Slipping on the rocky surface, Saddle reached them and Rory opened her arms. "Thank you," she cried, hugging him. "That bear could have killed you." The thought made her tear up again.

"Saddle's not exactly a knight in armor," Garth said to lighten her mood, "but he's a real dragon slayer. What in hell is keeping Paddy?" He handed her his Colt. "Use this only if you have to. Saddle, you stay here with her."

Garth jumped down and took off at a run, not seeing the man who suddenly appeared on the bluff above.

Rory watched with apprehension as the stranger climbed down to her. He had the same long-legged, broad-shouldered, and slim-hipped build as Garth. Straight dark hair hung almost to his shoulders beneath a sombrero, and a dark mustache dropped below his lower lip.

There was a warmth in his brown eyes that belied his menacing appearance as he patted Saddle on the head when he reached them. "¡Hola, amigo! You showed much courage, my furry friend." Saddle's tail wagged in response.

"He appears to know you," Rory said, keeping the pistol raised.

His teeth flashed against his dark skin. "Sí, señorita, the perro and I have become great friends since we met earlier."

"Who are you?"

The man removed his hat. "I am called Rico, señorita."

"Was Saddle your dog?"

"No, but we have met before on this mountain and know each other well."

"So it was you shooting at the bear."

"Yes, I did not wish to kill her, just drive her away. She was protecting her cubs. Who would protect them if she was dead?"

"She was about to kill *me*!" Rory exclaimed.

"Let me assure you, I would have prevented it. I see you have a problem."

"Yes, my foot's wedged between the rocks. Garth's gone to get some rope and his horse."

"Señorita, I would be grateful if you would lower that pistol you are pointing at me," he said with an engaging grin that reminded her of Garth's.

She raised the Colt higher. "Are you a bandit?"

"No, señorita. Will it offend you if I examine your foot?"

"No, but I don't think it will help. Garth tried to free it and couldn't."

His mouth curled into a smile. "And you have great trust in Garth."

"I do."

"That is good when two people are in love."

"In love? What gave you that idea, Rico? You don't even know us."

"I can tell from the way you speak his name."

He got down on his knees to examine her foot. After a short inspection, he said, "Your trust in him is correct. It is going to be very difficult to get you free." At the sound of a rifle cocking, he raised his hands in the air. "Do not shoot, Señor Garth."

"Okay, amigo, get up very slowly, and carefully turn around. One false move and I'll blow your head off. Who in hell are you?"

"Garth, Rico is the one who saved my life," Rory exclaimed.

"Yeah, and maybe *Rico* had other plans for you. Where's the rest of your gang, amigo?"

"I have no gang, señor."

"So you just came up here to admire the view?"

"No, Father Chavez sent me. Now, shall we get on with the task of freeing Señorita O'Grady?"

"Knowing the name of the priest is no proof that he sent you."

"Your name is Garth Fraser," Rico said. "The señorita is Rorleen Catherine O'Grady, and her father is Patrick Michael. You came here to find a gold mine that was discovered by your uncle Henry Fraser. The

O'Gradys filed a claim on it before you could. Is that enough proof for you, Señor Fraser?"

"I would say so." Garth offered his hand. "And we're grateful for your timely arrival, Rico. Do you have any idea how we're going to get her foot out of that rock? To make matters worse, it's the same foot she injured recently."

"A rope will snap before it even budges the rock, even if we had a way of connecting it," Rico said. "And there's no way of getting behind to try and shove it away, either."

"I agree," Garth said. "So if we can't pull it, or shove it, that leaves raising it or dropping it."

Amusement gleamed in Rico's eyes. "I think you have something in mind already?"

"To drop it," Garth said. "During the war we had a similar situation in Tennessee. There was a Yankee encampment below us, so we started a rock slide to get away. See how much smaller that bottom rock on the end is? If we could loosen it enough to get it to shift, the ones above it might shift enough to free her foot. We wouldn't have to even budge it an inch to make it work."

"And how do you plan on doing that?" Rico asked.

"I brought a shovel and pick. The object is to dig out the ground around it and let gravity take over. Those rocks are on an incline, so if we can get the bottom to start sliding, the others will, too."

Garth grabbed the pick and Rico the shovel, and they began to dig away the earth around the base of the smaller rock. They trenched and hollowed out an area about six feet deep to form a downhill chute.

Then they found an oak sapling that looked strong enough to use as a wedge. They dug around it to expose the roots, then tied one end of the rope to the roots and attached the other end to the saddle on Boots.

The horse's strength uprooted it and dragged the sapling over to the rock pile, where they trimmed it into a wedge and slid it under the rock.

Garth climbed up to give Rory her final instructions. "Honey, all we need is enough of a gap for you to pull your foot out. As soon as that bottom rock starts shifting, the others will follow, so your timing is critical."

"I understand," she said. "But what if the rock I'm on starts to slide?"

"There's no way it can. The gap next to it will only be open for a couple seconds; it can't slide right or left. We need two men on that wedge to loosen the rock, so neither of us can be up here to help you."

"I understand. Let's just get on with it," she said, her courage dwindling.

"Honey, you've held up this long, don't give in now." He kissed her and jumped down, then whistled for Saddle, who had lain with his head on Rory's lap throughout the whole procedure. To keep him from getting underfoot and possibly being injured, Garth tied him up next to Boots.

"Okay, Rico, let's see what luck we have."

Moving to the open side of the rock pile, they took a firm hold on the wedge and slid it as far as it would go under the bottom of the boulder, then began to rock it up and down. The effort was strenuous, and the fear that the wedge would snap was foremost on their minds.

Soon some of the earth under the boulder began to crumble, and the granite rock shifted slightly. They continued to jar it, and the rock shifted a degree deeper into the chute they had dug, which started a chain reaction in the ones above it. The instant the next rock shifted down, Rory yanked her foot free before the one above closed the gap.

As soon as the rocks settled again, Garth quickly scaled them, picked up Rory, and carried her down. Once a safe distance from the formation, he put her down.

He and Rico exchanged proud smiles, then reached out and shook hands for a job well done.

20

While Rico went back to get his horse, Garth insisted upon carrying Rory back to the mine. There he knelt and examined her foot to make sure there was no further injury. Smiling, he looked up. "Looks good, honey."

"It feels fine, too," she said.

He stood up. "And I've got more good news. The vein's run out, so there's no reason why we can't pack up and go back tomorrow."

"Hooray!" she shouted joyously, and threw her arms around him.

He kissed her, and the sound of Rico's return broke them apart.

"If luck is with us, Rico, by this time tomorrow we'll be at the mission with a hot bath and meal under our belts."

"Sí, amigo. I'm ready to leave any time you are."

"Let's eat early and then pack up everything we won't need on the trip back," Garth said.

"Good idea," Rory agreed.

"Where's Paddy, Rory?"

"He's off in the woods. He should be back soon."

Garth glanced at Rico. "We'll toss a coin to see who showers first."

"And I'll get dinner under way," Rory said joyfully.

"Oh, I can't wait to get away from here." She was so happy, she began to hum "Oh! Susanna" as she started to prepare dinner.

Captivated by her happiness, Garth grasped her around the waist, then lifted her up and twirled around. "For I've come from Alabama with a banjo on my knee," he sang in a rich baritone. Laughing, they continued the song and dance as Rico clapped his hands in rhythm.

"What's going on here?" Paddy asked, appearing on the scene. "And I heard some gunshots a while back."

"A good while back, Paddy," Garth said with a disgusted look in the old man's direction. "I'm getting rid of some of this dust." He headed for the waterfall.

"Pop, this is Rico," Rory said.

With a wary eye, Paddy scrutinized the young man. "Where'd you come from?"

"I live in the village, Señor O'Grady."

"How do we know that? Maybe you're one of them bandits figuring on moseying up to us, then stealing our gold."

"I can assure you, Señor O'Grady, I am not after your gold," Rico said politely.

Embarrassed by her father's rudeness, Rory said quickly, "Pop, Rico saved my life today, and we trust him completely."

"Whattaya mean, saved your life?"

"Just another time you were needed and nowhere to be found, Paddy," Garth said, drying his hair as he joined them. "Shower's all yours, Rico," Garth said.

Nodding, Rico moved away.

Paddy gave Garth a scathing glare. "I'm talking to me daughter, if you please, Mr. Fraser."

"And thanks to Rico, your daughter is still alive for you to be *talking* to."

"I met up with a grizzly bear, Pop, and Rico drove it off."

"And where was the likes of you, Mr. Fraser, when you was needed?"

"Working at digging the gold to finance your whiskey expenses, Mr. O'Grady. And the good news is that the vein has run out. We're clearing out of here to-morrow morning."

"How can you be so sure?" Paddy asked.

"I've been working that mine, Paddy. Perhaps there could be another vein farther in, but we don't have the tools to cut through that rock. And even if we had dy-namite, if we tried to use it, we could bring the whole top of the mountain down on us."

"I'm thinking you're bluffing, Mr. Fraser. I'm think-ing you might have it in mind to come back here after we're gone and mine some more."

Garth snorted. "Once I get off this damn mountain, I wouldn't step back on it for all the gold in the treasury, unless the whole United States Cavalry was accompanying me."

"Confederate cavalry," Rory corrected, and she winked at him.

The brief exchange between them was enough to cool his anger. What in hell did he care what Paddy thought?

"Paddy, due to your carelessness and setting the place on fire, every bandit for a hundred miles now knows we're here and is probably on his way to drop in. And unfortunately those shots today will let them know our location exactly. So we've still got the hardest job ahead of us: getting out of here alive. And since there's no longer any reason to remain here now, I'll hog-tie you to a mule if I have to, to get you out of here."

"I ain't asking you to stay, Fraser. I'll be glad to see the last of you. I've found me another source for gold."

"Really."

Rory had known this moment was inevitable, and she dreaded how it would end. "I think it's time you tell him, Pop."

" 'Tis none of his business," Paddy declared.

"Pop, we're all in this together, and Garth's got a right to know." Rory turned to Garth. "He's been panning for gold."

"Panning for gold!"

"Yes. There's a stream not too far from here. I saw him there this morning. I was on my way back when I encountered Mama Bear and her cubs."

"It's true, Garth," Rico said. "I've seen him there a couple times now. I followed Rory when I saw her follow him. That's why I was able to help her in time."

Garth shoved his hat to his forehead. "And all this was happening while I was back in that damn mine, scraping up the last grain of gold dust? I ought to kick your ass down that mountain, Paddy. Your greed almost got your daughter killed again!"

Paddy dug into a pocket, pulled out a tiny pouch, and poured out over a dozen small nuggets. "These are mine. I found them, so don't you be expecting any part of them because they've got nothing to do with the mine."

"It wasn't necessary to do it on the sly, Paddy. I wouldn't have touched any of your precious gold nuggets."

Rico went over and picked up one of the glittering stones.

"I'd thank you not to be touchin' me gold," Paddy said.

"I'm afraid this isn't gold, Paddy."

Paddy snatched it from his hand. "You're lying, hoping to keep it for yourself."

"Look at this closely. It's a common mineral, and this mountain is full of it."

"Are you talking about pyrite?" Garth asked. Rico nodded and Garth began to laugh. "He's been panning fool's gold—how appropriate!"

"What's pyrite?" Rory asked.

"It's often mistaken for gold by the untrained eye, but it's a combination of iron and disulfide," Garth said.

"You're lying. You're all lying just to cheat me out of me gold."

"You and your damn gold," Garth said. "For weeks now, I've watched you stumble around in a drunken stupor, making accusations, issuing orders or complaints, all of which are as worthless as you've been. In plain words, you're a pain in the ass." He turned to Rory. "I know he's your father and you love him, but we're wasting time with this argument. So let's eat and pack up."

No one had much to say throughout their meal.

After they finished dinner, Rico said, "You are right to get out of here in the morning. Do not let yourself be delayed from leaving. There's no way out if they get you trapped up here." He stood up. "I think I will go take a look around. We don't want to ride into an ambush tomorrow."

As Paddy sullenly headed into the mine, Garth looked at Rory. "If I were you, I'd get some sleep. We've got a rough trip ahead of us tomorrow."

He pulled her into his arms for a long, drugging kiss that left them both breathless.

As he gazed down into her mesmerizing eyes, he realized that all this time, he had been denying the truth. He loved her more than life itself.

He tenderly brushed her cheek. "Good night, honey."

Then he walked over and began to fill the canteens.

21

Garth's gaze followed Rory as she moved around the camp.

She had often joked about him being her knight, the one thing she wanted more than any gold. And with the love he felt for her, he *wanted* to be that knight.

But was his desire to roam greater than his love for her? Could he possibly live up to being that knight? He wanted to believe he could, because he loved her so much. He wanted to marry her and give her everything her heart yearned for.

When they got off this mountain, he'd ask her to marry him. *Somehow* he would live up to that knight in armor.

Garth had just finished filling the last canteen when Rico came hurrying back. He feared the worst when he saw the troubled look on the young man's face, and they stepped out of earshot of the others.

"There's a large party of banditos bedded down about a half mile below us. I heard that they're planning to attack at dawn.

"That means we'll move out tonight."

"But since there's only one way out, we can't get past them," Rico said. "They're camped right at that spot where the trail narrows to a footpath. We'd have to go single file with no cover. The way they're strung out, they'd spot us for sure."

"Then I guess that changes our strategy. If we can't slip past them in the dark, we'll need a diversion to draw them up here."

"A campfire won't do it, because they already know where we are."

Garth thought for a moment. "Do they have scouts out?"

"Yeah, there's one in those fir trees watching us right now. I figure we can get rid of him any time we're ready."

"How many are we up against?"

"I counted fifteen horses, and fourteen men below. The man up here makes it fifteen."

"Well, he might be the diversion we need. I figure once he sees us bed down for the night, he'll relax. That's when you get Rory and Paddy out. I'll give you enough time to get down there, then I'll take out that scout. That will draw the rest of them up here and give you a chance to get past them."

"And what about you?" Rico asked.

"I'll hold their attention as long as I'm able. Once you clear that narrow trail, don't stop. They'll be after you as soon as they discover you're gone."

"One man alone can't hold them for too long; you know that."

"I've got good cover here, and my rifle and Paddy's."

"But eventually they'll rush you."

"Not before you get a good head start."

Rico shook his head. "No, I'm staying."

"Rico, this isn't your fight. You've got to get Rory out of here. You know what they'll do to her if they get their hands on her."

"Then you take her back, and I'll stall them," Rico said.

"You know that trail better than I do. I've only been on it once, and that was in daylight. I'm counting on you to get her through. You'll have to travel light and on foot."

"You think Paddy can make it?" Rico asked. "It's a tough trail for an old guy on foot."

"He's going to have to. I hope to God he doesn't give you a hard time; you'll have enough on your hands to get them through as it is."

"I can handle him," Rico said. "You're the one I'm worried about."

"Forget me. Let's get moving. One canteen should be enough, and you'll have to take two pouches of the gold. I know he won't leave without it, and Rory won't leave without him. You'll have to carry one pouch, and he can carry the other. If they become too heavy and slow you down, pitch them or bury them, no matter what Paddy says. I'll try to bury the other two in the cave if I have time, and you can come back for them when this is over. Well, I guess we'd better break the news to the others."

He walked over to the fire. Rory had just finished washing up the dishes, and she looked up at him.

"Rory, we've got trouble. Paddy, come over here; you have to hear this, too."

He told them the situation and what they would have to do. "Now I want you all to act as if you're bedding down for the night while I put out the fire."

Throughout his instructions he had avoided looking directly at Rory, but he could feel her eyes on him. When he finished, she walked away and packed up the coffeepot.

Paddy came over to him, looking grim. "I'm not as drunk or dumb as you think, Garth Fraser. You'll not be following us, will you?"

"Paddy, Rory means more to me than life. When you get the chance, let her know how much I loved her."

"You're a fine man, Garth Fraser. I'd have been proud to have had you for a son-in-law, and 'tis shame I'm feeling for the hateful things I've said to you. Forgive an old man if you will, me boy. For a time, I let me greed do me thinking."

Garth slapped him on the shoulder. "I think it was more whiskey than greed, Paddy. Just give her the love she deserves."

"That I will, son." They shook hands and Paddy went into the cave.

Garth went through the motions and extinguished the fire. When he turned around, he was surprised to see Rory watching him. This was the moment he dreaded the most.

"Maybe Pop was right about you. You've been looking for an excuse to get your hands on the gold and get rid of us; now you've found one," she teased.

He knew she was just putting up a brave front, trying to make saying good-bye less painful.

He slipped his hands around her waist and drew her into his arms. "You could always figure me out, couldn't you, Miz O'Grady?"

Rory buried her head against his chest. "Oh, Garth, please don't make me leave. I want to stay with you."

"Hey, I'll be right behind you."

"No, you won't. You're going to stay here and get yourself killed."

"Now, why would I do anything that stupid just to get out of marrying you?"

"Because you're a hero at heart—my knight in armor. I know what you're doing. You're staying here to stall them, so the rest of us will have time to get away."

She clung to him and he couldn't restrain his feeling any longer. He kissed her with all the emotional passion these parting moments wrenched from him. Then he stepped away before he weakened any further.

"No regrets, honey, remember." He reached out and gently cupped her cheeks with his palms . "I love you, and you were right. You *are* the best thing that ever happened to me. I figured that once we got off this mountain, I'd marry you on the spot."

His fingers caressed her cheeks as he gazed into those beautiful, beautiful blue eyes, made even lovelier by the tears that turned them into shimmering pools.

Rico came to the entrance of the cave and nodded.

"Rory, it's time. The others are waiting," Garth said.

"But I can't leave you," she sobbed.

He held her closer and leaned his cheek against her soft hair. As he breathed in the sweet scent of her, felt the warmth of her, he knew he was losing her forever.

"Surely if we all remain, we could hold them off," she pleaded.

"We don't have enough ammunition, honey. Now, get out of here. Every moment counts." He kissed her again, and then she turned away and ran into the cave.

Rico came outside. "Are you sure this is what you want, amigo?"

"Yes. Get going when I go over to Boots. If they've been watching before, they'll know I take him inside at night. I'll start to make some kind of commotion with him, so sneak out when the guy's attention is on me. Then the rest is up to you. Good luck, Rico."

"May God be with you," Rico said.

"Same to you. Get going, pal. Time's awasting." Garth turned away and went over to where Boots was tethered.

"Sí," Rico repeated softly in his native tongue. "Que Dios esté con usted, hombre."

Garth untied Boots. "Come on, you dumb animal," he shouted. "You're as stupid as those mules." He hoped that in the darkness the guy couldn't see that he was holding the reins down; Boots had been trained not to move when he did that. "I'll leave you out here with these damn mules if you try that trick again!" he shouted.

After a reasonable pause, he led the horse inside and the cave was empty—except for Saddle, who had been leashed until the rest were safely away.

Garth listened for any possible indication that the others had been detected. Satisfied, he lit a lantern so that the scout in the trees would see the light and not suspect anything.

Then he dug a hole just big enough to hold the two pouches of gold. After filling it in, he had Boots trample it down until the surface appeared to be simply hoof marks from the horse.

"And if you choose to drop some manure on it, pal, it'll add an additional sweet touch—or should I say odor—to the proceedings."

Garth took the leash off Saddle, then gathered up the rifles, ammunition, and a canteen. He sat down at the entrance and checked the weapons to make sure they were fully loaded. Satisfied, he settled back to wait.

"Well, boys," he said to his two companions, "it looks like it's us against the world."

Suddenly Saddle stood up and moved outside. He stood with his ears and legs stiffened into his hunting stance as he sniffed the air. He'd either picked up the scent of the man in the fir trees, or that of some four-legged creature.

"Damn it, Saddle, get back here," Garth hissed. It wasn't wise for the dog to be out there chasing rabbits.

Picking up his rifle, he crouched down and stole outside.

It was time for him to go hunting, too.

Rory was shaking as the three of them huddled concealed in the trees, waiting for Garth's rifle shot.

"I'm going back, Rico," she said.

"I was afraid you would say that. Then we'll go back with you."

"No, three of us can't make it past them without being seen. I can make it to the trees nearest the mine without being observed. That just leaves a couple of exposed yards to get to the entrance, and in the dark they might mistake me for one of them."

Rico took off his hat. "Here, maybe this will help. Put this on and tuck your hair under it."

Garth's gunshot finally came; it reverberated like thunder. The sleeping bandits jumped to their feet, and one of them shouted out orders as they hurried to their horses and saddled up. Within minutes, they all rode off toward the mine.

"Now get out of here before it's too late," she said.

"Vaya con Dios, Rory."

"And you, too, Rico."

"I'll not leave without you," Paddy said.

"Please, Pop, this is what I want. I love Garth, and my place is with him now."

"But you know he doesn't have a chance, darlin'."

"More reason for me to be there with him."

"We must hurry," Rico warned.

Tears streaked Paddy's cheeks when she kissed him,

and Rico led the heartbroken man away. Rory watched for a moment, then turned and raced back to the mine. She was breathless when she neared it, and stopped to catch her breath. Upon hearing the sound of horses and voices nearby, she started to run again, but tripped over a fallen timber in her path and landed hard on the ground.

Dizzy from the fall, she got to her knees, and a pair of boots appeared in her blurred vision. Rory raised her head and looked into the leering face of one of the bandits.

"So, chica, why are you in such a hurry?" Smirking, he tried to yank her to her feet.

Suddenly a hundred pounds of fur and snarling teeth sprang on him, and his rifle flew out of his hands as the bandit was knocked to the ground. As the man fought off Saddle, he reached for the machete looped to his side.

In desperation, Rory grabbed the rifle and pulled the trigger as he was about to strike. The machete dropped to the ground and the outlaw pitched forward.

"Come on, Saddle, let's get out of here!" They raced to the entrance of the cave and she dashed in on the dog's heels, which was what saved her from being shot by Garth.

"My God, Rory, what are you doing here?" he asked, stunned. "And where did you get that rifle?"

Rory looked astonished at the weapon in her hand. She hadn't even realized she was carrying it. "I just shot a man, Garth."

"Why did you come back, honey? I wanted to get you out of this mess and know you were safe and . . ."

The words choked in his throat as he looked at her standing before him, rifle in one hand.

He murmured helplessly, "Don't you know that we haven't a prayer of getting out of here alive?" He opened his arms, and she dropped the weapon and ran to him. For a long moment he held her, and then lowered his head and kissed her.

A barrage of bullets bounced off a nearby rock, jolting him back to reality. He shoved her away. "Get over against that wall and stay down."

The attack had begun.

22

The two riders slowed at the outskirts of the town. They both rode tall in the saddle, with a casualness that reflected confident skill.

Colt Fraser shoved his Stetson to the top of his forehead. "Well, here we are. Sign says Hope. Why Garth would want to come to this godforsaken town is beyond my understanding."

"Uncle Henry's map, remember?" his brother said.

As they rode slowly down the street, Colt continued, "Look at this place. There's not a decent-looking building in the whole damn town. They should have named it Hopeless."

"Tierra de Esperanza," Clay Fraser replied. "Land of Hope."

"You speak that Spanish lingo pretty good, Brother Clay."

"I've lived in California for over a year now. 'When in Rome, do as the Romans.' "

"Romans? I thought these people were Spanish," Colt said, tongue-in-cheek. He pointed. "Hey, that must be the mission we're looking for, up there."

"El Misión de La Dueña de Esperanza—the Mission of the Lady of Hope," Clay said, unable to resist the temptation of getting another rise out of his brother.

"All right! I'm impressed! Enough!" Colt reined up at a hitching post in front of the cantina. "Let's stop for a drink, and hopefully something to eat. I'm hungry."

The saloon was empty except for an old man behind the bar. They sat down at a corner table and the old man came over to take their order. He didn't speak English, but Clay managed to make himself understood.

"So what did you order?" Colt asked when the man shuffled away.

"Beers and a couple of sandwiches."

"What kind of sandwiches?"

"I hope it was chicken, but I'm not making any promises," Clay said, chuckling. "I told him to just make sure it's cooked."

"You had me believing you spoke their lingo."

"I'm *learning* it. Actually, it's a beautiful language, Colt. Kind of rolls right off the tongue. You ought to try and learn it, too."

"I don't expect to be in California that long—any more than I expected to spend my honeymoon with *you*, stumbling over loose rocks, choking on dust, and bathing in frigid water. Nothing personal, Brother Clay, but I can't wait to get back to New Mexico and settle down on the Lazy B."

"I thought you wanted to be a lawman. Since when did you take up ranching?"

"Cassie's family owns a cattle ranch. It's not real huge, like some there, but it's beautiful. Rolling hills, streams to fish in, plenty of graze for the cattle."

"And Indians running wild and massacring the settlers," Clay added drolly.

"Remind me to tell you about my encounter with Cochise sometime," Colt said.

"You mean that Apache chief who's been stirring up all that trouble in Arizona?"

Colt nodded. "One and the same, Brother Clay."

"My God, the newspapers are full of him." He reached over and patted his brother's shoulder. "Now *I'm* impressed."

"Clay, have you thought about going back to Fraser Keep?"

"As things stand now, I don't think so. Becky and I have put a lot into planting the vineyard and getting the winery built. We've just bottled our first wine for commercial sale. But once the railroad is completed, I promised to take Becky to Virginia to see the plantation."

"When you do, Cassie and I will go with you. She wants to see it, too."

"Will's last letter to me said that Jed's gone to sea. I guess he has no heart for plantation life, either."

"He's always loved the sea. But I think the South has changed so much since the war that we're all looking for something different."

"That's for sure. But I'm willing to bet nothing would ever get Will away from there."

"And shouldn't," Colt said. "Fraser Keep is his heart and soul. He worked his ass off to preserve it. Thank God one of us did."

Suddenly a young boy dressed in a choir robe burst through the door. "Abuelo, abuelo!" he shouted, and began to wave his hands and talk excitedly to the old man.

"What's his problem?" Colt asked.

"He's talking so fast I can't follow it. Apparently the old man is his grandfather, and I made out the word *muerto,* which means dead, and *bandidos,* which are bandits. He keeps pointing to the mission."

"Maybe some bandits killed someone at the mission?" Colt said.

When they heard the word *Fraser* come out of the boy's mouth, both men jumped to their feet. They exchanged startled looks, then ran outside and galloped up to the pink stucco wall at the top of the road.

As they dismounted, they saw a priest standing over a gray-haired man sitting on a bench fanning himself with his hat. A younger man stood beside them.

A door slammed and a mature woman came out of the rectory and handed the older man a glass of liquid. He took a drink, then handed it back to her with a twisted expression of disapproval.

"Excuse me, who's in charge here?" Clay asked.

They all turned around, except for the old man, who sat slumped and continued to fan himself.

"I am Father Chavez. If you will excuse us, gentlemen, I cannot be of service right now. We have a serious problem to deal with at this time."

"That's what we're here about, Father Chavez," Clay said. "We heard in the cantina that there was trouble here at the mission; and we believe our brother's name was mentioned."

The younger man spoke up immediately. "Are you the brothers of Garth Fraser?"

"Yes, we are. Where is he?"

"I have some bad news for you."

Colt stepped forward. "He's not dead!"

"Not when we left him, señor, but his situation was hopeless."

"What do you mean? Was he ill? Wounded? We heard the mention of bandits?"

"Rico, why don't we go inside where you can explain everything," the priest said.

"There isn't time for that," Rico said. "If there's any hope for Garth and Rory, we must get help back to them as quickly as possible."

"You just got it," Colt said. "You can tell us the details on the way."

"I'm afraid three of us will not be enough," Rico said.

"There'll be four, countin' me. Me daughter's up there, too," the gray-haired man said.

"Damn it, will somebody just tell us what happened?" Clay asked.

"Garth and Rory have been mining for gold," Rico began. "Yesterday the vein ran out, so we packed up and were going to leave this morning, but bandits discovered us last night. Garth stayed behind to stall them and give the rest of us a chance to get away. Rory went back to be with him, and I don't know if she even made it."

"How many of them are there?" Clay asked.

"Fifteen for sure. There could be more."

"How was Garth set for ammo?" Clay continued.

"He had his pistol, and his and Paddy's rifles. About a half a box of cartridges for the rifles and a couple dozen for the pistol."

"And the cover?"

"The cover's good. There are rocks around him for protection. If we leave now, we could be back there by morning."

Clay opened up a folded sheet of paper he'd pulled out of his pocket. "Is this the same mine we're talking about?"

Father Chavez glanced down at it. "I believe so. That is the same map he showed me."

"Garth made me a copy before he left the Napa Valley. He wired me once a week to let me know where he was, and the last wire was from Sonora. The sheriff there remembered him asking about this town. When I didn't hear from him for a while, we figured we better start looking for him."

Rico pointed to the map. "The mine here is a natural cavern in solid rock. There's no further trail beyond a waterfall that is right next to the mine. The waterfall drops sharply off the edge of the mountain for at least a thousand feet and forms a stream below, so the only way to reach the mine is from this trail that ends at the waterfall. And the only way to go higher would be to try and scale the wall above it, but it's a solid rock surface with nothing to grab."

"So the cover sounds good, as long as he can hold them off," Clay said.

Colt was not as optimistic. "It may be good cover, but the only way out is the same way he got in. If they rush him or he runs out of ammo, it sounds like Brother Garth's rode himself right into a box canyon. Let's move out."

"We must travel light," Rico said. "Just a canteen, blanket, a rifle, and all the ammo we can find."

Paddy stood up to follow.

"You're not coming, Mr. O'Grady," Clay said. "It's clear that you're physically exhausted."

"That's me daughter up there," Paddy declared.

"I understand your feelings. But frankly, you can be more helpful to your daughter by remaining behind. You'll only slow us down."

Father Chavez patted Paddy's arm. "They are right, Paddy. The job is for the young men who have the energy and strength. Let us go to the sanctuary and pray for our Lord to give them His helping hand." He put his arm around Paddy's shoulders and led him away.

Colt glanced back at the mission as they rode out. The woman at the mission was standing at the gate watching them. A breeze suddenly caught her dark hair, lifting it off her shoulders like a black silk flag fluttering in the wind.

Was it a good omen or a bad one?

The climb was strenuous for both man and horse, made more difficult by their attempt to hurry. Jagged crags and narrow trails slowed their progress as the trail snaked up the side of the mountain. It was made more treacherous by deep hollow clefts on the rocky trail, where one misstep could send horse and rider plunging into the narrow canyon below.

Occasionally they paused briefly on a level woodland to rest and water their horses.

Time and again they had to dismount to duck under an overhanging precipice, moving from the shade of a bluff into the blazing sun reflecting off the bald face of a granite wall.

"And you traveled this in darkness, supporting that old man?" Colt asked during one of their rare rests.

"Sí, Señor Colt, but think of how much worse it would have been if I had to carry him."

"You think we'll find him alive, Clay?" Colt asked as they mounted up and followed Rico.

"You know that if Garth has good cover and his ammo holds out, he's an army unto himself."

"I wonder if O'Grady's daughter made it back to him? Sounds like it could be serious, if she had the chance to get away and turned back to be with him."

"Sounds like she's in love with him. I could see Becky doing the same thing if she was in the same situation."

"Yeah, I can see Cassie doing the same thing, too."

The sudden sound of gunfire caused them to rein up, and Clay and Colt exchanged looks of relief.

"He's still alive," Clay said, and he dismounted. "Let's see what we're up against."

They tied their horses to a shrub and moved stealthily through the trees, then stopped at the sight of some tethered horses.

"I count fifteen," Colt said. "And no picket. These aren't the smartest fish in the pond, are they?"

"I figured that out when they took on Garth," Clay said.

They moved closer and saw that the bandits were stretched out in a semicircle from the trail to the waterfall.

"So if the mountain drops off at that waterfall," Clay said, "they can only attack him from two directions: Garth's left flank or the front. Have I got that right, Rico?"

The young man nodded.

"If one of us covers his left flank and keeps them from getting to their horses, and another gets behind them in those fir trees opposite the entrance, we'll have them surrounded," Clay said.

"Surrounded!" Rico exclaimed. "Señor Clay, how do the three of us *surround* them?"

"That's only five to one," Colt said. "Those are better odds than we had during the war."

"Yes, but did you not lose the war?"

"Sure, but when Garth jumps in, that'll be another gun." He slapped Rico on the shoulder. "See, the odds are better already."

"The way I figure it," Clay said, "one of us will have to get to the cave in case they try to rush it. If Garth is low on ammunition, he won't be able to hold them all off."

"I'll do it," Rico volunteered. "The entrance is a narrow crack and I know where it is. I can get to it quickly."

"You'll need a diversion," Clay said.

"I suggest we stampede some of these horses into the clearing between those fir trees and the entrance," Colt said. "The confusion should help prevent one of them getting an easy shot at Rico."

Clay nodded. "Good idea. Okay, I'll hold the left flank, and the front one is yours, Colt. Rico, when I stampede those horses, you go in with them and get to Garth. When you reach him, the two of you come out, and these bastards will be in the squeeze of our crossfire."

"I'd say it's got a good chance of working," Colt said.

"What do you think, Rico? You've got a dog in this hunt, too."

Rico flashed a grin. "I'm still trying to understand what you meant by *surrounded*."

"Just make sure that you stampede *all* the horses," Colt said. "I don't want any of those men getting away and picking us off on the way back."

Clay nodded. "Give me a signal when you're in place." The two brothers shook hands. "Watch your back, Brother Colt."

"Same to you, Brother Clay. See you when it's over." He shook Rico's hand. "Keep your head down, amigo."

"Usted también, Capitán Colt."

Colt slipped away into the trees.

23

Throughout the night and most of the day, the bandits had not tried to rush as a gang. Garth had picked off or held back any of the more daring ones, but in another few hours it would get dark, and the bastards would surely rush them then.

Garth spun the chamber of his pistol. He had three rounds left, and he'd used up all the bullets in his and Paddy's rifles. He glanced at Rory, sitting nearby with her back against the wall. Her eyes never wavered from his, but he knew she suspected the time was drawing near.

"Soon be dark, honey."

"Garth, you know why I came back. I want us to be together at the very end."

"For God's sake, Rory, think about it. They won't kill you right away. I know what they'll do to you will be horrible, but if you could just hang in there for a couple hours, Rico should be back with some help."

"It doesn't matter. I love you, Garth. I wouldn't want to go on without you."

"You've got a whole life ahead of you, regardless of what happens here. If you don't care about yourself, think about Paddy."

"Garth, I knew what the outcome would be if I came back, and I don't have any regrets."

"Baby, I can't do it."

"Then give me the gun. I'll do it."

He felt as if he was going to blow apart. "God, if only we could have had more time together."

Her smile was tender with love. "I'm grateful for the time we did have, and I wouldn't trade one moment of it for a lifetime."

"But think ahead, Rory. With the gold, you'll be able to have a better life than you've ever thought you could." His eyes were full of poignancy. "Picket fence and all, honey."

"That picket fence included my knight in armor."

"I love you, Rory. That's why I want you to live. Nothing else matters."

"And nothing else will matter to me if you don't," she said.

"Oh, God, baby, I was such a damn fool in the beginning. I kept telling myself I couldn't trust you, when my heart told me differently."

"We must have been the two biggest fools on earth, my love. Always bickering with each other like children."

"And now we have to try to squeeze everything we should have said to each other into a few minutes." He looked longingly at her. "Rory, when did you realize you loved me?"

"Who can say the exact moment a person falls in love? I think in the beginning, what I felt was the concept of you more than anything else—what I wanted my knight in armor to be like. Gradually my knight took on more and more of your attributes, and sometime between then and now, he became you.

"It was the night I spent in that black hole, waiting for you to come and rescue me." Her eyes glowed with worship as she gazed at him. "Because I knew you would come."

"Funny how your heart knows what your mind refuses to recognize."

She nodded. "I kept telling myself you were out of the reach of a girl like me, and that your only intentions were to have sex. And so I tried to will myself not to be foolish enough to fall in love with you. But I failed miserably at the attempt."

Then her mouth curved into that gritty little grin he loved so much. "Your turn, Fraser. When did Cupid's arrow strike you?"

He marveled at her. Even now, facing death, the spunk and courage that he admired so greatly never faltered.

He chuckled. "Lord, how I fought it. I tried to convince myself you were a liar, a thief, a trollop. That the only thing I wanted was to get you into bed. Yet despite all that I believed, I liked you. I was captivated by your wit, and your mood changes fascinated me. And those blue eyes of yours mesmerized me every time I looked at you." He grinned. "And the sex sure didn't hurt, either.

"It got to the point when I thought of nothing but you, and wanted to be with you every waking moment.

"You're the most incredible woman I've ever met, Rory. I never had a chance from the beginning."

Their love arced between them, as tangible as the rock beneath their feet, and they reached out and clasped hands.

"Any regrets, Rory O'Grady?" he asked tenderly.

"No regrets, Garth Fraser."

One of the bandits suddenly appeared in the doorway, and Garth reflexively stepped in front of her and fired a shot. "Get down, Rory." He kicked the dead man's body away from the entrance.

Now you've only got one more shot, Fraser. Then there'll be one left to . . .

He suddenly had a glimmer of hope. Maybe they didn't know Rory was with him. He looked around in desperation. If they didn't know, maybe they wouldn't think of looking in the darkness at the rear of the cave. They might not even check out the mine at all, if he went outside and surrendered. The sharks would be too occupied with their bloodletting. So how was he going to convince Rory to get back there?

The idea became academic when the hoot of an owl sounded from the fir trees. From the trees nearest the trail, he heard a similar hooting.

Then something clicked in his mind. He hadn't seen or heard an owl the whole time he'd been up here. If he didn't know better, he'd think it was Indians, or the signal he and his brothers used to make when they were hunting back in Virginia. But there were no Indians around here, and it sure as hell couldn't be his brothers. It had to be a signal the bandits were getting ready to rush him.

He tightened his grasp on the pistol and started to back up slowly toward Rory.

Take only one shot, Fraser. You have to save the last one for her.

Suddenly the famous Rebel yell rent the air, and gunshots exploded from all directions. Racing wildly, a slew of riderless horses thundered into the clearing as all hell broke loose. Many of the bandits, flushed out of concealment, began running around as helter-skelter as the horses, shooting wildly at unknown targets.

One of the horses raced directly toward the entrance, a crouched rider hanging low off the side of the animal. Garth took aim.

"Don't shoot, it's me, Rico," the rider shouted. He jumped free and made it behind a rock as bullets ricocheted off the surrounding rocks.

Garth handed Rory his pistol. "Honey, the cavalry's just arrived! There's one bullet in there. Get into that corner and stay there until I tell you to come out. And if any of those bastards comes through this entrance, shoot him." Garth pointed a finger at the dog, and Saddle trotted back and lay down at Rory's feet.

Garth ran to the entrance and grabbed his empty rifle. "Rico, I need ammo."

Rico tossed Garth a box of cartridges. "We figured you could use these."

Garth saw several of the bandits fall to the ground. "What the hell is going on?" he shouted.

"I've brought some help. One's in the fir trees over there and the other one is near the trail, so pick your target carefully, amigo." His shot took down one of the bandits. "We're supposed to move out to outflank the bandits and catch them in a crossfire."

As Garth loaded his rifle, Rico sent a steady stream of fire at the routed outlaws, while Clay and Colt picked off the bandits who were running amok trying to escape. Garth took cover behind the same boulder as Rico, and added his fire power to the rout.

When the shooting finally stopped, Clay and Colt came out of concealment.

Garth was beside himself with exhilaration. "What in hell kept you guys? I was down to my last round," he grumbled, to disguise his real emotions.

"We figured you could handle them alone, Brother Garth," Colt said. "There were only fifteen of them."

Then the three men broke into laughter, followed with hugs, handshakes, and back slaps until Rico joined them, looking grave.

"Garth, I have some very bad news. Rory did not go back to the mission."

"I know. She's in the cave, safe and sound."

"Thank God," Rico said, crossing himself.

"What about Paddy?" Garth asked.

"He's with Father Chavez."

"We convinced him to stay behind," Clay said.

"If you won an argument with that stubborn old mule, that's more than I could ever do. Colt, I hear you got married."

"Wait until you meet Cassie, Garth. You'll love her," Colt said.

"I'll go get Rory. She's probably wondering what's happening."

"Is she wounded?" Clay asked.

"No, I just told her to stay where she was. She's the most remarkable woman I've ever met." He raced away.

Colt looked at Clay. "You thinking what I'm thinking?"

Clay nodded, and they turned to Rico with questioning looks.

Rico nodded. "Sí, caballeros, he is in love. Muy enamorado."

"I suggest we get out of here before any more of those bandidos show up here," Colt said.

"How many are dead?" Clay asked.

"I counted fourteen, so one got away," Rico said.

"I don't think he'll give us any more trouble. But I'm for getting out of here, too," Clay agreed.

Garth found Rory sitting where he'd left her. He rushed over, picked her up, and spun her around. "Honey, you aren't going to believe this! My brothers, Clay and Colt, are the ones who came with Rico to our rescue."

"Your brothers! Where did they come from?" she asked, happy to see his pleasure. "What about Pop—is he safe?"

"Yes, he's at the mission. I've got a dozen questions for them, but I'm holding off until we get out of here." He grabbed her hand. "Come on and meet them."

"This is Rory O'Grady, the woman I hope to marry," he announced when they rejoined his brothers.

Rory was as stunned by Garth's announcement as his brothers appeared to be, but she managed to smile.

Both men doffed their hats. "Pleasure meeting you, ma'am." Clay said.

"It certainly is," Colt said.

"I don't know how to begin to thank you. You saved our lives."

"Miss Rory, the pleasure was all ours," Colt said.

Clay nodded. "Yes, ma'am, it sure was."

Rico led Boots over to them. "Rory will have to ride a mule, or ride double with you."

"We'll ride double," Garth said. "Did you dig up the gold?"

Rico nodded. "It's in my saddlebags."

"You mean you actually struck gold?" Clay exclaimed. "Looks like we all have a lot to talk over—so let's get moving instead of standing and gaping at each other."

Colt winked at Rory. "You have to excuse Clay's shortness, Miss Rory. He's always been the serious one in the family." He hoisted her up to Garth, who set her in front of him.

As they started to move out, Clay leaned over and

whispered to Colt, "Rico's got that right. Muy enam-orado. Brother Garth's in love."

"What about burying those dead men?" Rory asked.

"Let their friend come back and bury them," Garth said. "We need to get as far down as we can before it gets too dark."

As Garth glanced back and thought about how close he had come to losing the woman he loved, Father Chavez's words echoed in his memory.

Montaña del Diablo. Mountain of the Devil.

Soon the trail became too dangerous in the dark, and with the experience of three veteran soldiers—who insisted Rory sit down and rest—within minutes they had a pot of coffee brewing on a campfire.

Garth discovered a few sticks of jerky in his saddle-bags and Rico and Colt had filled the canteens before leaving, so there was plenty of water for everyone, including the horses and mules.

Garth stretched out with his head in Rory's lap, the other three men sitting or lying nearby.

"At least the coffee's hot," Rory said as they chewed on the jerky.

Colt winked at Garth. "We could slaughter one of those mules of yours if you're hungry, Miz Rory."

"Don't you dare! The poor things have suffered on this wretched mountain the same as we have."

The men broke into laughter, and she realized Colt had just tried to get a rise out of her. "All right, Clay, tell me the truth. Which one of your brothers has the most devilment in him? Garth or Colt?"

"Hmmm," Clay pondered. "I'd have to say they're a matched set."

"Listen to him, Brother Colt," Garth said. "Seems to me, our brother Clay was never the last horse to the trough."

"Now, Colt, you know Mama never raised any son to speak disrespectful of a lady," Garth replied.

"Did I say I was referring to Ellie Deveraux?" Colt asked in an innocent voice, with twin devils dancing in his eyes.

Clay groaned. "You boys just aren't going to let me forget that, are you?"

"Well," Colt said, rubbing his chin reflectively. "It's like having a good knife, Brother Clay. You've got to keep honing it to keep it sharpened."

Rory stood up. "I think on that happy note, I'll go to bed." She bent down and kissed Garth on the cheek. "Good night. And good night to the rest of you. These last couple of days have been rather tiring, and once again, I can't tell you how grateful I am to all of you."

"You're safe now, Rory, so have a good night's sleep," Clay said.

Colt grinned. "Good night, Rory."

Rico echoed it, and stood up. "I think I will do the same. Buenos noches, amigos."

Sublimely contented, Rory lay down on her bedroll and smiled as she listened to their soft voices. When she was with them, she could feel their love and loyalty for one another. And all the teasing and joking was part of it, because they were friends as well as brothers.

"Rico's a good man," she heard Clay say.

"I'd say a good friend, as well," Colt added. "How long have you known him, Garth?"

"Just a short time. He showed up just when a bear was about to rip Rory apart. Funny how someone like him shows up when you need him the most. There's no doubt that Rory, Paddy, and I would be dead by now otherwise."

"It sure gives a person food for thought."

"About what?" Clay asked.

"Oh, divine intervention. Providence. One's own mortality."

"I thought about those things during the war," Clay said. "Whenever the guy next to me took the bullet or was blown apart. I never could figure out why him, not me?"

"I did, too," Colt said. "Though deep down you're relieved that it *was* him, not you, it makes you wonder why."

"It's not only about life and death," Clay said. "It's about falling in love with that special woman. For instance, in Independence, with all the men there who were heading west, why did Becky pick me?"

Garth snorted. "If I recall, Brother Clay, you asked yourself that same question—but with a lot less awe at the time."

"Yeah, I was damn pissed then." Clay chuckled. "But thank God He did pick that feisty Yankee for me."

"That's how I feel about Cassie," Colt said. "Fate put us together on that stagecoach the day it was being robbed. I jumped in front of her and took the bullet that would have hit her. Not that it would have killed her, any more than it did me. But *what* set up that whole chain of events, which caused me to stay in Arena Roja rather than go on to Santa Fe? And you don't have to tell me about feisty Yankees, Brother Clay. I'm married to one."

"And she's much too good for you," Clay quickly interjected.

Colt nodded in agreement. "I won't give you an argument on that point."

Listening to them had eased Rory into a blissful peace. Surrounded by her four knights in armor, she felt safe and secure.

Garth and his brothers were wonderful men, decent men, and not embarrassed to admit to one another how much they adored their wives. Thank God there were such men in the world.

"Speaking of the subject of wives, what about you, Garth?" Clay asked. "You said you intended to marry Rory."

"If she'll have me."

"You mean you haven't asked her yet?" Colt said.

"No. But I know she loves me, and I love her."

"Are you sure you know what you're doing?"

Rory sucked in a breath at the challenge in the question.

"What the hell are you getting at, Colt?"

"Well, you always said that about *any* girl you were with."

"I did love all of them, but I never wanted to marry any of them. Rory is the only woman I ever thought about marrying."

She exhaled the breath she'd been holding.

"Well then, Brother Garth, I suggest you ask her before you start making wedding plans."

Rory thought her heart would burst with joy.

"Was Rory born in Ireland, too?" Clay asked. "I didn't notice any brogue."

"No, she was born in California, around Sacramento."

"Gentlemen," Colt said, "I see a definite pattern here. We've all chosen Yankees for wives."

"California didn't enter the war," Clay said.

"They didn't join the Confederacy either, so as far as I'm concerned, they're Yankees," Colt said.

"It is a coincidence, though," Garth agreed. "What do you suppose is the reason?"

"I think the Yankees are still fighting, only this time they're using women instead of men. They hornswoggle us by letting us win the skirmishes, but *they* win the war," Colt said.

Garth said, "But if we're the losers and they're the winners, how come we end up getting the better end of it when they marry us?"

"Elementary, Brother Garth. Isn't the claim, 'To the victor falls the spoils'?"

"That's what I'm getting at," Garth said.

"Since they're the victors, the spoils fall to them. They're stuck with us," Colt said. He poked Garth in the arm, and they all broke into laughter.

Rory closed her eyes. It was going to be so easy to love Garth's family.

*　　　*　　　*

As the night deepened, one by one the men moved to their blankets until only Garth remained, with Saddle beside him.

"If you could only talk, Saddle," Garth murmured softly as he stroked the head of the big, shaggy mutt. "I bet you have a story to tell as good as any of us.

"When I was handing out thanks tonight, I forgot to thank you. She told me what you did, Saddle. Don't matter to you whether it's a bear or a man with a machete. I owe you the biggest thanks for saving her, boy. If you hadn't, none of the rest would matter to me.

"I wish I could have met the man who trained you so well. I bet that you miss him, pal," he said as he hugged the dog at his side. "And if he's alive somewhere, I know that he misses you."

Garth banked the fire for the night, then moved his blanket beside Rory's. He lay down and gently gathered her into his arms, careful not to wake her. She cuddled against him in her sleep, and he held her tighter as he thought of how close he had come to losing her.

He'd always depended on his own strengths to get him out of difficult situations, but today, in what he believed to be their final moments, he had prayed desperately for God to spare Rory.

With a sheepish smile Garth glanced heavenward. "Thank you, Lord. I guess you're another one I neglected to thank today."

Then, holding the woman he loved close to his heart, he closed his eyes and fell asleep instantly.

*   *   *

Garth awoke to sunlight teasing his eyes and the aroma of coffee. He sat up and looked around. Everyone else was up and busy breaking camp. The mules were packed, and the only thing that remained was the coffeepot on the fire, and his cup.

"It's about time," Colt said when he saw him. "The rest of us have been up for an hour."

"Why didn't you wake me?" Garth pulled on his boots and scrambled to his feet.

"Because Miz Rory threatened to shoot anyone who went near you," Clay groused, joining them. "She said that you needed your sleep."

"Good morning, sweetheart," he said, when Rory came over and handed him a cup of coffee. He slipped his arm around her and kissed her.

"Can you two delay the smooching for a few more hours?" Clay said. "You've got a lifetime ahead for that, and we've got a half day's ride ahead of us with almost nothing in our stomachs!"

"Yes, but soon we can eat my madre's enchiladas. No one can make them like her," Rico boasted. "I can taste them now—the corncake stuffed with chicken and cheese, dripping with hot chili. And if we're lucky, she'll have made us a special treat."

"What's that?" Colt asked, begining to salivate.

"A cherry pie."

"That's it, I've heard enough. Gag him or shoot him," Colt declared.

Clay mounted his horse. "Yeah, let's get the hell off this mountain. If I'm going to commune with Nature,

I prefer it to be the Shenandoah Valley with the river flowing through it."

Garth mounted Boots, hugged Rory against his chest in the circle of his arms, and nuzzled her cheek as they moved down the trail.

Rico followed, leading the pack animals. He grinned. "Sí, muy enamorado."

24

Paddy had been pacing the mission's patio for hours. He felt helpless and frustrated, not knowing if his beloved daughter was dead or alive.

Elena Chavez came out of the rectory and walked over to the man. "Would you like a glass of lemonade, Señor O'Grady?"

He looked at her, appalled. "No thank you, Miss Chavez. The drink's not to me liking."

"I'm sorry I have nothing else to offer, except water."

"That's not to my liking, either. Now, if you were to be having a wee nip of whiskey—"

"Oh, Father Chavez does not permit alcohol here. We only have wine—used mainly for Holy Communion."

"A glass of that would do," he said. "Rory's me only

child, and me nerves are unsteady with the worrying of her."

"I understand, Mr. O'Grady. I understand better than you might think."

Now what did the woman mean by that? Paddy pondered. Friendly enough, she was, but she was not saying what she was thinking. And this was no time for him to be without whiskey. Perhaps if he went down to the cantina and had just one drink, it would help.

He thought of the last argument he'd had with Rory over whiskey. And he might never have the opportunity to ever quarrel again if those murderous heathens had discovered her.

"Oh, darlin'," he began to sob, "why did you go back? What will I do without your sweet smile and loving ways?"

Suddenly several people began yelling at the gate. Elena came rushing out of the kitchen door, and Father Chavez hurried over to him.

"They've been sighted, Señor O'Grady," he exclaimed.

"How many made it back?"

"I don't know. They should reach us—"

"I can see them!" Elena cried out.

"How many?" Paddy asked again.

Elena put a hand to her eyes to block out the sun. "I make it out to be four horses and a couple mules, and . . . Rico! Father Chavez, I see Rico," she cried out joyously. "He's leading the mules."

"What about Rory? Is Rory with them?" Paddy asked anxiously.

"The first two riders are men," Elena said. "Oh, there she is! Now I see her. She's riding double with somebody."

"Saints preserve us!" Paddy exclaimed. "That must be Garth Fraser. They all made it."

Ten minutes later, the weary group rode through the gates of the mission.

Paddy watched tearfully when Garth lowered Rory from his horse, and she raced to him with open arms. He held her for a long moment and then stepped back and looked into her face, streaked with tears like his own.

" 'Twas a fright you gave me, darlin'," he said, trying to sound stern.

"I'm sorry, Pop."

"Well, you're alive, and that's all that matters. But me heart is still aching from the worry of it."

Having shaken the hand of Father Chavez, Garth walked over and joined Rory and Paddy. He slipped an arm casually around her shoulders.

"I knew you were trouble when I first lay me eyes on you, Garth Fraser. I'm beholden to you for saving me daughter's life, but if it weren't for you, she'd never have gone back to that mine. Now I'm caught with the problem of whether to be shooting you or kissing you."

"Shall we just settle for a handshake, sir?"

Paddy clasped his hand and shook it. "And I'm beholden to you for saving me gold."

Colt, who was standing aside with Clay watching the tearful reunion, put a hand to his mouth and whispered aside to him, "Does he mean the dust or his daughter?"

"I was wondering the same thing. And look at that other reunion." He nodded to where Elena was crying and hugging Rico. "Did Rico ever tell you his last name?"

"No. Never thought to ask," Colt said.

"But Father Chavez introduced his sister as Miss Chavez, didn't he?"

"Thought so. Maybe he said 'Mrs.' "

"Hmm, interesting, isn't it?"

"Clay, I know what you're getting at, but it's none of our business. Let's go and check out those enchiladas that Rico claimed are so good."

"Unfortunately, the cook looks occupied at the moment."

"I think you're right. So let's take care of the horses, then head for that cantina. I don't know about you, Brother Clay, but I could use a drink."

While Rory was enjoying her first hot bath in two months, Garth went searching for his brothers and found them at the cantina.

"You plan on marrying her?" Clay asked when the subject got around to Rory.

"Yes."

Colt shoved his hat to the back of his head. "But you actually haven't asked her yet. What's the problem? If she loved you enough to go back to die with you, I can't believe she wouldn't marry you." He slammed down his glass. "God, this tastes like swill! How do you say sheep's piss in Spanish?"

"*Whisky*," Clay said drolly, trying not to laugh. "They merely drop the *e*."

"I don't trust your Spanish. I wish Rico had come with us. Hey, abuelo," he called, and motioned for another round of drinks. "Whiskey this time, abuelo. Okay?"

"Colt, abuelo means grandfather; it's not the old man's name," Clay said.

Colt got up and went over to the bar to demonstrate what he wanted.

"Garth, are you really sure you're in love this time?" Clay asked, resuming their conversation.

"Lord, yes," Garth said. "I love that woman beyond words. I think my world would collapse if I lost her now, after all we've been through. I was down to my last bullet and was on the verge of shooting her when you showed up."

"Would you have done it?"

"I don't know. I can't get past that moment."

Colt came back and put a bottle down in front of them. "Okay, this should be it. I read every damn label on those bottles," he said. He refilled their shot glasses, and then picked his up, gulped it down, then shoved the bottle aside. "Sheep's piss," he murmured in dejection.

Benito Morales kept his head down on the table and continued to pretend he was asleep as he listened to the gringos' conversation. He recognized them at once as the ones from the battle at the mine. His eyes burned from the force of his hatred. They had killed his father, his brother, and the rest of his friends. He was the only one who got away, and now it was up to him to avenge their deaths.

He snarled in frustration. He had lost his rifle when he escaped, and had only a knife as a weapon. The gringos were all wearing gun belts, and even if he killed the gringo Garth, who was their leader, the others would kill him before he could get away. He had to get him alone, but how? They were always together.

Benito's heartbeat quickened when he thought of another idea. What if he killed the gringo's woman? That would be the sweetest revenge of all. To kill the woman the gringo loved more than anyone else. He must think of a way to do it.

He waited until the gringos left. Then he got up and followed.

Later that evening, after their stomachs were filled, Garth led Rory outside. He set her down on a bench, sat beside her, and drew her into his arms.

"We still have some unfinished business to attend to," he murmured in her ear.

She sighed and closed her eyes as his mouth toyed with her ear. "My love, I'd say we've *resolved* that unfinished business time and time again."

"That's not the business I'm referring to. Will you marry me, Rorleen Catherine O'Grady?"

Rory looked at him, perplexed. "I thought that's what we were going to do. At least, that's what you said yesterday."

"I said I intended to marry you. I never asked if *you* wanted to marry me."

"You're crazy, Garth Fraser. Of course I do."

"Hallelujah! Then let's go visit Father Chavez."

Hand in hand, Garth and Rory tapped on the door of the priest's office.

"Father, if you're free, Rory and I would like to speak to you for a few minutes."

"Of course, my children, come in. What is it?"

"Rory and I wish to marry."

The old priest broke into a smile. "That does not come as a surprise to me. What I find more astonishing is that when you left here, Garth, I feared you might injure this woman."

"Father Chavez, I would never injure *any* woman."

"That is true, Father Chavez," Rory interjected as some of her earlier nervousness began to ease. "Garth claims he has never met a woman he didn't love."

The priest raised an eyebrow and turned to Garth.

"She's taken that out of context, sir. What I meant by it was that I hold all women in high esteem, and admire and respect them for how they turn a wilderness into a civilization."

At the twinkle of amusement in the priest's eyes, Garth quickly added, "Or some sour berries on a shrub into a delicious pie."

Father Chavez reflected for a moment, then nodded. "I must agree, Señor Garth. So what is your problem? You are in love with her, but the young lady does not hold the same affection for you?"

"No, I love him desperately, Father," Rory said.

"As you know, I'm not a Catholic," Garth said, "and Rory wants to get married in the church."

"You can convert to Catholicism, as your uncle did."

"I'm not prepared to do that at this time, Father Chavez. Besides, we want to get married tonight. We're intending to leave here in the morning."

"Tonight! That is impossible. Even if you were Catholic, there are banns to be posted, instructions to be given, papers to sign."

"Banns? Good grief, Father, Garth and I are both strangers here. Who among your congregation could possibly care about two strangers getting married?"

"Rory, my dear, nothing would give me greater pleasure than to join you two lovely people in the bonds of matrimony. But you know as well as I that the church has definite rules on the issue of marriage."

"Father Chavez, I intend to marry Garth with or without the church's consent. And Garth and I have become very fond of you, and hoped you would be the one to read our vows."

"I see. And what of the children who will follow after this union?"

"I swear to you, Father Chavez, our children will be raised in whatever religion their mother wishes them to be," Garth said. "Rory and I may not pray in the same pews, Father Chavez, but we both pray to the same God."

"In the past there have been exceptions to the rules, but . . ." Father Chavez clasped his hands together and bowed his head deep in thought.

Garth met Rory's worried glance. He could tell how

important it was to her to get married in the church. He reached over and squeezed her hand.

After a long moment, the priest raised his head. "There are times when one must look beyond one's church's canons. I believe the Lord has spared your lives for a Divine purpose and would want me to bless this union. Therefore, I will administer your oaths."

"Thank you! Then we can marry tonight?"

"Not tonight, my son. I will administer your oaths tomorrow after the morning Mass. Let us say ten o'clock."

Garth jumped to his feet. "Thank you, sir."

"Oh, thank you, Father," Rory cried. Tears of joy rolled down her cheeks.

"And, Señorita O'Grady," the priest said, shaking a finger at her, "I want to hear your confession before ten o'clock tomorrow morning."

"Yes, Father." Rory threw her arms around his neck and kissed him on the cheek. "No time like the present."

While Rory remained at the church, Garth told his brothers of his wedding plans for the next day. When Rory joined them, they were unmerciful in their teasing and advised her that she could make a better choice for a husband.

Even Paddy joined in the razzing, taking the news in good humor.

Rory and Garth bore their teasing, and when she decided to go to bed in order to be rested for the big day to follow, her future brothers-in-law hugged and kissed her and whispered in her ear that she was marrying a great guy.

"I like your brothers, Garth," Rory said, as they strolled hand in hand across the darkened patio to the quarters she and Elena were sharing.

"And I can tell they like you."

"You, my beloved, are the only woman I have ever wanted to marry, the way Emmaline is the only woman Will ever loved, and I'm sure Cassie is the only woman Colt ever thought of marrying.

"Have to say I can't say the same about Clay. He fancied he was in love with this girl back home. We all told him time and time again it would be a disaster to marry her. Then the war broke out, and they decided to get married when the war ended. Clay even bought her a ring and carried it all through the war."

"So he listened to all of you, and didn't marry her?"

"No. Two months before the war ended, Ellie up and married Elias Buford, a no-good Yankee sympathizer who had inherited a lot of money from a Yankee aunt who lived in Vermont. He and Ellie moved up there."

"Sounds like that should have made all of you happy except Clay."

"It did."

"Then hold up a minute, Garth. I don't quite understand this. You seem to have accepted your sister's husband—who actually served in the Union army—but you haven't a good word to say about this Elias Buford, who's responsible for preventing this so-called disastrous marriage Clay might have made."

"You would, too, if you were a Virginian. The cowardly bastard pretended he was too ill to join the army.

Didn't raise a hand to defend Virginia throughout the whole war."

"So poor Clay had a broken heart when the two of you left for California."

He chuckled. "Yeah, for about two weeks. Then he met Becky."

"I'm eager to meet your brothers' wives. Do you think they'll like me, Garth?" she asked worriedly.

"Of course they will." He grinned mischievously. "They're all Yankees, the same as you are. Besides, you're easy to love, sweetheart." He pulled her into the deeper shadows and kissed her.

"I want to make love to you so badly, I ache," he whispered, sliding his hand to her breast. He kissed her again.

The fervor of his kiss aroused her passion, but she pushed his hand away. "It would be sinful, Garth," she whispered breathlessly. "This is a holy place, and we are guests here. We must honor that."

"What's sinful about two people in love, making love? Especially when we'll be man and wife in twelve hours."

He trailed kisses down the slim column of her neck as his fingers freed the buttons of her shirt.

"You must stop, Garth," she murmured weakly, and drew a gasping breath when he slid his hand under her camisole and its warmth cupped a breast.

At that moment, Saddle began to bark and ran over to investigate.

"What the hell!" Garth grumbled. "The damn dog never uttered a bark until now. If that mongrel doesn't shut up, he'll have everyone in the mission out here."

The door to the rectory opened and a light pierced the yard from the lamp Father Chavez held above his head.

"Quiet, you four-legged Benedict Arnold," Garth hissed, and stepped out of the shadows. "Sorry if we disturbed you, Father Chavez. I was just stretching my legs. Saddle must have seen something."

"A kitten in the shadows, perhaps," the priest said. "Garth, my son, you are the very person I wish to talk to. Will you join me?"

"Yes, Father."

"If you will excuse us, Miss O'Grady?"

Flushed with embarrassment, Rory stepped out. "Of course, Father." She sped off to the privacy of her room without a backward glance.

Benito hugged the shadows of the wall. The dog had almost betrayed his hiding place. Since nightfall, he had hidden behind a tree to observe the whereabouts of the others.

He would never have a better chance than now. She was alone. The jefe gringo was with the priest, the housekeeper, and the man they called Rico. The old man was with the other two gringos in a room at the end of the building. And the dog had trotted off to the stable.

He would strike swiftly and be gone before they even suspected that he was there.

Pulling a knife from the top of his boot, he stole stealthily through the shadows toward the rear of the house.

25

Garth was surprised to see Elena and Rico when he entered the rectory. Both looked grave and he began to have an uneasy feeling.

The priest indicated a nearby chair. "Please sit down, my son."

"If you don't mind, Father, I think I'll stand."

"As you wish."

"Is there a problem?" Garth asked. "You haven't changed your mind about marrying us, have you, Father?"

"Nothing like that. But what I have to tell you might possibly be disturbing to you. It concerns Henry Fraser, Garth."

"Uncle Henry? What is it?"

"I told you your uncle visited the mission many times, and that he converted to Catholicism. There is one other thing I did not tell you." He opened a drawer and extracted a thick ledger. "Please read this, Garth." He pointed to a line in the ledger dated Mayo Dieciséis, and the year 1847, followed by the names *Henry Fraser* and *Elena Chavez.*

"I'm sorry, Father, I'm very limited at reading Spanish. What does it mean?"

"It's an entry registering the marriage of Henry Fraser and Elena Chavez on May 16, 1847."

Garth snapped up his head in surprise and looked at Elena. "You mean my uncle married your sister?"

Father Chavez nodded.

As the full significance sank in, Garth looked at Elena and broke into a wide grin. "Then that makes you my aunt." He walked over and hugged her, then pressed a kiss to her forehead. "Welcome to the family, Aunt Elena." Struck by another realization, he straightened up and slapped Rico on the shoulder and extended his hand. "Guess that makes us cousins, Rico."

"Does that disturb you, Primo Garth?" Rico said as they shook hands.

"*Primo*?" Garth asked.

Rico's teeth flashed in a grin. "*Primo* means cousin, Cousin."

"Why would it disturb me, Primo Rico? I'm proud to call you cousin, and indebted to you for saving our lives."

"Elena and I were startled by the family resemblance between you and Rico when you first arrived," Father Chavez said.

"I never noticed it. But come to think of it, Rory

once mentioned she saw a resemblance between us. I thought she was talking about our personalities." He teased, "Don't tell her I told you, Rico, but she once said a woman would find you very handsome. So I guess it's flattering for me to know there's a family resemblance between us."

Elena's eyes glowed with pride and love as she looked at her son. She said, "Yes, he resembles his father greatly. Henry was a tall and handsome man. Rico was born five months after his father died."

"Aunt Elena, you speak English very well."

"Thank you. Your uncle taught it to me, as my brother and I did to my son. I wanted Rico to know his father's language, so that Henry would always be a part of both of us."

"Wow, this is an amazing revelation," Garth said. "But why didn't you tell me this when I first arrived, Father Chavez?"

"I was uncertain of your intent at the time, or whether you would even return from Montaña del Diablo."

"We never would have, had it not been for Rico," Garth said.

"My nephew knows the mountain well. That is why I summoned Rico to follow and keep a watchful eye on you."

Some of the mysterious events that had happened became clear to Garth. "Rico, it was *you* who fired the shot that saved my life that first time, when bandits attacked the O'Gradys, wasn't it?"

"Yes, Cousin."

"I've always wondered what happened to the wounded bandit who escaped from that fight."

"His wound was minor but enough to fool Paddy into believing he was dead. I had to dispose of him when he escaped, or he would have returned with others."

"And that time at the fish stream, or when—?"

"I swear on the holy book, Cousin, I was always discreet when any situation called for privacy."

"Good Lord, if Rory knew all this, she'd never be able to look you in the eye again."

"The truth will never go beyond this room, unless you are the one to tell her."

Garth grinned. ""Let's go and tell my brothers! After all, you're their cousin, too."

"Which may not please them, Garth."

"Why would you think that?"

"You are Anglos, amigo, while I—"

"Just tell me one thing, Rico? Did you serve in the Union army?"

"No."

"Good! It was beginning to look like there'd be more Yankee Frasers in this family than Confederate ones."

After the two men departed, tears of joy glistened in Elena's eyes, and she smiled at her brother. "Él es un buen hombre."

Father Chavez nodded and patted her hand. "Sí, hermana. Garth Fraser *is* a good man."

Clay, Colt, and Paddy were engrossed in a game of three card monte when Garth and Rico joined them.

Recalling his conversation with Rory, Garth said, "You fellows shouldn't be gambling; this is consecrated ground."

"That's why we're not using money," Clay said. He threw down his cards in disgust and got up. "I can't believe my luck. You must have stacked the deck."

"Aha, fresh blood!" Colt exclaimed, raking in the winning pot of dried beans. "Sit down and join the game, gentlemen. You must excuse my brother's outburst; these are the two biggest losers I've ever seen. It's a good thing we aren't playing for money, or I'd be the owner of a winery now and our friend Paddy here a poor man."

"I think he's cheating," Clay grumbled. "I just haven't figured out how."

"You mean you just haven't figured out how to play three card monte," Colt rebutted.

"Well, put aside the cards, Midas. I've got something important to tell you boys."

Paddy stood up. "I'm going to bed. And I'll be thanking you to hold down the noise, so's a man can get a decent night's sleep."

"Well, what's so important you have to tell us?" Clay asked, as soon as Paddy left. "You aren't going to bore us with a big thank-you speech for saving your ass, are you?"

"No. I figure that was payback for all the times I saved yours. But I think a welcome to the family is in order. Gentlemen, may I introduce *our cousin*, Enrico Fraser, the son of Henry and Elena Fraser."

"What?" Clay asked.

"Uncle Henry and Elena Chavez were married shortly before he died."

Both men broke into wide grins and pelted Rico with backslaps and handshakes.

"This is great! I can't believe it!" Clay exclaimed.

"Wow! A cousin *and* a new sister-in-law. Cassie's never going to believe me when we get back," Colt said. "To think I once told her the Fraser family was dwindling. Welcome to the family, Rico. We've got a lot of catching up to do."

"Are you forgetting about our new aunt, too?" Garth pointed out.

"That's right! Let's go and find her," Clay said. The two men hurried out the door.

Garth and Rico exchanged amused grins. "What did I tell you?" Garth said.

Then he and Rico followed behind them.

Benito ducked back quickly when the door to the rectory opened and the gringo Garth and Rico came out, crossed the court, and joined the other men.

After a short wait, when it seemed they were remaining there, he moved on. When he reached the rear door, he opened it cautiously and stepped inside into the kitchen. A dim light shone from under a door directly off the kitchen. That had to be the housekeeper's room, where the woman was staying. He tightened his grasp on the knife and crossed the room.

Then he heard approaching footsteps and ducked into a closet, just as the housekeeper entered the kitchen. He watched through the open crack in the closet door as she lit a lamp. Now he would have to kill her, too. She started to walk to the closet, and he raised the knife to strike.

Suddenly the two gringos burst into the room. Shouting joyously, one of them lifted her off her feet and carried her into the other room.

It was too dangerous to attempt his plan. A lamp was lit in the other room and the two men gathered around her, then the gringo jefe and Rico joined them.

Benito cursed the bad luck that had fouled his scheme. But the night was still young; there would be another opportunity.

He stole out the back door and into the shadows.

That night, with thoughts of his wedding in the morning and the revelation about his uncle on his mind, Garth was unable to sleep. He pulled on his boots and went outside.

It was past midnight and all the lights had been extinguished except for a single one at the gate, and one in the sanctuary.

Garth drew a deep breath. The cool mountain air was a welcome relief from the stuffy room. He sat down on the stoop and gazed up at the stars. Funny, how much closer and brighter they appeared in the mountains, as if he could reach up and pluck one out of the sky.

Saddle had been lying by the door and came over and lay down beside him. Garth began to stroke the dog's head. "Can't you sleep either, pal?"

Then recalling the earlier incident, he withdrew his hand. "I forgot, I'm mad at you. I thought you couldn't bark. You sure picked the wrong time to prove me wrong."

Then he began to stroke him again. "But you were right, pal, and I *was* wrong. There's a time and place for everything, so thank you for reminding me." Then he grinned. "But you didn't have to alert the whole place when you did."

Then after a short pause, Garth added, "Just the same, I miss her, Saddle. You do, too, don't you? We've gotten used to her sleeping beside us, haven't we?"

Garth got to his feet and, drawn by the light, he strolled aimlessly over to the sanctuary. The door was open and he stepped inside. With head bowed and deep in prayer, Father Chavez was on his knees at the altar. So as not to disturb him, Garth sat down on one of the wooden pews and glanced around.

The pews were scarred from two hundred years of wear and the center aisle was worn from the thousands of feet that had trampled its length. No costly statues or icons adorned the plain wooden altar, covered by a white cloth hemmed with gold fringe. No fancy tapestries or paintings decorated the plain adobe walls; a huge wooden crucifix hung above a large Bible that was set on the altar.

And yet Garth sensed an aura of reverence that rivaled many of the splendorous cathedrals he had seen in large cities throughout England, France, and the United States.

When Father Chavez finished, the priest rose and left the altar. He stopped in surprise when he saw Garth sitting in the pew.

"Garth, what is wrong, my son? Do you have a problem?"

"Nothing serious. When I saw the open door, I came in. Guess I've too much on my mind to sleep. Must be bridegroom nervousness."

Father Chavez sat down beside him. "It's not unusual for a man to have second thoughts about getting married."

"I have no reservations about marrying Rory. I no longer can even imagine a life without her."

"Then what is disturbing you, Garth?"

"I wish I knew. But don't worry about me, Father Chavez. I think I'm just a nervous bridegroom."

Father Chavez sighed deeply. "I, too, have a problem I am struggling with."

"You, Father? So many others turn to you for advice that no one thinks about who you have to turn to."

The priest's face softened in a kindly smile. "I turn to God for guidance, my son. That is what I was just praying for." He gazed around with reverence. "El Misión de La Dueña de Esperanza: it means 'the Mission of the Lady of Hope' The story is told that two hundred years ago, a small party of Spanish missionaries were being pursued by an overpowering band of Indians. Their situation was hopeless until suddenly a young Indian maiden appeared and led them to this spot, where they met up with a force of conquistadores. The soldiers succeeded in winning the battle, and the priests erected this mission in memory of that young woman."

"How long have you been at this mission, Father Chavez?"

"Almost sixty years. I was just a young man fresh out of the seminary in Madrid when I came here to assist Father Howard. Tierra de Esperanza was a thriving town then.

"Now our town is dying. So many of the parishioners have moved on, and they grow fewer with every passing year. Those that remained are poor peasants. They give what they can afford, but their donations are small, so we depend greatly on the support of the diocese. I received a troubling letter today, which is why I have sought guidance at this late hour. The archbishop feels the mission is too costly to maintain and he is considering closing it."

"Where would you go, Father?"

"I suspect they will retire me and transfer me to a parish in Sacramento or Stockton to live out my remaining years."

"But what about Aunt Elena? This mission has been her home since she was a child, too. What will happen to her?"

"That is what lies so heavily on my heart—as well as what will become of my poor lambs. Who will teach them the holy word? Pray with them? Hear their confessions or give them communion? There will be no one to marry them, baptize their children, or bury their dead." He shook his head. "What will become of them?" he repeated sadly.

The priest stood with a sigh. "Perhaps we both can think clearer in the morning, after we get some sleep. Good night, my son."

26

After the priest left, Garth thought for a long moment, then shot to his feet and strode to Elena's door. Clutching a belted robe around her, Elena opened the door to his steady rapping, and her eyes widened in surprise at the sight of him.

"Aunt Elena, I'm sorry to have wakened you, but I must talk to Rory."

"She is asleep. And at this hour it would not be proper, nephew. Have you not heard it is unlucky for a man to see his bride on their wedding day before they exchange their vows?"

"But this is important and can't wait. It would be more unlucky if I waited until after the wedding to tell her."

"Oh, you are so much like your uncle," she said affectionately. "Henry was always so urgent. Wait here, I will wake her."

She closed the door and a few minutes later, sleepy-eyed, hair tousled, and wearing a robe twice her size, Rory appeared in the doorway.

One look and his heart swelled with love.

"What's wrong, Garth?" she asked worriedly.

"I have to talk to you privately."

"That is not proper," Elena said, appearing beside Rory.

"I swear on my uncle's grave, Aunt Elena, I won't do anything you'd disapprove of. We won't budge from this porch."

"Then I will allow it, but only for a few moments."

"Thank you, sweetheart. I love you." He clasped her cheeks between his hands and kissed her.

"Now I am *sure* you are just like your uncle," Elena said, trying not to smile. She closed the door.

Garth took Rory's hand and led her to the stoop. "Sit down, honey."

"What is this all about, Garth?"

"It concerns something that might affect our getting married. Rory, how much do you love me?"

"I thought I have made that very clear."

"But what if I gave you the rest of the gold? If I were penniless and you were wealthy, would you still want to marry me?"

"Of course I would. I'm in *love* with you! Garth, stop talking in riddles."

"I think we should give the gold to Elena and Rico. They're my Uncle Henry's proper heirs."

"What are you talking about now?"

"Did Elena tell you what Father Chavez wanted to talk to me about tonight?"

"No, I was sleeping when she returned to her room. I remember waking up once and hearing your brothers making a lot of noise on the patio, but I was too sleepy to find out what all the whooping and hollering was about. I thought you all were getting a head start on the wedding celebration."

"Well, we were celebrating a wedding that happened twenty years ago."

When he finished telling Rory the whole story, she sat in silence for a long moment.

"I knew there was a family resemblance," she said, when she finally spoke.

"Is that all you've got to say about it? I just told you I want to give away our share of the gold. That mine no more belongs to me, than it did to Paddy and you. It belongs to Uncle Henry's wife and son."

"And you're willing to give up all that gold that you worked so hard for?" she asked.

"Let's be realistic, honey; I didn't work that hard. Plowing, planting, and harvesting a field is a lot more work and takes a damn sight longer to do. That's why I want to know if you're still willing to marry me—because we won't even have two pennies to rub together."

Her eyes glistened with tears as she slipped her arms around his neck. "If that's the only problem, I can come up with two pennies. That's a start, isn't it?"

"Sweetheart, I love you!" Unable to resist the temptation of her nearness, he kissed her, but pulled away before he let himself get too fired up to stop.

"It would be nice if Paddy turned over his gold to them, too. I know they'll donate most of it to the church, to prevent the mission from closing down. Father Chavez said the diocese is threatening to close it because it has become too costly to finance. Honey, they'll retire him and send him away. He's dedicated his life to this mission, and it will break his heart."

"Won't our gold be enough, if Pop does refuse?"

"I suppose so. But Paddy's share of the gold still belongs to Aunt Elena and Rico."

"You had me scared there for a moment. I thought you were trying to weasel out of marrying me."

"Weasel out of it! What choice do I have? Didn't you once tell me that you were saving yourself for the man you married?"

"Yes," she eyed him warily. "There you go again. What's that supposed to mean?"

He grinned, and hugged her tighter. "You *did*, sweetheart. You did." Then the grin faded, replaced by a tender smile. "I love you, Rory. And some day I'll give you that happy home and security you've always yearned for. But for now, I can only promise you a husband that loves you very much."

"That's all I've ever really wanted. And I could never know more security than I do when you hold me in your arms."

Rory gazed into the warmth and love in his beautiful brown eyes. She loved this man beyond reason, and whatever he wanted for their future would be her wish, too.

She gently stroked his cheek. "But what of your dreams, beloved? The pot of gold you dreamed of finding at the end of the rainbow? Are you certain you're ready to give up that dream?"

"I'm holding the greatest treasure I could ever hope to find in my arms right now."

"Not anymore, nephew," Elena suddenly declared behind them. "She is coming inside and going to bed. The poor dear needs her sleep." She took Rory by the hand. "I am putting her to bed again, and then I want to speak to you. Wait until I come back."

"Good night, sweetheart," he said.

Rory smiled, waved good-bye, and allowed herself to be led back inside.

"Oh, boy, Saddle!" Garth moaned. "I'm already in hot water with my brand-new aunt."

Elena returned within minutes and took a ring out of her pocket. "This was my wedding ring." She handed him the plain gold band. "Your uncle forged it himself out of the gold he had discovered."

"I can't take this," Garth said, stunned.

"I want you to, and I know Henry would want you to have it."

"But Rico's his son. It should be passed on to him."

"Rico is the one who suggested it, my nephew. He respects the traditions that meant so much to his father, and he knows how much these traditions mean to you, as well. This will be passed on for generations, and as long as it is passed on, the memory of the man who made it will be, too.

"I remember how Henry's eyes shone when he told me how your mother's wedding ring had been passed down to her from your grandmother, who in turn had received it from your great-grandmother. And now, passed to your older brother, his wife wears it, and will in turn pass it on to the next generation. It is a wonderful tradition, and it pleases us to think that the ring Henry had made will be passed on to the bride of his favorite nephew. Both Rico and I want that for him. Not only will it always be a link to him, but it will always be a link to us, as well."

Garth could not refuse. He hugged and kissed her. "I can't thank you enough, Aunt Elena. And I hope one day, when we pass the ring on to our child, Rory and I can tell them the amazing story about their Granduncle Henry, and how his dream had brought their mother and father together."

He put the ring in his pocket and started to walk away, then drew up sharply when he saw Saddle poised in hunting position, looking at the rear of the house.

"Saddle, what is it, pal? Did you flush out a—"

A scream rent the silent night, and barking, Saddle raced to the house as Garth dashed after him.

Benito was running out of time; it would be daylight before he knew it. Then there would be no chance to kill her and get away. Throughout the evening, the woman had not been alone. Either the old woman or the gringos were with her. And even though none of them were wearing gun belts, he would never be able to get near the woman without them interfering.

He watched the housekeeper take the girl inside, and come out again to talk to the gringo. This was the chance he was waiting for.

Benito slipped in the back door into the dark kitchen. As he moved toward the bedroom door the floor creaked loudly underfoot, and he paused to be sure no one had heard.

The old priest's quarters were on the far side of the building; he could hear the murmurs of the gringos and housekeeper's voices coming from outside, but where was the dog? He could not remember seeing it outside with the jefe. What if it was in the room with the girl? He would have to take the chance.

He turned the doorknob, and the door creaked as he opened it.

Rory lay thinking about marrying Garth. She still couldn't believe that in a few hours she would be his wife. She never thought it was possible to love someone so much that you willingly would die for them— or with them.

But that was behind them now. Tomorrow, a future together lay ahead of them.

When she heard the door creak open, she turned her head, smiling. "Elena, how long does a wedding . . ."

She screamed at the sight of the man in the doorway. He leaped at her, and she rolled off the bed and escaped the knife thrust meant for her. Elena came running with a lamp just as Saddle burst through the door, Garth at his heels.

Benito grabbed Rory and yanked her to her feet. Using her as a shield, he held the knife against her throat.

"Stay back, or I will kill her," he warned.

Teeth bared and snarling, Saddle edged forward, threatening to strike, but Garth ordered the dog to be still.

"If you draw one drop of her blood, I'll let him rip you apart," Garth said.

"Tie up the dog, mujer," he said to Elena.

Garth nodded. "Go with her, Saddle." Elena quickly put the dog in the closet and closed the door.

"Move away, jefe, or I kill her now. *¡Dése prisa! ¡Dése prisa!*"

"He wants us to hurry," Elena said.

Garth could see the man's hand was shaking; any slip could injure Rory. "Honey, just stay calm. Nothing's going to happen to you." He stepped aside.

"Hey, what's going on?" Colt shouted from outside.

"Tell them to get back," Benito ordered, "or else the woman dies."

"Back off, we're coming out," Garth shouted, then glared at him. "I warned you; one drop of her blood and you're dead!"

He and Elena stepped outside, followed by Benito, still holding Rory as a shield with the knife against her throat.

His brothers and Rico each had pistols in their hands.

"Give him room, boys, I don't want Rory hurt."

Paddy stood speechless, seeing the peril his daughter was in.

"Please, no shooting," Father Chavez said.

"No offense, Father," Clay said, "but we're not going to just stand here and watch that bastard cut her throat."

"No, we promised Father Chavez, no shooting," Garth said, moving a step closer to the outlaw.

"My son, let the woman go. Nothing will be gained if you harm her," Father Chavez pleaded.

"They will kill me if I let her go, and if they don't do as I say, I will kill her now. Put your guns down."

"Garth, I can put a bullet between his eyes before he even knows what hit him," Colt said.

"No, just do as he says," Garth said, taking another step closer.

Rico spoke to the man in rapid Spanish, and when they were finished, he said, "I asked him why he's trying to kill Rory. He said for revenge. We killed his father and brother."

"What's he talking about?" Garth asked.

"He was one of the bandits that attacked you on the mountain."

"My God! They were trying to slaughter us, and he wants revenge!"

Garth was incensed at the thought that this was the second time this man had tried to kill the woman he loved. He would have raped her to death, along with his father and brother and their twelve other companions. The son of a bitch had just signed his own death warrant.

He was within striking distance of the man now, and he glanced at Rory as Rico continued to ask him questions in Spanish. The fear in her eyes turned to understanding when she read the message in his. Without moving his hand, he raised three fingers slightly. Her look told him she understood.

He raised one finger, then another, and on the third he dove for the man's arm as Rory shoved her elbow into the man's rib.

Garth twisted the man's arm until he screamed with pain and dropped the knife. The he punched him in the jaw, sending the bandit reeling. Out of control now, Garth drove him back and slammed him into the wall, then began to pummel the man.

"Stop him! Stop him!" Father Chavez cried out in despair. "He's killing him!"

It took all the strength of the three men to pull Garth off the man.

Rory ran into his arms and he held her quivering body, unaware that he was shaking equally as much.

Sobbing and bloody, Benito staggered over to Father Chavez and sank to his knees, crying and begging for help.

The priest talked to him in low tones for several moments, then raised his head and looked at the group a short distance away.

"I told him he could leave," Father Chavez said.

"You mean let him go?" Clay said. "Father, he came here to kill Rory."

"I know, but can't you see he's a broken man now? I don't believe he will ever try to hurt anyone again."

"That's naïve, Father," Clay said. "You don't know how many other innocent people this man has murdered. He should be locked up, tried for murder, and hanged."

"We have no sheriff here, no jail. Are we to be this man's judge and hangman?"

"Does that mean you allow murderers to run free?" Colt asked.

"What do you suggest we do, Colt?"

"Since I don't shoot unarmed men, I don't know. You shouldn't have stopped me while he was holding the knife to Rory's throat."

"What do you suggest, Garth?" Clay asked.

Garth went over to Benito, who was huddled on the floor weeping. "Get out of my sight. And if I see you again, I'll strangle you with my own two hands."

"You figure he might be back?" Clay asked.

"Not if he enjoys breathing," Garth said. "He's terrorized Rory two times; if he tries a third, he's not going to walk away from it."

Elena came over and clasped Rory's hand. "Come, dear, and go back to bed."

"I'm not letting her out of my sight, Aunt Elena."

"She needs sleep, nephew."

"I'm not letting her out of my sight, Aunt Elena," Garth repeated firmly. "We'll just sit on the stoop for a little while. Aunt Elena, will you let Saddle out of that closet before he suffocates?"

"Sí, sobrino," Elena said, hurrying off.

Garth put his arm around Rory's shoulders and they started to walk away.

With a savage cry, Benito snatched the knife from the ground and lunged at Garth.

Bullets from three guns slammed into him, and the madman was dead before he hit the ground.

Garth spun around and looked at his brothers and Rico; their smoking guns were still in their hands.

He nodded in gratitude. "Thanks for the wedding gift, fellas."

He lowered himself onto the step of the stoop and pulled Rory down beside him.

A short time later, Elena came out to once again insist Rory return to bed. She found the girl curled up on Garth's lap with her head against his chest. Both of them were sound asleep.

Elena smiled down tenderly at the couple. Henry's nephew had the heart and the soul of a saint. And she marveled at the physical resemblance between Garth and his uncle and Rico.

"Sí, mi querido," she whispered, "su sobrino es un buen hombre."

Saddle, who had been lying at the foot of the stoop, lifted his head with a single bark, as if to say he agreed—or perhaps merely to display his newly discovered skill as a watchdog.

Elena put a finger to her lips. "Hush, perro, or you will wake them," she scolded softly.

Then Elena glanced across the patio to where her son and his two cousins were keeping a vigil in the event Benito had any accomplices.

She smiled with tenderness. "They, too, will not let anything happen to them, little perro." She went back inside and quietly closed the door.

The following morning, Elena helped Rory dress for the wedding. She wanted the young woman to have a proper gown for such an important occasion in her life. When Father Chavez had informed her of the forthcoming wedding, Elena had unpacked, laundered, and pressed the gown.

Elena had made the gown for her own wedding when she married Henry Fraser. With shuttle and thread, she had woven the white tatting that formed the neckline and cap sleeves of the dress, as well as the matching lace that adorned the hem. Elegant in its simplicity, the white muslin gown dropped in delicate folds to the tips of the satin pumps that Rory had saved from her dancing days in saloons.

Having shampooed Rory's hair with rosewater, Elena brushed it until the scented strands glistened like a gold mantle down Rory's back.

"This is the mantilla my mother wore on her wedding day," Elena said as she placed a white lace mantilla on Rory's head.

She stepped back to admire the outcome. "You look lovely, querida. My nephew has chosen wisely. You will have handsome children."

Rory couldn't believe it was her own image she was viewing. Never one who ever lingered at the sight of herself in a mirror, she felt lovely and twirled around as she viewed herself from all angles. "Oh, the gown is so beautiful! What a lovely bride you must have made, Aunt Elena." Rory turned in consternation. "Do you mind if I call you Aunt Elena? It is bold of me to take such license, as if I were already one of the Fraser family."

"It pleases me that you do so. This Fraser family is just as new to me. And since my mother died, I have known and lived with only male family members, so I enjoy sharing these moments with a woman again."

"I can't thank you enough, Aunt Elena. The only family gown I have is the red one I wore in the saloon. I want Garth to be proud of me."

"I don't think you have to worry, my dear. The love and pride he feels for you is very visible when he looks at you."

Rory sighed with happiness. "I love him so much, Aunt Elena. I never knew how loving someone can swell the heart with so much joy. A simple smile or touch from him makes me feel precious and sheltered. I ask myself over and over what I have done to deserve such happiness. Is that how Uncle Henry made you feel?"

Elena smiled in remembrance. "That is how I still feel, little one, because his smile still lingers in my memory and his voice in my ears."

At the sight of the tears misting in Rory's eyes, Elena said quickly, "Now, have we forgotten anything? It is said on her wedding day a bride must wear something old, something new, something borrowed, and something blue."

"My shoes are blue," Rory said. "And the gown is borrowed, and the mantilla is old."

"Then let us think what we have that is new for you to wear."

"Must one wear it?" Rory asked.

Elena thought for a moment. "I really don't know. What do you have in mind?"

"I was thinking of *new* hope. I can feel it, Aunt Elena—not only in my life, but in all our lives."

"Then wear that new hope, querida. Wear it with the faith and assurance you carry within you."

Rory hugged and kissed her. "I love you."

"And I you, little one. Now, we must not keep your handsome groom waiting." Merriment danced in her eyes. "We are all aware of the groom's impatience to get on with the pleasure of the wedding bed that follows."

"Aunt Elena!" Rory cried, embarrassed.

"Aha, let us hasten; the blush now on your cheeks has made you even lovelier."

Elena took her by the hand, and they hurried to the church.

27

Garth nervously rose to his feet when Rory and Elena entered the sanctuary. He looked at Rory with awe, then drew her hand to his lips and pressed a kiss to the palm.

"You're the most beautiful bride a man could ever dream of having," he murmured, and handed her a nosegay of poppies to carry.

"And there will never be a more handsome groom, my love," she replied.

Father Chavez stood behind the altar with one of the altar boys near by. The Fraser brothers and Rico were seated on one side of the aisle, and her father sat in a pew across from them, dabbing at his eyes.

Elena sat down next to Paddy.

Colt winked at Rory as Garth led her to the altar, and suddenly all her jitters dissolved.

She had been blessed not only with the finest man she had ever hoped for, but had gained wonderful brothers, a cousin, and an aunt who was more like a mother to her.

As she gazed into Garth's eyes when he slipped the small gold band on her finger, Rory knew that this moment would be etched on her heart and mind forever.

When the ceremony ended, Rory was deluged with hugs and kisses from her two brothers-in-law and their more reserved cousin. Elena had prepared a savory meal of chicken and rice for the occasion, topped off with a two-tiered wedding cake.

When they finished their meal and the wedding toast offered by Clay, Garth stood up with Rory at his side.

"Ladies and gentlemen, my wife and I would like to thank our hostess for the delicious meal and her successful efforts to make our wedding special for us.

"Everyone in this room is related either through blood or marriage, and other than the sanctity of marriage, nothing is more inviolable than family loyalty. We are indebted to my brothers and cousin for risking their lives to save ours.

"I came here as a stranger, in search of a gold mine, and discovered a much greater wealth—an aunt and cousin that I never knew existed. Why my quest should lead me to a mission in this small village can only be due to God's design." He grinned at Father Chavez. "I'm sure you would agree, Father.

"And that is why Rory and I have reached this decision. We feel the gold we discovered belongs to the rightful owners—the wife and son of Henry Fraser. Therefore, we are giving them our share of it. And we hope Paddy will do the same."

For a long moment, the room remained silent as all those present absorbed the full meaning behind Garth's words.

Rico was the first to speak up. "We can't accept such a gift. You were almost killed mining that gold. Why would you give it away?"

"Because, just as Garth said, the gold doesn't belong to us," Rory answered.

"I could never consider accepting it."

"Nor I," Elena said, in support of her son's decision.

"Would you consider accepting it to save this mission?" Garth turned to Father Chavez. "You haven't told them, have you?"

"Told us what?" Elena asked.

"That the diocese is considering closing down this mission for financial reasons. It has become too costly to run."

Shocked, Elena asked her brother, "Is that true? Why didn't you tell me?"

"I was waiting until our guests departed," Father Chavez said. "You were so happy and excited over this wedding, mi hermana. I haven't seen such happiness in your eyes for years, and I didn't have the heart to diminish that enthusiasm."

"Will they really close down the mission, Uncle?" Rico asked.

"I am afraid so, my son."

"Does that make your decision easier to make, Rico?" Garth asked. "It certainly did for Rory and me."

"Well, it doesn't change *my* mind," Paddy suddenly spoke out. "I'll not be giving away the gold that I worked so hard to get. Me and me daughter filed the claim on that mine, so I'm the one to be having the say of it."

Clay and Colt stood up. "This is a personal issue between you, so we'll clear out," Clay said. He shook Garth's hand. "You've done the family proud, Garth."

Colt nodded and slapped him on the shoulder as they departed.

"And I'll be taking me leave as well, for I've had me say. I'll not be giving up me gold." He strode from the room.

"God bless you," Father Chavez said. "The love and generosity of you two young people will live in our hearts forever."

Garth clasped Rory's hand. "Come on, sweetheart, let's go and find my brothers. Lord only knows what kind of trouble those guys have gotten into."

Rory looked askance at him. " 'Physician, heal thyself!' "

Father Chavez burst into laughter. "Garth, my son, you have your hands full. This truly is a union made in heaven."

Upon returning to his quarters, Paddy dug in his pack and pulled out a pint of whiskey he had purchased at the cantina, then took a deep swallow. "Well, I guess

I'll be going me way, and she can go hers. She has a husband now to be looking after her needs."

Paddy sat down on the edge of the bed and once again dug through his pack. He withdrew the two green pouches of gold and held one in each hand. "These are mine; I've earned them." Returning the pouches to the pack, he reached for the whiskey bottle.

"Helping the poor, indeed! Why don't they help themselves, like I did? All me life I've been poor, scratching and scraping enough to keep food in me daughter's stomach or a roof over her head. You know I'm right, don't you, Katie? Now I have a chance to live out the rest of me life not having to worry about our daughter, or where the next pint is coming from."

As if seeking reassurance, he took another swig of the whiskey. "And I'll not be feeling no guilt or shame over it. Feeding the poor and saving the mission doesn't fall on the shoulders of Patrick O'Grady. The mine really belonged to me."

He finished the whiskey and sat with the empty bottle dangling from his fingers.

His voice softened. "She has a husband now to be tending to her needs, and a good job he'll be doing of it. He's a fine man. Surely a finer man than Paddy O'Grady, though it hurts me to be saying so. We've had many a cross word between us, but I'm not one to bear a grudge. I know a real man when I see one.

"So there's no further need for me. No need a'tall. I'll have me gold and me pint, so I'll have no need of her, either."

He wiped the tears off his cheeks, and lay back with his head on the pillow. Paddy closed his eyes and the bottle slid through his fingers. "No need a'tall."

It was late when Rory slipped into her father's room, and she shook him gently to wake him.

Paddy opened his eyes to the sight of his beautiful daughter clad in white. "Faith and begorra, 'tis an angel," he murmured. "I've died and gone to heaven."

"Are you okay, Pop?"

"Aye, darlin'."

"I just came in to say good night. Garth wants us to get an early start in the morning."

"Aye. 'Tis the smart thing to do."

"Pop, I was upset about your keeping the gold, but you have every right to do what you want with your money. Father Chavez and Garth said the same thing. Now go back to sleep. We've got a long trip ahead of us tomorrow." She kissed him on the forehead, and started to leave.

"I'll not be leaving with you," he said.

She turned around. "What do you mean?"

"I'm thinking of staying here for a few more days."

"Pop, we can't do that. Everyone is packed and eager to get back to their homes. Rico is even going with us. He has to take the gold to the bank, where it will be safe, so we all thought it wiser if he travels with us. And I won't think of leaving you here, either."

"You have no need for me, darlin'. You have a fine husband who loves you and will take good care of you."

"But that doesn't mean I don't need you, too, Pop. I'll always need you."

She knelt at the bedside and clasped his hand. "Clay told Garth there's good land available right next to his. It sounds like a wonderful place to build our home and raise our children.

"But we can't be a family without you, Pop. Garth wants our children to grow up knowing their grandfather, their uncles and aunts, and their cousins, the way he did. He said that's what family is all about, and it's something I never had.

"He said we'll build a special place that will be yours alone. Even under a separate roof, if you prefer, where you can sit on the porch every day and have your pint, teach your grandchildren and their cousins how to stack a deck of cards, or tell them those wonderful stories about Ireland. They'll need you as much as I do, Pop."

Paddy thought his heart would burst with joy. He brushed the tears out of his eyes. "Well, now that I have the money, I've been thinkin' of taking a trip back to Ireland, so let me think on it again."

"There's nothing to think about, you old curmudgeon. You're coming with us. I won't have it any other way."

"You've a strong will, daughter. Just like—"

"My Grandmother Finn," Rory finished for him. She got to her feet. "I love you, Pop." She kissed him again, then went out to join Garth.

There was no sign of him with the others, and after several minutes Rory realized where she would find him. She went to the small cemetery and stood back as he said his final good-bye to his uncle.

"We're pulling out at first light, Uncle Henry, and I don't suppose I'll be back this way again, so I guess this is good-bye. We got your gold back for you, and I'm sure Aunt Elena and Rico will put it to good use.

"I know you'd be proud of him, Uncle Henry. He looks like you, too. And Aunt Elena is wonderful. I wish the two of you could have had more time together.

"She gave us the wedding ring that you made for her, and it will always be a memory of you.

"Thanks for everything, Uncle Henry. I never forgot you, and I never will."

Rory walked up and slipped her hand into his, then leaned down and laid her wedding bouquet on the grave.

Slipping an arm around her shoulders, he drew her to his side. "I wish you could have known him, honey."

"I think I do know him through you and Rico, my love."

"He was my hero. I realize now that it wasn't his dream that drew me to him—it was the man."

He smiled and kissed the top of her head. "I suppose you're wondering right now if the man you married is a little soft in the head."

"More like soft in the heart, my darling. One of the things I love most about you is how you embrace whomever you love, whether it's a brother, Father Chavez, or even a dog or horse."

Garth chuckled. "I hope there's a wife included in

there, because I can't think of anything or anyone I love more."

He turned her in his arms and kissed her, then tenderly caressed her check. "Lord, I love you, Rory."

A mischievous gleam flashed in his eyes as they turned to go back. "Is it permitted for a man to make love to his wife on consecrated ground?"

"If it's not, it should be," she said.

"Well, I think we might not be the first." He looked back and winked. "Right, Uncle Henry?"

"You're just the one we're looking for," Colt said, as they crossed the patio and joined him and Clay. "The others have all gone to bed, but we thought we'd have a final toast before we do the same."

"Honey, do you mind?" Garth asked.

"Not at all. Good night, all." She managed to escape from under the hugs and kisses on the cheek from her new brothers-in-law.

Smiling, Rory returned to the small room Elena had prepared for them to spend their wedding night. She opened the shutters to catch the evening breeze and stood in the darkness, gazing out with love at Garth as he shared this final drink with his brothers before they retired for the night. She could see how happy he was to be with them again, and her heart swelled with love for all of them.

"How long has it been since we've all stood together in a toast?" she heard Colt ask.

Clay spoke up at once. "At Fraser Keep, the night before we left to join our regiments."

"My God, that had to be almost seven years ago," an astonished Colt exclaimed.

"You're wrong, Brother Clay," Garth said. "The last time was when the war ended and we'd come back to Fraser Keep. Remember, Clay? It was the night before we left for California."

Clay shook his head. "No, I'm talking about the last time we *all* stood in a toast together. When, Dad, Will, Andy, and Jed made that toast with us."

"Yeah, I guess you're right. This sure isn't the same, is it?" Garth conceded.

"And never can be again," Colt added sadly.

"But nor are we the same fellows who stood in that circle and made that toast," Clay reminded them. "There've been many changes in all our lives since then—some painful, many joyous. We've all traveled long and different roads since then."

"None as long and different as the one the three of us had to travel to get us here to California," Colt interjected, in an effort to lighten the mood.

"I sure agree with that," Garth said. "And when we get back to Clay's house, we can stand all night making toasts with his wine, compliments of our vintner host. But now, as much as I enjoy your company, I would like to spend my wedding night with my wife. So let's get on with this toast."

Colt nudged Clay's arm. "Does that sound like the brother Garth we grew up with? He never passed up having a drink with us to be with a woman before."

Clay chuckled. "That's the pot calling the kettle black. Before Cassie brought you to your knees, you and Garth were like two peas in a pod. How often did we hear that a woman would never tie down either one of you?"

"I don't recall making such naïve statements, do you, Colt?" Garth asked, tongue in cheek. "But at least Colt and I were sober when we said our I dos, which is more than you can say."

"You know very well the explanation for that," Clay replied in an effort to defend himself.

"Which I listened to for four months on the trail and do not care to hear again." Garth slapped his brother on the shoulder. "Can we get on with this toast? My wife awaits her lord and master." He was immediately rewarded with groans and pummels to his head from his two brothers.

Rory couldn't help smiling. *You're going to pay dearly for that, Garth Fraser. We'll just see who's the lord and master.*

Clay cleared his throat, "All right, a toast." He raised his glass and Colt and Garth followed suit.

"To the newlyweds, Garth and Rory. I can't think of a more sincere wish for their marriage and future, than the hope that they'll know the happiness Colt and I have found with Cassie and Becky."

"We all got far more than we deserve," Colt said, after they downed their drinks.

"I agree wholeheartedly, Brother Colt," Garth said. "So now, one last toast: the most important one. Do us the honors, Clay."

Colt refilled their glasses and Clay raised his in the air. "To the incredible women who have honored us by becoming our wives, and given us the richness and blessing of their love. May we never betray that trust."

The Fraser brothers clinked their glasses together in accord.

Epilogue

The rising sun barely streaked the sky as Father Chavez watched the Fraser party, his beloved nephew among them, ride away. When they disappeared from sight, he turned away with a heavy heart. He would miss them all.

And now, due to the honesty and generosity of Garth Fraser, not only would Rico be able to afford to attend the university in Sacramento, but the mission would be solvent far beyond his own remaining years.

He went into the sanctuary and knelt at the altar. After finishing the morning breviary, he said a special prayer that the newlyweds would know a long and happy life, blessed with many children.

On this day there was much for which to give thanks. He thanked the Lord for bringing Garth Fraser to their humble mission, and for the happiness it had brought to his sister and nephew, and the many others who would benefit from that generosity.

And he thanked his Maker for bestowing the opportunity for this son of a humble sheepherder to have served Him through the years.

When he finished he rose from the altar, and as he walked to the door his attention was drawn to the wooden box set on a carved base in the corner.

He drew closer, and stared in puzzlement at the two green pouches that lay on the top of the box for donations to the poor.